THE UNKINDNESS OF RAVENS

THE
UNKINDNESS
OF RAVENS

A Greer Hogan Mystery

M. E. HILLIARD

CROOKED
LANE

NEW YORK

Published in the United States by Crooked Lane Books, an imprint of The Quick Brown Fox & Company LLC.

Crooked Lane Books and its logo are trademarks of The Quick Brown Fox & Company LLC.

Library of Congress Catalog-in-Publication data available upon request.

ISBN (hardcover): 978-1-64385-694-0
ISBN (ebook): 978-1-64385-695-7

Cover design by Kara Klontz

Printed in the United States.

www.crookedlanebooks.com

Crooked Lane Books
34 West 27th St., 10th Floor
New York, NY 10001

First Edition: April 2021

10 9 8 7 6 5 4 3 2 1

For Mark

Chapter One

❦

Growing up, I remember liking Trixie Belden better than Nancy Drew because she got into more trouble. Plus, Trixie had a better boyfriend than Nancy. Jim Frayne was much hotter than Ned Nickerson. I'm not convinced Ned Nickerson was anatomically correct—I always pictured him looking like a Ken doll. Jim Frayne had red hair and a working-class background, but turned out to be related to an eccentric millionaire, and came into a pile of money at an early age. He was a prototype Nora Roberts hero—well-mannered, financially secure, comfortable in a tux, but still able to fix things around the house and radiate alpha maleness at the drop of a hat. Jim was the beginning of a lifetime of crushes on blue-eyed redheads who looked great in Levis and opened doors for me. I might envy Nancy's wardrobe allowance and covet her convertible, but I was a Trixie girl at heart.

Trixie and Nancy were part of the reason I ended up a librarian. It was my second career. Circumstances were such that at the age of thirty-seven I had needed a change.

A big change. So, I went to the place where I always felt safe and happy—the library. More precisely, library school. Armed with a master's degree, I could spend my days ferreting out information without actually having to deal with bad guys. I was a girl detective with a laptop instead of a roadster. I spent much of my time in charge of the reading room, sitting at the reference desk, answering questions and pimping books to readers eager for something novel. Even on those days when the computers and copier were at their most uncooperative, requiring knowledge that two years of graduate school had failed to impart, I was still queen of all I surveyed.

When I'd arrived for my job interview at the Raven Hill Public Library the previous October, I had spent a few minutes staring at the building in awe. It had such a Gothic, Jane Eyre feel that I expected to see the first Mrs. Rochester glaring at me from an upstairs window. I knew that Raven Hill Manor had been deeded to the village for use as a library decades before by the last of the Ravenscroft family. The result was a brooding exterior that greeted new arrivals with some suspicion. The resident ravens were icing on the cake. While I had yet to meet any of the Ravenscroft family ghosts, I remained hopeful. Now that I had six months of employment behind me, I thought of it as my home away from home.

The interior of the manor was like any old house, with inefficient heating and temperamental wiring, and inexplicable noises that echoed through its high-ceilinged rooms. Nonetheless, it retained an air of shabby gentility.

Retrofitting the place as a library had resulted in odd nooks and crannies and strangely repurposed artifacts. Some village residents found this outdated and irritating, while others felt it had a quirky charm. I was in the latter camp. The place was full of small mysteries and historical oddities. Nothing was as it first seemed in Raven Hill Manor, and I loved that.

I planned to take advantage of the first sunny day in an exceptionally rainy spring by having lunch on the roof terrace. I used the old servants' stairs, working my way up and away from the busy reading room into the areas used only by the staff. The worn wooden banisters always warmed and hummed beneath my hand, releasing the scent of lemon polish. Not today, though. Today the wood remained cool beneath my fingertips. I felt no happy hum. The place was unnaturally still. No dust motes danced in the watery sunlight. The expectant silence was broken only by the occasional protesting squeak from the wooden floor beneath my feet.

By the time I reached the small anteroom that led to the attic stairs, I heard nothing but my own labored breathing. Vowing to get more exercise now that spring had finally arrived, I stopped to catch my breath. I turned the knob of the final door. It stuck. Thinking the wood must have swollen from all the wet weather, I braced myself and pulled. It opened with a groan and an exhalation of cool, damp air.

A body landed at my feet.

The air compressed around me, sucking the breath from my lungs. A convulsive shudder rolled through me. I stared down at the broken thing in front of me. Twilight shades of gray and black drifted across the scene.

A man's dark hair and pale skin, stars of broken glass across the midnight blue of his tie.

No.

I closed my eyes and forced myself to breathe. In, out, and again.

I looked down once more, and the room came back into focus. Not a man, a woman. A woman I knew. Joanna Goodhue, president of the Friends of the Library and the closest thing I had to a friend in Raven Hill. My mind raced, denying what I saw in front of me and searching for a rational explanation. CPR dummy? No, it's Joanna. She's slipped and fallen, but she's okay. But she wasn't okay. I had to acknowledge what the primitive part of my brain had known instantly.

Joanna was dead.

I knew I should check for a pulse, or breathing. Something. Anything. Just to be sure.

I reached down, knowing what I would find.

White fingers, red-tipped, reaching out, hesitating, and then contact. So very still, and cool.

Cold. There was nothing where Joanna's pulse should be but a bone-chilling cold. I snatched my hand back so quickly I lost my balance. I grabbed the door to keep from falling backward, pulling it and the body, toward me. Then I saw the blood.

I scrambled away, putting as much space between me and Joanna as I could. I landed against the windowsill and stared at the ceiling, trying to think straight.

I needed to tell someone. Call an ambulance. The police.

This could not be happening. Not again.

I didn't kill the guy. I swear it. He was alive when I left him.

My husband's death was case closed, as far as the police were concerned. But here I was, with another body, my thoughts whirling and scattering.

I had to do something.

"Cell phone," I said out loud. My cell phone was in my lunch tote, right where I had dropped it.

Next to the body.

I could do this. I pushed off from the window, focusing on the lipstick red of my bag. I grabbed it and scuttled back to the sill. I pulled out my phone and paused.

If I dialed 911, there would be sirens and flashing lights around the building in no time. In any emergency, we were to clear the library immediately. I looked out the window at the parking lot. We had a good crowd. I might be able to buy some time to pull myself together before I had to talk to the police.

I dialed the library's main number, turning my back on the ugly tableau in the stairwell.

"Raven Hill Village Library—Circulation. How may I help you?"

Mary Alice. Thank God. The woman could think on her feet and was unflappable.

"Mary Alice, it's me, Greer. I have—um . . ." *A dead body at my feet.* "I have a situation, and I need you to send

Helene up. I'm okay, but she needs to hurry. Third floor. Attic stairs. And keep everyone else away."

There was a brief pause, and then, "Okay, honey, I'll send her."

I leaned my head against the cool glass of the window and waited. It wasn't long before I heard the sound of hurried footsteps. As I turned, Helene Montague, Library Director, stepped into the dim room.

"Greer, what—?" she said, and stopped as she looked past me.

"Joanna Goodhue. Dead."

Saying it out loud made it horribly real. I turned. The surreal, nightmare quality of the scene dissolved and I saw only Joanna, impossibly still and silent. I gulped for air and put my hand over my mouth. Helene looked at me and without a word reached past me and unlocked the window. Pushing it up, she spun me back toward it.

"Breathe through your mouth," she said.

I stood inhaling the fresh spring air. I could hear Helene moving behind me. Then she used her own phone to call Mary Alice, giving instructions to close the library. After that she called the police.

"Greer." Helene was back at my side. "I need to check the attic entrance in the archives and then help Mary Alice secure the building. I want to make sure no one comes up. Can you stay here and wait for the police? Will you be all right?"

"I'll be all right enough. We don't have a lot of options. I'll wait right here."

She gave me one last searching look, then disappeared back into the darkness of the stairwell. I closed my eyes and tried the measured breathing I'd learned in a long-ago yoga class.

No good. The scene on the landing seemed burned onto my eyelids. The sight of my husband's lifeless body kept swimming up out of the dark pool of memory, superimposing itself over Joanna's. Blonde, brunette. Blue eyes, brown. But Danny's wounds seemed somehow worse. Vicious.

Maybe that was it. Danny had been murdered. His death had looked violent. The scene around him had spoken of rage. I could be overreacting now, seeing more than was there because I somehow expected to see it. Joanna could have fallen, hit her head, and broken her neck. The door was stuck. Could the impact have killed her? Possible, but something niggled. Something was off.

Whatever it was, I wasn't going to figure it out standing here with my eyes closed. In my previous, corporate life, I'd been known for my cool, analytical thinking. Now I was behaving like the heroine in a Victorian novel having a fit of the vapors. Time to put on my big girl panties and deal. I hadn't spent my entire life reading mysteries for nothing.

I turned around and moved toward the stairway, stopping near the body. Trying to remain dispassionate, I studied Joanna. Greer Hogan, girl detective, on the job. Joanna was lying half on the landing, half on the floor of the old box room between the two stairways. Her legs were still on the stairs, her head on the floor at my feet. Clotted blood matted her carefully highlighted blonde hair. There was a dark smudge on her bright blue Raven Hill hoodie, and another where her head must have rested against the door. I followed the line of her body up into the dim stairwell.

On the best of days, the old servants' stairs were not well lit. Each had a single bulb at the top and bottom landings, with a long stretch of darkness in between. At the moment, I had nothing more than the light from the window behind me, and some filtered sunlight from the attic above.

I could see the stair just above Joanna's feet, and then nothing until the top few steps and the short, spindled railing that separated the stairs from the attic, where a window on the upper landing provided some light. I leaned sideways, craning my neck. Objects were scattered at the top of the stairs, some wooden toys, an old-fashioned spinning top, and what looked like a doll's leg sticking out from under something large and dark.

What was that? I reached automatically for the light switch and stopped. I had to leave things as they were. The light was off. I pulled my hand back slowly.

If the light was off, how had Joanna gone up to the attic? Must have been during the day, or for some reason she turned the light off at the top. Why? I studied the scene on the upper landing, trying to make out what the shapeless dark thing was. I was reaching for my phone with its flashlight app when I heard a gentle creak above my head and froze. A few seconds passed in silence. Maybe I had imagined it, that sound where no one should be. And then once again, the slight protesting noise of an old floorboard in the attic above.

An electric zing of fear shot through me. I eased back, out of sight of anyone who might look over the stair rail. I managed one deep breath before I heard a clatter behind me. I whirled to see Helene, followed by two people I didn't know. Helene was flanked by a tall, solidly built man with salt-and-pepper hair and a younger blonde woman, who eyed me with some suspicion. The police had arrived to find me standing over the body of a dead woman, and they did not look pleased.

"I heard something," I said, pointing at the ceiling. It was both the truth and a good excuse for stepping all over the crime scene. The woman went into high alert, almost vibrating with energy. She motioned me back, moving across the floor to take up the position I had just vacated. As she leaned forward to look up the stairwell, I heard the man ask Helene, "There's another way up, isn't there?"

Helene nodded.

"Anything, Jennie?" The blonde officer leaned back, shaking her head.

"The other entrance is in the archives. I'll show you," Helene said.

"Take Officer Webber. I'll stay here with Ms . . .?"

"Hogan," I replied. "Greer Hogan."

Helene gave a brief nod and the two women left. I resumed my place at the window, leaning against the sill on legs that had begun to tremble.

"Sam O'Donnell, Ms. Hogan," he said, walking past me. He stood unmoving in the center of the room, carefully studying the scene. Without turning, he said, "You found her?"

"Yes."

"Recognized her?"

"Yes."

"Know her well?"

I hesitated.

He turned his head and raised an eyebrow. "Ms. Hogan?"

I didn't want them to associate me too closely with Joanna, but I didn't want to break one of my cardinal rules: Never lie about anything important. My relationship with the victim of an unexplained death was important, especially to the police at this point in their investigation. So, appear forthcoming, but stick to the facts.

"We first met in college. I was her RA. Then we lost touch. We reconnected a few years ago on Facebook. The job here threw us together again. So, we were friendly, but I can't say I knew her really well. I'm not on the mommy circuit, you know? Besides, I've only been here since October."

"Right. Thought I recognized the name. You're the new librarian."

Which was how every village resident I'd met had referred to me since the day I had arrived, and would until I left. Or passed away quietly at the reference desk, as my elderly predecessor had done. But O'Donnell seemed satisfied, for the moment at least. He turned back to Joanna's body. I edged closer, straining to hear any activity in the attic. Was Webber there yet? Was anyone else? I was leaning toward the door when O'Donnell's radio chirped. I jumped. He turned and raised an eyebrow.

"Was there something you wanted to tell me, Ms. Hogan? Anything you'd like to discuss?"

I wanted to know what was going on in the attic, but he wasn't going to let me check, and it wasn't in my best interests to have a lengthy chat with him at this point. Someone else would know if they found someone. Helene, certainly.

"Um, no, I'm fine. Really."

He held my gaze for a moment, then nodded. "Good. Go downstairs, Ms. Hogan. You'll find an officer in the main hall. We'll need to talk to you when we're done up here. And please don't discuss this with the rest of the staff."

I fled.

Chapter Two

An hour later I was in the staff room, having been deposited there by a young and nervous uniformed officer. The room was part of the original manor kitchen. Running the length of the building on its lowest level, the old kitchen had been divided in two. The front half, with its enormous fireplace and a row of small, high windows, was now used for book discussions and meetings. And today, for corralling witnesses. Except for me. Apparently, I was the star of the show and so was stashed in the back half. Used by the staff for lunch and breaks, it had been retrofitted with modern kitchen appliances donated by the Friends of the Library. The furnishings were odds and ends from elsewhere in the building, creating a *Food-Network*-meets-the-*Addams-Family* ambience. The only windows were at the back, the largest being the door to the former kitchen garden, permanently fastened shut. I leaned against the frame and kept an eye on the comings and goings. Sequestered I might be, but I was armed with a powerful curiosity and a smart phone, and used both.

I started with O'Donnell and Webber. Neither had a social media presence, which I chalked up to departmental policy. Not surprising, but I'd hoped to find something that would give me some idea of what I was dealing with. I moved on to Joanna. Facebook and Instagram. She didn't tweet. I ran through the Friends of the Library pages, looking for anything that would help me make sense of her death. She was so vivid, her energy endless. It seemed impossible that she was gone.

I was so lost in my thoughts that I jumped when the hall door opened. Mary Alice slipped in, closing the door quietly behind her.

"Anything going on out there?" she asked.

"People coming and going. I don't recognize most of them."

"Well, you wouldn't. I would, but I've been shut up with the rest of the staff next door. If I have to listen to Dory's wild speculations for another minute, I'll scream." Dory Hutchinson was another member of the Circulation staff. She was a lifelong village resident, knew everyone, gossiped freely, and supplemented what legitimate information she had with the products of her vivid imagination. By contrast Mary Alice, who knew almost as many people, listened far more than she talked. She was observant. Both would be good sources of information, though I'd have to take what Dory said with a grain of salt.

"I told Helene you probably hadn't eaten anything," Mary Alice said. "You'll be no good to anyone if you faint."

"I never faint. I'm not the type." I was the type who drank too much and made inappropriate comments. Fainting would be better.

"Neither am I, but you've had a shock."

She handed me a cup of tea liberally laced with milk and sugar. I never took it that way, but it did the trick. After a few sips I was able to eat the snack she put in front of me.

"I left my lunch bag upstairs." The thought of eating anything that had been sitting next to Joanna's body, however briefly, made my stomach roll. Mary Alice nodded.

"I'm not supposed to say anything, but . . . someone was up there. In the attic. Do you know where Millicent was?" I said.

Millicent Ames was our archivist. She'd been a fixture in the library for decades.

Mary Alice raised her eyebrows.

"She was helping me, but it's possible. She wasn't in sight all the time, and she did clear the second floor. But all those stairs that fast at her age? I just don't know. The police arrived in waves, and then herded us all down here. She was one of the last to appear. What do you think happened?"

"It could have been an accident, but I don't think so."

"Something stinks," Mary Alice said shaking her head. "Joanna hadn't been herself."

"And where's Vince Goodhue in all this?" I asked.

"Good question." She was about to say something else, but we heard voices in the hall. By the time the door opened, she was at the sink and I was back at the window.

"You can talk to people individually in here," Helene was saying. "The staff is next door. Greer is here. Mary Alice brought her some lunch."

"Thank you. We can take it from here." O'Donnell said. "Ask the rest of the staff to wait next door. They can go as soon as we're done talking to them." He gave Mary Alice a pointed look. "We'll see you as soon as we're done talking to Ms. Hogan."

"Certainly, Sam," she said, "glad to help if I can." And as she followed Helene out the door, "Remember, she's had quite a shock."

I busied myself making another cup of tea at the little machine on the counter, using the time to collect my thoughts. By the time I turned around, they were seated at the table, notebooks and extra-large Java Joint cups at the ready. Nothing like being half a mile from the only coffee shop in town to insure there was always a cop around when you needed one. No wonder they had gotten here so fast. I fought the urge to make a donut joke. Pleasant and cooperative, but just the facts. That was my plan. Keep it brief. What they asked, or didn't, might be enlightening. I seated myself. First things first.

"So, who did you find in the attic?"

Webber's eyes narrowed. O'Donnell sighed.

"Tell us how you found Mrs. Goodhue. Start from when you decided to go upstairs," he said.

It had been worth a try.

I recited the events of my lunch hour, pausing occasionally to picture the scene in my head. They didn't jump in with any questions. I wound up with my call to Helene.

"So, you knew she was dead when you saw her?"

I shook my head. "She practically landed on me. She was cold when I touched her. I tried to find a pulse. And when I saw the blood . . ." I stopped.

When I saw the blood, I started seeing things I'd only seen in nightmares since Danny died, and I decided someone had killed her. This was not a story I wanted to tell.

O'Donnell tried again. "I know it's tough, the first time you see a body, but please try to focus."

"No," I stared into my tea, seeing the dark stairwell. Joanna. The dark apartment. Danny. Better they heard it from me first.

"Not the first body." I took a sip of my tea, not sure how to begin. "My husband."

Silence.

"My late husband," I added, "obviously."

I gripped my mug, returning O'Donnell's level stare. Out of the corner of my eye, I could see Webber giving me a cool look. Both remained silent.

Do not babble, do not babble, I chanted silently. That's what had gotten me in trouble the last time. I'd wait them out. For a while there was no sound but the ticking of the hideous cuckoo clock on the wall.

O'Donnell and Webber exchanged a look. Then Webber spoke.

"I'm sorry for your loss, ma'am." A brief pause. "How did he die?"

"He interrupted a robbery in our apartment."

"And you found him?"

"Yes."

More silence. Finally, she circled back around.

"Cause of death?"

Here we go.

"Blunt force trauma."

O'Donnell shifted in his chair.

"Blow to the head?"

It wasn't really a question. I could tell by the way he asked. I nodded. "He was struck from behind."

Another image of Danny flashed into my head. Bruising along his jaw. I frowned. That couldn't be right if he'd been hit from behind. He was lying on his back when I found him.

"Like Mrs. Goodhue," Webber said.

That got my attention.

"So, she was, too?" I asked. "Not just a fall?"

Webber flushed. O'Donnell stepped in.

"We haven't determined that," he said. "Jennie?"

Webber flipped some pages in her notebook.

"You lived in New York City, is that correct?"

She was going to check my story.

"To find one dead body, Ms. Hogan, may be regarded as a misfortune; to find two looks like carelessness." Or homicidal tendencies. What would Oscar Wilde have made of my sad little tale? At least it had taken place in his kind of neighborhood.

"Upper East Side," I said. She could look up the precinct herself. Would the neighborhood mean anything to her? Probably not.

"And you know Mrs. Goodhue from there?"

"No," I said. "I met Joanna when she transferred to NYU. I was her RA for a year, as I told you earlier," I added, turning back to Sam O'Donnell. "Are there any other questions I can answer for you about this afternoon?"

"A few," he said. He asked about other staff members, how many people used the roof for lunch, general traffic in the building, and the like. He wound up with the obvious.

"When was the last time you saw Mrs. Goodhue?"

"It was yesterday afternoon. She was using one of the computer stations."

"Was that typical, ma'am? Didn't she have a computer at home?"

Webber looked curious. She probably did everything on her smartphone.

"If she was here with the kids, or on Friends' business, she'd use them. We also have databases that you can't access from home. I think she used some of them for her business. I know she did some research here."

And her browser history would be wiped as soon as she signed off. I wouldn't have thought that would matter to her, but now I wondered. She'd been in more than usual lately.

"What time was she in yesterday?"

"I'm not sure when she arrived." I'd been flying around the reading room, retrieving books and filling in displays, and spotted Joanna in the stacks. She waved and headed toward the computer stations. She caught my eye once or twice, but I was swamped. She was still there when the shift changed at four, engrossed in whatever was on the screen. I had bolted for the quiet of my office.

"She was there at four. I don't know when she left. I didn't see her again, but I didn't go back into the reading room."

"What time did you leave the building?"

"Five. I had a haircut scheduled, and I didn't want to be late."

I gave them the details of my evening. Salon appointment, dinner at the little soup place, and some shoptalk in the bookstore, all in the same plaza. All verifiable, up to when I left the bookstore. I was home alone after that. The worth of my alibi would depend on the time of Joanna's death.

"Thank you, Ms. Hogan," O'Donnell said. "That will be all for now. We may ask you to take a look at the attic tomorrow. You might notice something out of place, something that may explain how Mrs. Goodhue ended up going down the stairs the way she did. You weren't planning any time off? Trips, anything like that?"

"No, I'm not going anywhere," I said. Which was just as well. It's not like the police could keep me here, but I sensed a hastily scheduled vacation would be frowned upon.

I walked to the door, then paused with my hand on the knob.

"Just one more thing," I said, "I was wondering—why didn't her husband notice she was gone?"

My question was answered by silent stares. I stared back.

"Why don't you leave that to us, Ms. Hogan?" O'Donnell said.

I'd had my Colombo moment, so I nodded and left.

Chapter Three

When I arrived at her office, Helene was leaning back in her office chair, eyes closed, cheetah print glasses sliding down her nose. Her short silver hair stuck up in spikes. She'd been running her hands through it, something she only did when agitated. Helene Montague was no one's idea of a stereotypical library director. A fit sixty, she was always both stylishly and impeccably turned out. Having spent many years traveling the globe with her husband, a university professor of some wildly esoteric subject, Helene had a fashion sensibility with an international flair. I suspected it was our mutual love of clothes that had tipped the hiring decision in my favor. My interview had been on a cool September morning. I'd broken out one of the classic designer pieces from my high-paying corporate days. Helene greeted me at the rear door of the manor, introduced herself, and with one quick survey of my black sheath dress and jacket, said without preamble, "Is that Prada?"

This afternoon we had more important things to discuss. Like what they found in the attic. And whether or not she considered me a potential murderer. Equally important, what the board thought of the situation. I knocked gently on the open door. Helene opened her eyes and gave me a small smile.

"Greer. Come in. Have a seat. How did things go with the police?"

"About as well as could be expected." I seated myself in one of the chairs opposite her desk. "I couldn't tell them much. Of course, finding the body puts me at the top of the suspect list, if all the cop shows are to be believed. Unless they found someone labeled "first murderer" lurking in the attic?"

"For better or worse, they did not, and I don't see you as the type to throw a friend down a flight of stairs. Besides, we don't know what happened, and won't for a while yet."

"So now what?"

"We'll keep the library closed for the rest of today and all of tomorrow. Friday is up in the air. The police will know more once they've finished talking to everyone and going over the building. Hopefully, they'll have something definitive by tomorrow. I've informed the board we'll have to play it by ear."

"That must have gone over well. What did Anita say?"

"Essentially, that if I were a better library director dead bodies wouldn't turn up in the library, and if the police were more competent, dead bodies turning up in the library would be dealt with efficiently and our patrons wouldn't be inconvenienced."

I was relieved she hadn't included, "and lunching librarians who find bodies should be suspended without pay until cleared of all wrongdoing." But that could still happen.

"Ah," I said, "that sounds very much in character." Anita Hunzeker chaired the board of trustees. She was petite, so thin she seemed pointy, with an excruciatingly exact haircut. She was never without her signature accessory—a colorful scarf. No matter the weather or activity, the casually draped scarf never moved. It wouldn't dare. Anita had all the people skills of a rabid wombat and was often referred to as "Attila-the-Hunzeker" by the staff.

"Well, she's looking at it from a liability standpoint, not to mention PR. This isn't good no matter what the cause, and she's determined to get a new library building."

"True." Sudden, unexplained death wasn't going to increase public confidence in the library or its board. Murder even less so. Anita was determined that her legacy to the town would be a brand new state-of-the-art, high-tech library building. She was correct that we needed a new building, but there were many village residents who were quite attached to the old manor and who were willing to fight tooth and nail to keep things the way they were. Chief among these was Millicent Ames. The hostility between the two women was palpable. If it had been Anita at the bottom of the stairs I would have known exactly where to look for answers.

"Well," I said, "is there anything you'd like me to do?"

"Go home and get some rest. I'm sending everyone home as soon as they're done with the police. I'll call you once I know what's going on. I need to talk to Sam O'Donnell before I make any plans."

I left Helene, secure in the knowledge that my boss didn't think I was a killer and my job was safe, at least for now. Not only did I not want to be a murder suspect, I needed the paycheck. Danny had been working for a start-up when he died and didn't have life insurance. I'd sold our apartment for enough to pay for grad school and maintain a small emergency fund, but that was it. I didn't live an extravagant lifestyle, but any loss of income, even a brief "administrative leave," would be a problem.

I took a circuitous route back to the library offices, curious as to what the police were doing and where, confident I would hear them before they spotted me. The force was small, and the manor was big. The main floor was quiet. A uniformed officer stood outside the front door with his back to me. The small vestibule was empty, the interior fire doors propped open. Sounds of footsteps and muffled voices drifted down the main staircase. The reading room was strewn from one end to the other with items abandoned when the building was evacuated. Everything was turned off. No sign of police activity, the action was confined to the upper floors.

Nothing to see here, folks.

This morning the main hall was bright and bustling with activity. Now it was dim and hushed, the only illumination provided by jagged shards of light stabbing through the leaded glass window above the front door. I padded down the hall, my reflection moving beneath the rippled surface of the antique mirrors that lined the walls, interspersed with portraits of Ravenscroft ancestors, whose disapproving gazes followed my progress.

My desk was piled with books, copies of Publisher's Weekly, catalogs of upcoming releases, and files. I'd barely been at my desk in the last two days, yet the mess had somehow grown. My organized chaos was disordered. Had the police been through it? No. I was pretty sure they'd need a warrant, even if it was library property. I eyed my jacket and bag. Everything I'd brought today was where I had left it that morning. But things on my desk were not where I'd left them last night. The changes wouldn't be noticeable to anyone but me, but a couple of piles had shifted.

Someone probably just needed to borrow a stapler or something, I thought. I'm overreacting. But my sense of unease grew. Feeling all of eleven years old, I placed some innocuous items—paper clips, a red pen, a bookmark—in places where they'd be moved if someone went through my desk. Then I gathered my belongings and left.

My short trip home was uneventful, but that didn't stop me from looking in my rearview mirror at frequent intervals. By the time I got home, the adrenaline that had fueled me since finding Joanna's body had run out. I changed my clothes and stretched out on the couch, telling myself it was just for a few minutes.

Three hours later I woke up with a scream, heart pounding, gasping for air. It must have only been a dream scream, or my landlord's Frenchie, Pierre would be barking. I sat up, still a little disoriented.

The dream was always the same, but today there was a variation. I was in my apartment in New York, standing over Danny. I had the phone in my hand, our old-fashioned landline that we never got rid of, but I couldn't get a dial tone. My cell was in my tote bag, by the door where I dropped it. I couldn't get it because someone was outside the door, just out of sight, waiting for me to come close enough to grab. That's when I usually woke up.

Today's dream went further. I looked around and saw Joanna sitting at my desk with her back to me. I knew she would help if I could only get her attention. But no matter what I did she wouldn't respond. I couldn't move my feet. I couldn't move at all. I finally tried to scream her name, and woke myself.

I got up and put on some lights, then headed for the kitchen. Comfort food time. I pulled out my laptop to do some more digging while I ate my grilled cheese. Various news sites had developing stories about the body of a woman found in Raven Hill, but the information was sparse. The police were keeping a tight lid on things, which would make the board happy.

I did a more detailed study of Joanna's social media, but found no convenient death threats. Ditto the library page, though Joanna was involved in some heated discussions about the new building proposal. I jotted down the names in those threads. She was also involved in a long debate on the PTA page regarding the message sent to children about healthy food choices if chocolate milk was offered in the cafeteria. Joanna was pro-chocolate. As a child-free city girl, the things suburban parents got upset about mystified me, but I added the names from that thread to my list, and circled the ones that overlapped.

At the end of this exercise, I didn't have anything I thought would motivate a murderer, chocolate milk aside. Midsomer County we were not. Was the fact that it happened in the library related to why Joanna was killed, or was it convenient? Planned or opportunistic? If it was the latter, it must have been someone she knew, or someone with a reason for being there late or after hours. Joanna would have noticed anything out of the ordinary. She noticed everything.

Maybe that was it. She was a detail person. She noticed everything, and she filed it away. She never forgot. If she thought it was important, she never let it go. What had she seen that someone didn't want her to know?

I always thought you'd marry Ian. Her voice whispered through my mind.

So did I, Joanna, at least for a little while. That mad, hot love affair my senior year had ended badly.

Ian wasn't a subject I wanted to revisit, but denial and avoidance were beginning to fail me. The dreams had started after Christmas, the first I'd spent at home since Danny died. Seeing everyone from the neighborhood where we grew up, Danny's parents at midnight Mass—I thought I was keeping it together. Then my mother started nagging me about all the stuff I had stored in the basement.

"You've got to go through all those boxes eventually, Greer. You can't avoid it forever."

Watch me, Mom.

I didn't want to open those boxes full of tangible reminders of my old life, but the box I really wanted to keep a lid on was the one in my head, where I'd stored the memories of Ian, and of Danny, the murder, and the trial. Everything that went on in the months before I left New York for Philadelphia and graduate school. The first morning I woke up in my new apartment, in a city where no one knew me, I felt a guilty, giddy sense of freedom, and decided I would never think about the whole ugly mess again. It was a new life, a new me.

Or so I thought.

I shut the laptop and went to the kitchen. Sherlock had his opium pipe; I had my martinis. I was a fan of the traditional five-to-one ratio, stirred, with a twist, and as ice-cold as I could make it without actually chilling the gin. By the time I gently twisted the lemon rind over the glass and dropped it in, the familiar soothing ritual had calmed me down.

I moved out onto the porch, leaving the lights off to enjoy the peaceful twilight. I could make out the manor roofline through the trees, a dim glow in the top story. The police were still there.

Three years since that scene in the living room. The end of my enviable life in Manhattan. The perfect marriage to the handsome boy from my old neighborhood, the one I met in high school and reconnected with after college. He was in finance at what turned out to be a lucrative start-up. Or would have been lucrative, if he'd lived through the IPO. I had a six-figure job in marketing at a prestige brand cosmetics company. We shared a light-filled two-bedroom apartment on the East side. Active social life.

I'd been bored insensible.

It's not that I didn't love Danny. I did, but he had always loved me more. What seemed like a feature turned into a bug. It's a great responsibility, being loved like that. Danny was busy and distracted with the new venture. My job had gotten stale. I needed a change. I needed something. Ian Cameron was unfinished business. I hadn't seen him in fifteen years. In my defense, Danny was supposed to be with me that night. But he wasn't, Ian was, and there was an open bar. An empty conference room. A closed door. An unanswered question.

"Haven't you ever thought about it, Greer? What you would do if we were both free?"

Only twice. Whenever Ian got divorced. And the third time on the long taxi ride home. Right up until I walked in the door and found my husband dead.

It's not like I made it happen. I didn't wish it, even for a second. I didn't.

A fox barked. The short, sharp yips snapped me back. I blinked into the darkness, aware of the silence of the nearby woods. The nocturnal creatures had gone quiet. I heard the rhythmic footfalls of an approaching jogger. Not uncommon at this time of year, but unusual on this little dead-end street. I sank back into the deep shadows of the porch. Word would be out by now, and I didn't want to talk to anyone. The jogger paused, lingering at the edge of the woods. Lost? I thought of slipping to the corner and peeking around, but then I heard the crunch of gravel. The driveway and path leading to the stairs up my apartment. A rattle as someone pushed at the gate.

Pierre began to bark furiously downstairs. No one he knew, then. I stayed still. Pierre's barking became intermittent. I heard the sound of someone jogging again, and then that faded as whoever it was rounded the corner toward Main Street. I let out a long breath. The night noises started again. Maybe I was paranoid. But I remained in the shadows.

Three years, I thought again. Three years I'd played the part. No one knew about me and Ian but me and Ian, and he wasn't talking. But now a new set of cops would be looking into Danny's murder. A woman I'd known and liked was dead. The job I enjoyed and the paycheck I needed were threatened. My nightmares were getting worse. I couldn't even have a quiet drink on my own porch without feeling hunted. The new life I'd created and liked was being upended, and I was being forced to take a good, hard look at the old one.

For all of that, someone would have to pay.

Chapter Four

❦

Noon the next day found me back at the library. An early morning phone call from Helene informed me there would be a midday staff meeting, and I should plan to stick around in case the police had additional questions. We would reopen the following day on our usual schedule.

I sat with the rest of the staff in what we called the community meeting room. This was on the second floor at the back of the building, directly over the offices. At the moment we were all seated around some folding tables that had been pushed together to form a large circle. Anita was there, flanked by Helene and Sam O'Donnell. I spotted Officer Webber by the door, half hidden by a coatrack. She leaned against the wall, scanning the crowd. I turned my attention to Anita.

"I'm sure many of you are wondering why I've asked you here today," she began. If the woman had any sense of irony, I'd swear she used that line on purpose. I stole a glance at Mary Alice. She rolled her eyes.

"Unfortunately," Anita continued, "yesterday afternoon an employee discovered the body of Joanna Goodhue on one of the upstairs landings." Anita's phrasing and delivery made it unclear what she found most unfortunate—the fact that Joanna was dead or that I'd had the temerity to discover her body on library premises.

"Most of you know Joanna through her work with the Friends. She was also active on the new building exploratory committee, and in various other village organizations. She was a great supporter of the library," here Anita's voice softened, "and she will be greatly missed."

But not by everyone, I thought, discreetly evaluating the expressions of the staff. They all looked appropriately distressed. Webber was looking at me.

"I heard she tripped and fell down those stairs and broke her neck." Dory Hutchinson piped up. She fixed Anita with a bright-eyed stare over her omnipresent knitting. "I've always said those stairways are dangerous—too dark, and most without railings." Her needles clicked as she spoke. "I also heard that maybe somebody pushed her."

That was Dory, never hesitating to lob a conversational hand grenade into the middle of any gathering.

"Dory," Helene began but Anita beat her to it.

"This building conforms to all county codes," she snapped, nostrils flaring. "I would be happy to speak with you privately about any safety concerns you may have. In the interim, I would like us all to refrain from gossiping about Joanna's unfortunate accident. Now," she went on, "Lieutenant O'Donnell will bring you up-to-date on the police investigation, which will conclude shortly."

O'Donnell's eyebrows went up. Apparently, this time frame was news to him. Anita sailed on. "The board appreciates the cooperation you have shown the sheriff's department thus far. With few exceptions," she eyed me with disapproval, "I don't think they will need to bother you further. Lieutenant?"

O'Donnell stood and launched into standard police-speak about the deceased, the incident, the premises, and so on. He was informal about it, not surprising given that he was on a first name basis with half the people in the room. He wound up by stating that since autopsy results were pending, the cause of death was still undetermined. While it was possible Joanna had died of injuries sustained in a fall, he stated the police would continue to investigate as they would with any unattended death. He then requested that all employees who were in the building between one o'clock on Tuesday and one o'clock on Wednesday make themselves available after the meeting. He thanked us all and left. Officer Webber detached herself from the coatrack and followed.

"Well," Anita said, "I'm sure we would all like to put this tragic accident behind us, so as long as I'm here I might as well update you on what was discussed at the last board meeting." And off she went, as though nothing untoward had happened. The woman was a force of nature. No wonder she ran every committee in town. The mind boggled at what she might accomplish if anyone actually *liked* her.

When Anita finished, Helene went over the logistics of the library reopening, and we dispersed. I headed to the kitchen, as did most staff members who would be staying. It was nearly lunchtime, and I had learned during my short tenure that the staff of the Raven Hill Library put almost as much emphasis on food as they did on books. There was no program not accompanied by refreshments and no book sale without a bake sale. It was my best opportunity to find out who knew what. I'd toss out a little bait and do some fishing.

Dory was already holding court at the coffee machine.

"Did you notice Sam never said Joanna died because of an accident," she said. "He never said *accident*, he only said injuries sustained in a *fall*. I think he knows something."

"Oh, for Heaven's sake, Dory!" Mary Alice said. "I should certainly hope he knows something. He's the investigating officer. If he doesn't know quite a bit by now, he needs to hang up his badge. The police department had people here half the night."

Dory was unfazed. "Well, I think the whole thing is suspicious. If they don't think she was murdered, why are they spending so much time here, asking questions and trying to figure out where everyone was? Alibis, that's what they're after. And," a note of triumph entered her voice, "they had people guarding the place all night. I wouldn't be surprised if we saw the state police if this goes on much longer."

How Dory knew about the guard was a question mark, but I was going to trust her sources on this one. It made sense. Raven Hill didn't have its own police department. We shared a force with several other towns near the

Helderberg Mountains. Not a large population, but a lot of ground to cover. The state police had more resources and more experience with violent crime. O'Donnell didn't seem the type to get caught up in a turf war with another law enforcement agency. He'd call in help as needed. Maybe this would be wrapped up quickly. That would be good for me, as long as they got it right. I'd do my part to make sure they didn't waste time looking in the wrong direction. At me, for example.

"But why would anyone want to murder Mrs. Goodhue?" This from Anne Marie, a library school student intern who was with us for a semester. If this was murder, we might never see another.

"Well," said Dory, clearly enjoying herself, "I really don't like to say. But there were plenty of people she rubbed the wrong way with her opinions about how things should be done in the village. Particularly about the new library." She cut her eyes toward Millicent Ames, who had joined us and was fixing herself a cup of tea. Fortunately, Millicent had her back to the room, and Anne Marie spoke to me before Dory could go on.

"Didn't you find her, Greer? That must have been creepy. I would have fainted."

"I never faint," I said. "I'm not the type."

"So, what do you think happened?" Dory asked me. "You must have a theory, Greer. You found her, and the two of you were friends."

Time to redirect, and maybe get an answer to a nagging question.

"I really don't know what to think," I said, which was true. "Though I do wonder . . ." I paused, as if I was hesitant to say what was on my mind, and waited until I had everyone's attention.

"I do wonder why Vince didn't come looking for her. Didn't he notice she wasn't home?"

I could almost hear mental gears shifting as the group thought about this. Dory was the first to speak.

"Maybe he didn't want to leave the girls?" Dory sounded doubtful. "Though he could have called someone."

"The girls are with their grandparents this week," Anne Marie said. "Sophie, the younger one, told me at story hour. But she didn't say why."

"If you want to know what I think," Dory began, but at that moment the door opened. Officer Jennie Webber stepped in. The room fell silent. Millicent spoke first.

"Good afternoon, Officer Webber. Can we be of some assistance?" Millicent had the kind of low, cultured voice that brought to mind silver tea services and carefully cultivated rose gardens. Her tone, while pleasant and correct, implied that it was a lucky police officer indeed who received aid of any sort from Millicent, and by extension, anyone else in the room.

"Good afternoon, ma'am," Officer Webber replied. "I was hoping to find you here. If you could spare a few minutes this afternoon, I have some questions about the archives. But first I need to spend some time with Ms. Hogan."

"Of course." Millicent inclined her head regally. "You'll find me at my desk." She glided past Webber and swept out.

"Lieutenant O'Donnell has a few more questions for everyone. Please wait here for him," she said to the group and then turned to me. "Ms. Hogan? Please come with me."

Once the door closed behind us, she turned to me and said, "We'd like you to take a look at the attic and the stairs where you found Mrs. Goodhue. You're familiar with them—we're hoping you might notice something that would explain how she ended up going down the stairs."

Again, the word "fall" did not come into play. Did she fall or was she pushed? Inevitably, she was pushed. That was my theory, anyway. It was the little things that didn't jibe. The light switch. The odd assortment of things at the top of the stairs. It looked like a stage set, the things that were there and the things that weren't.

I was suddenly back in my apartment in New York, doing the post-police clean-up and inventory. The things that were taken, and the things that weren't. It didn't make sense. But I wanted to be done and gone, and the friends helping me didn't seem to notice.

"Ma'am?" Officer Webber was looking at me.

"Yes, of course. I'll do what I can. Do you want to go up the back way?"

"Whatever you did yesterday. I'd like you to retrace your steps. I understand you often go up to the roof to eat your lunch?"

"Depending on the weather. It's nice to get outside, out of the building for a bit." I headed toward the back stairway as we spoke. It went from outside the kitchen to behind

Helene's office on the main floor, twisted back on itself and ended behind the archives on the second floor. When I reached the second floor, I crossed the hallway and started up another set of stairs that began behind the community meeting room.

"Isn't there another way up from this floor?" Officer Webber asked.

She already knew this. "Yes, there is. The way you went yesterday—through the archives."

"I'm just wondering why the stairs don't connect. And why you used this one, ma'am."

What was she after? And what was all this "ma'am" business? Professional courtesy, I guessed, but it made me feel elderly. It's not like I was that much older than she was. Maybe five years. I scanned her face. All right, maybe ten. But still. I turned back to the stairs.

"I'm not sure why the stairs don't connect. This floor has been renovated to create larger rooms. The servants' stairs stop and start at odd places up here. And I use this stairway because Millicent doesn't like people trooping through her archives, particularly if they're carrying food or drinks. We all use this stairway."

"Mrs. Ames was always fussy. Even when she was only in charge of the raven room." Officer Webber said.

The raven room was what kids called Horatio Raven-scroft's study. I loved that room. It was a period piece, set up exactly as it was in the time of old Horatio, gentleman farmer and collector of rare books and Poe memorabilia. The smell of old books, leather, and furniture polish soothed me every time I stepped into it. Sometimes I even got a whiff of pipe smoke. If the reading room was the heart of the manor, the octagonal study was its brain, the bookshelves and dim recesses holding esoteric knowledge and the collective consciousness of the manor. An enormous stuffed raven presided over the room. The thing was a marvel of taxidermy. Glossy, black, and bright-eyed, it always seemed to be looking at you. Generations of local children grew up under its watchful eye. You couldn't walk into the library without seeing the raven.

"I wasn't aware you were a native of Raven Hill," I said to her as we reached the landing. "I don't think I've ever seen you in the library."

"I'm not, but I spent summers here with my grandparents when I was a kid."

"What brought you back?"

She took a second before answering.

"Family. And what brought you here, Ms. Hogan? Quite a change from what you're used to."

"Paycheck. I left the city for grad school. But you already know that." I wanted to see how much digging she had done. Her face remained impassive. "Anyway, it seemed like a nice place. I thought it would be peaceful. Had I but known." I trailed off. Still no expression. The Mary Roberts Rinehart reference was clearly lost on her.

The door to the attic stairs was closed as it had been yesterday. I stood before it, remembering how I'd yanked it open. I hesitated, knowing there would be nothing on the other side this time, but still fighting a sense of dread.

"It's been cleaned up," Jennie Webber said. She moved next to me as I reached for the knob and opened the door. It swung out soundlessly. I looked up the dark passage. Once again, nothing but murky shadows until very near the top, and then flickering daylight.

"The light was off yesterday, too," I said. "I thought that was odd."

"Why is that, Ms. Hogan?"

"She would have needed it to go up. Unless she went up when the sun was coming straight in the window. I don't think that's possible if I saw her in the reading room at four. What was the time of death?"

"We have to wait for the autopsy. How late could she go up these stairs without turning on a light?"

Wait indeed. I'd put money on the police having a best guess on the time of death before Joanna's body left the building. But after her slip yesterday, Webber was giving away nothing.

"I'm not sure at this time of year. I'm usually not up here much later than one."

I flicked the light switch and climbed into the attic. In front of me was a large window with an old-fashioned shade, both of which were usually closed. Today the shade was only halfway down. The police must have needed the light. To the right was a wall of floor to ceiling bookshelves. The heavy wooden shelves were on sturdy brackets and were usually stacked with odds and ends collected throughout the year for the Friends' annual jumble sale. Today a shelf was missing. I studied what remained and recognized the doll and top I had seen yesterday as well as other familiar items. There was a small embroidered footstool on the floor next to the shelves that had never been there before. It was faded and threadbare, the carved wood frame worn. It must have come from another part of the attic. The doll and the spinning top must have, too, I decided as I surveyed the items on the shelves again. They were the only things that looked like they were from a previous era. Everything else fit the Friends' "current and gently used" request. So, why were they there? I turned and took a few steps into the room.

The attic was a set of interconnecting rooms filled with the detritus of several generations of Ravenscrofts. Anything of known value or historic interest was downstairs, but Millicent still occasionally unearthed something worth cleaning and adding to the local history collection. She had ceded space to the Friends grudgingly, roping off the sections that still contained Ravenscroft possessions. Right now, I was interested in things that looked out of place. As I stared into the dim room, I heard a window open behind me. I raised an eyebrow at Webber.

"It was open yesterday," she said, "Is that typical?"

"No. Not only has it been raining for weeks, Millicent would have a fit at the very thought of sunlight or bugs or damp air. She sees the attic as an extension of the archives."

Officer Webber looked around. "Looks like the stuff we cleaned out of my grandparents' barn."

"Well, she has found a few things of importance, and the terms of Horatio Ravenscroft's will make it hard to get rid of anything related to the manor."

"So, does anything seem out of place?"

I gestured to the shelves.

"The footstool, two of the toys. They don't go with everything else. They had to have come from another part of the attic."

She studied the assortment.

"I see what you mean. Couldn't someone have just put them in the wrong place?"

"Unlikely. The Friends want to stay in Millicent's good graces, so they're pretty careful. Maybe someone put them there to draw Joanna's attention? She'd climb up to get them to put them back. It's one way to make sure she'd be at the top of the stairs."

Webber raised her eyebrows but she didn't argue.

I walked farther back into the attic, following a path cleared through all the junk. I swung left and entered a short hall connecting the two sides of the house on this floor. To my left were casement windows, which gave access to the small roof deck we called the terrace. It had been added by a Ravenscroft with a passion for astronomy. Not easy to access, but the view was spectacular. No way to get to it from the outside unless you were Spiderman, so no chance someone had gotten in that way.

Ahead was another doorway to a room similar to the one we had just left, and immediately off that were the stairs from the archives. I walked the full length of the hall and peered into the gloomy interior of the next room. All the windows were shut, their shades drawn. The archive stairway was equally dark, though I could see the faint outline of the door at the bottom. I'd done some poking around up here when I first started, looking under dust sheets and into old trunks, but the light was poor and there wasn't anything of interest. I hadn't paid much attention since.

"Anything else out of place?" Webber asked.

"It's hard to tell, but other than the area at the top of the stairs, everything seems to be just as it was the last time I was here."

"When was that?"

"Couple of weeks ago. Someone had left a box of donations outside before we opened. Sports equipment." I looked around and pointed. "There."

There was a sharp crack from the front room. We both jumped, and Webber pushed past me and eased carefully into the doorway. She peered around the corner. The cracking noise repeated. I had the satisfaction of seeing her flinch. Not so unflappable after all.

"It's the window shade," she said as she moved into the next room. I was conscious of a slight draft through the hall. Odd. It felt like something had opened behind me. I looked, but all the windows I could see were still shut. I followed Webber, rounding the corner as she reached for the sash. Another gust of wind set the shade flapping, and again I felt the draft. The air moved past me, weaving through the room, lifting the doll's hair ribbon, gently stirring papers, and setting a tiny rocking horse into motion. The horse nodded at me, the light winking off its bright glass eyes as it rocked gently. I heard the window close, and everything was once again still.

Cross-ventilation. Somewhere else in the attic, a door or window had been opened. The archives? Too far, I thought. It must be something closer. I started toward Webber. I didn't want to call out and alert anyone who might be in the attic with us. The floor creaked beneath my foot. I stopped, lifted my foot and set it down again. Creak. This was the noise I had heard yesterday. I was sure. Then another creak, faint, from behind me, and a stirring of air like a slow exhalation of breath. I felt a crawling sensation on the back of my neck.

I turned my head and took a brief look over my shoulder.

Nothing.

The window rattled. Officer Webber was playing with the shade.

"This must be what you heard yesterday" she said, moving the shade back and forth. She caught my eye. "Wouldn't you say?"

"No," I said. "Listen."

I moved foot and shifted my weight. The floor creaked.

"See?" I said. "Come over. You can hear it better."

She gave me a puzzled look, but came closer.

"Something opened, then shut. Back there." I jerked my head. "Didn't you feel the air movement?"

She shook her head, then looked back toward the window. With the breeze from outside, she probably wouldn't have noticed anything. Webber must have reached the same conclusion, because she turned sideways and slid past me. She moved like a cat, not making a sound. She took up position a few feet away, back to the wall, where all the rooms intersected. She did a quick scan, and then looked back at me.

"Other than the light and the window, does anything else seem strange to you, Ms. Hogan?"

"Where's the missing shelf?"

She debated with herself. Her usually impassive face tightened in every feature. I guess she decided she would get better information from me if she offered some herself.

"Forensics. We're examining the possibility it fell and hit her."

"Or she reached for something, lost her balance, grabbed the shelf, and it came down on her."

Another internal debate. "That's one theory."

I rolled my eyes.

"Don't you think this all looks a bit staged? There were things on that shelf that shouldn't have been there. I'd put money on it." I kept my voice pitched low, conscious that somewhere else in the dark attic, someone might be listening.

"You're very sure this is a crime, Ms. Hogan. Why is that?" Her voice was just as low, and she did another quick scan.

Because someone went through my desk.

Because of the dog that barked in the night.

Because I feel like we're being watched.

And because the manor doesn't feel right.

She would think I was nuts. Or making it up. But I did have something a little more solid.

"Joanna noticed things. She never forgot a detail. She was here more than usual, lately. She didn't seem herself. Mary Alice thinks so, too."

"What do you think she noticed that might have gotten her killed?"

"I have no idea."

It was true, and I didn't want the police or anyone else to think otherwise. But I intended to find out.

"Well, if you think of anything else, please call immediately. Anytime. I've added my cell number." She handed me her card. I stuffed it in my pocket.

"That'll be all for now, Ms. Hogan." Her attention had gone back to attic. She was practically sniffing the air.

I was being dismissed.

I left Webber on her own. Not regulation, investigating on your own. She wasn't the rules girl I pegged her for. We might have something in common after all. That could be useful. Maybe she'd find whoever had been listening to us in the attic, because I had no doubt someone was. Millicent was the most likely suspect, both yesterday and today. Based on timing and the direction the draft had come from, though, she was not a sure thing. Which meant that someone else was moving around undetected.

It was time to hunt down the manor floorplans.

Chapter Five

~

I considered my options while making my way back to the
main floor. The police might be playing along with Anita's
accident story for now, but they were looking for a killer, and
I was still on the suspect list. The person who finds the body
usually is, especially if that person has found a body before.
My movements after I'd left the library that night were easily
traced, but I still didn't know what time Joanna had died. My
landlord might be able to vouch for what time I got home, but
I didn't know how much weight that would carry. Until the
killer was found, I'd be in for some intense scrutiny.

During the interview process I had told Helene and the
board that my husband had been killed during a burglary
gone bad, and that's what had prompted my career change
and move. Any conversation that begins, "My husband was
murdered, and then . . ." is awkward at best. I gave a brief,
subdued recital of facts and the subject was dropped. Since
being involved in two murders couldn't be good for anyone's career prospects, I wanted it to stay dropped. So, a
two-pronged plan. Diversion and detection.

I found Mary Alice behind the Circulation desk, hip deep in returns and checking in books with practiced efficiency. Come murder, mayhem, hell or high water, the book drop must be emptied.

"Need a hand?" I asked.

"Sure. If you could get through that pile right there, and shelve the new books, it would be a big help. Helene told the pages not to come in today. I can't blame her, but without them we have no one to shelve."

Nearly all of the grunt work in our library was handled by the pages, mostly high school students starting out in the workforce. They shelved books, fetched things from the far reaches of the building, and tidied up before we closed. Most were regular library users since their story hour days. I could understand why Helene didn't want them in the middle of the police investigation, but it did throw a lot of work back on the rest of the staff. On the other hand, it gave me a reason to be in places I usually wasn't. And when they returned, it would be worth checking to see if they had noticed anything unusual in the days leading up to Joanna's death.

"So, did the police have any more questions for you?" I asked Mary Alice.

"Sam ran me through the whole sequence of events yesterday, from your phone call to their arrival. He asked me about the previous day, too, but I couldn't tell him much. We were swamped. All that sunshine. It's been such a rainy spring, and it looks like we're getting back to it. Anyway, I didn't really have anything tangible to tell him."

"Do you have something intangible in mind?"

"Well, it's what I started to tell you yesterday. I'm usually here on the night the Friends meet, and they've been meeting more often the closer we get to the sale. In the last couple of months there's been something strange in the whole dynamic. A kind of tension I've never seen before. Some odd pairs with their heads together before or after the meeting."

"Who?

"Joanna and Felicity for one. That attorney who just joined—Julia something-or-other. The Barrett woman. Different combinations. Something's off, but I just can't put my finger on it. So, I couldn't say anything to Sam. I don't want the police to think I'm imagining things."

Join the club.

Mary Alice sighed and shook her head.

"Did you learn anything from Jennie Webber?" she asked.

"She told me next to nothing. She's cool, closemouthed, and seems to suspect the worst of everybody."

"Well, I guess two tours in Iraq will do that to a person. Too bad. She was always such a nice, helpful little girl." Anne Marie approached the desk and Mary Alice stepped away to speak to her. I continued to clear books. So, Jennie Webber had been a soldier. That explained a few things— the detached demeanor, the tendency to go from zero to red alert in the space of seconds. I still didn't like her, and based on her response to me, the feeling was mutual. She had immediately cast me in the role of first murderer. I tried to picture her as a little girl, the blue eyes more trusting, the ash blond hair in pigtails, but I couldn't get there.

Mary Alice reappeared and we continued to work. I would have liked to hear her theories on Joanna's death, but other staff members were coming in and out of the reading room. I saw Webber and O'Donnell go by in the main hall at separate times, but couldn't tell where they were headed. Everyone was buzzing about the investigation. Some discreet eavesdropping was in order. I finished checking the books in front of me and loaded the newer releases onto a cart. As I pushed it toward the stacks, Helene drifted over.

"Why don't you let me do that, Greer? I feel like I've been at my desk for days."

Foiled. I relinquished the cart. I considered asking Helene if she knew where I could find a comprehensive set of manor floorplans, but I couldn't come up with a reasonable excuse for needing them. There were a few places I could check first.

With no excuse to linger, I went back to the offices. I stood in front of my little cubicle and studied the mess. None of my strategically placed items had been disturbed. Still convinced someone had rifled through my desk between the time I left on Tuesday and when I packed up to go on Wednesday, I tried to create some order. Something missing might be significant. Something added less so, as bags of donations and books recalled for weeding were dropped off as they came in, but it was worth taking a look.

I did a Post-it purge and turned to my files. I was sorting through articles and e-mails on upcoming programs when I came across a folded note handwritten with a

Sharpie on yellow legal paper. It was clipped to an e-mail dated three days earlier. I smoothed out the paper and read:

Hi Greer!

Thanks for the book list—this is <u>exactly</u> what I was looking for! The anti-princess project has begun! I decided to buy some of these for the girls, but I'm having them sent to you here at the library. I didn't think you'd mind—I want them to be a surprise. There's some other stuff going on related to what we talked about, and I need your help with some research. I know I can trust you to be discreet. I'll fill you in when I see you.

Thanks again!
Joanna

The e-mail was a booklist I had sent to Joanna on Monday morning. Several items had been highlighted. She'd asked for books for her daughters that featured girls who accomplished more than simply catching Prince Charming. Joanna had come in late one night the previous week, cheeks flushed, eyes bright, radiating righteous indignation. She marched up to the reference desk and promptly launched into a diatribe against fairy tales, kids' movies in general and Disney in particular, the prevalence of purple, pink, and sparkle in little girls' clothing, and marketing aimed at children. She wound up with a brief thanks for Hermione Granger, "a smart, competent character the girls can grow up with," and bemoaned the fact that it would be years before her kids were ready for Katniss Everdeen.

Once Joanna was on a roll, there was no stopping her. I waited for her to wind down. Once I could get a word in, I agreed with her about Hermione and Katniss and asked how I could help.

"I need some books for the girls, as many as you can find, about girls who actually DO something. Save their village from a dragon, start a business, solve crimes, stand up to bullies, stuff like that. None of this Prince Charming nonsense."

This was going to be no small task. I wasn't a children's librarian, so my knowledge of the literature was limited. My personal favorite, *Fancy Nancy*, was clearly not going to cut it. *The Paper Bag Princess* would work, but it was all I could think of and I wasn't going to be able to pull a book list out of the air in the twenty minutes I had until we closed.

"Hmm," I said, "that's interesting. I don't get a lot of requests like this, but I'm sure I can find some things for you." This was librarian speak for "I've got nothing."

"I have a few ideas," I said, "but I'd like to check with Jilly." Jilly was our Youth Services librarian. She was a walking encyclopedia of children's literature. I smiled at Joanna. "We can look for a couple of things tonight, and I'll get you a more extensive list in a few days."

We chatted as we moved through the stacks. I tried to remember our conversation. Had she said anything significant? I didn't think so, but she surprised me at the end. She thanked me for my help, and said she didn't want her daughters to ever put their dreams on hold for a man. Odd, because I was sure she hadn't. If she had her way, her girls wouldn't either.

Except she wouldn't have her way, because she was dead.

Who would save Sophie and Olivia from Prince Charming now?

I always thought you'd marry Ian, and go off and have all kinds of adventures.

Joanna's voice again. Well, I hadn't married Prince Charming. I'd married Danny, the best and truest friend I'd ever had. Now both Danny and Joanna were dead. Last night had brought another round of nightmares. The lid I'd kept on my emotions was being blown off with a vengeance. Grief and guilt were there, but the overwhelming feeling was rage. I was irrationally angry at Danny and Joanna for being dead, and livid at their killers. What could merit such a thing? Though if I were honest, at that moment I could have killed someone myself.

I put aside thoughts of Danny. Joanna was my immediate concern. I would miss her. We were unlikely friends from the beginning. I was the cool, detached New Yorker, a senior serving as RA to a bunch of transfer students. She was a sophomore from the western part of the state, full of ideals and energy. But we both had a fondness for the underdog and a willingness to bend the rules in the interests of justice. She talked me into helping with various projects, like getting donations for a West Village food pantry that served out-of-work actors, AIDS patients, and the elderly. We lost touch when I graduated, but she was kind to me when I first arrived in Raven Hill, inviting me for coffee and introducing me to people. We fell into an easy, casual friendship again, sharing laughs about village life, our outsider sensibility setting us apart. She could be a maniac, but she was a principled, funny maniac.

Had her latest crusade killed her?

What was that crusade? She had a lot of irons in the fire at any given moment. I had no idea what she might have wanted my help with. Joanna had majored in journalism, she'd been in the news business, and she was no slouch when it came to research. Why did she need me?

"I need your clever, twisty mind, Greer."

Danny's voice intruded, our last real conversation playing back in my head.

"Why do you need my help, Dan? You know that business better than I do."

"I'm missing something. There's something off and I can't see it. You will. It's not in the numbers, it's in the people, I think. You watch for a little while and you make all these crazy connections and suddenly they make sense. Please, Greer."

"All right, all right. Fine. But not now, I've gotta go. Later, maybe after dinner."

After dinner was too late for Danny. And I had raced out the last time I saw Joanna, too.

My eyes started to well up. I've always thought tears were the only thing standing between me and homicidal mania. When I was mad enough, I cried. But this was not productive. I unclenched my fists and started looking for tissues. When I felt a hand touch my shoulder, I nearly levitated right out of my seat. I slid a folder over Joanna's note and twirled around in my chair.

"I'm sorry," Jilly said, "I didn't mean to startle you."

She held out a box of tissues. I took a handful. My nose was dripping.

"It's all right. I'm being silly."

"No, you're not. We're all on edge. And you and Joanna were friendly." She sat at her desk and swiveled around to face me.

"This is awful," she said.

"I know. I was just thinking of her kids."

"I feel terrible for them. And as petty as it sounds, I feel terrible for all of us, too."

"You mean the library staff?"

"Yep. Everyone is upset, and a little afraid. We're all toeing the party line on Anita's accident theory, but no one truly believes it. We'll be inundated with people tomorrow, and probably all weekend. Morbid curiosity. And I've already gotten seven e-mails asking for recommendations for books on bereavement for children."

"Oh, great. I hadn't thought of that. Do we have many?"

"Not enough. I'm going to pull together what we've got and request anything else I can find in the system. I'd like to give Vince Goodhue first dibs, but I'm not sure how to broach the subject with him. He used to drop the girls at programs when Joanna was working, but he never stayed or chatted."

Too busy and important.

"Maybe one of the other parents?"

"That's what I'm thinking. The Prentisses, probably. He and Matthew Prentiss have known each other for ages, and they're in the Road Runners Club. Though truth be told, I've actually seen him more often with Felicity. I think those two have known each other just as long. All of them grew up here. I'll figure something out. Vince might not be interested, but I feel I should try."

She pulled a reference book off her desk.

"Will you be all right?"

"I'm fine. Just a bad moment. But thanks for checking."

I turned to my desk. Picking up Joanna's note, I scanned the contents again. A fine, upstanding citizen would undoubtedly hand it over to the police, just in case the "stuff" she referred to had something to do with her death. I was not a fine, upstanding citizen. The note was vague. Not a lead the police were likely to pursue, unless they pursued it right back to me thanks to Joanna's "what we discussed" and her trust in my discretion. Since I had no idea what she meant, it would only be a distraction for them and an irritation for me. No. Better to hold on to it, produce it later if the situation warranted, and claim I had just discovered it.

Now to find a place to stash it, near at hand but out of sight. I paper clipped the note behind the book list and folded the two together, list facing out. Eyeing the tickler file on the top of my desk, I chose a folder labeled "Information Literacy—Best Practices" as most likely to remain unmolested and popped in the little packet I'd made. I pushed it all to the back corner of my desk.

I stood back and studied my handiwork. I murmured, "Must have gotten put into the wrong file," and turned my attention to the rest of the mess.

I ran through my suspect list as I sorted through papers. Usually the first person suspected was the husband. Vince Goodhue was a native of Raven Hill, a local boy who made good, married well, and came back to raise a family. In my few interactions with him, I pegged him as a supercilious twit, the type who "watched films" while those of us less evolved merely went to the movies. But that didn't make him a murderer. Joanna's death meant he'd be raising two little girls alone. She helped him run his business, a small film production company, though she had a full-time gig as a producer for the local 24-hour news station. Between work and the kids, he'd have his hands full. How old were they? Around six and four, I thought. I couldn't rule Vince out, though. The kids were with their grandparents the night of the murder, according to Anne Marie. Of course, it would help if I knew what time Joanna had died.

I moved on to a stack of Publisher's Weekly. Dory had implied there were plenty of people who weren't too wild about Joanna, and though she did tend to exaggerate, there was truth to her statement. Like me, Joanna was a newcomer to the Village of Raven Hill. Unlike me, she hadn't bothered to hide the fact that she found some of its customs more antiquated than quaint. From the PTA to the library building committee, she made her presence felt. But had she angered anyone enough to inspire a shove down a flight of stairs?

That brought me to Millicent, who had my vote for most likely eavesdropper. She and Joanna had been on opposite sides of the new library issue, but their paths didn't cross elsewhere that I knew of, and I'd sensed no personal animosity between them. I also couldn't see Millicent resorting to physical violence. She was more the poisoned petit four type. Of course, I would have said listening in on other people's conversations was beneath her, too, but knowledge is power.

I considered that. Joanna was in the news business. There was always the possibility this was related to her work, though from what I understood she was more involved in production than investigation. Still, she was in a fiercely competitive business, full of people with big egos and a strong sense of entitlement. Professional rivalry? Was she in a position to fire anyone?

What about a love triangle? Was there another man? Could Vince have a little something going on? It seemed like I'd heard something. What had Jilly said? Vince and Felicity?

I grabbed the PW's I was done with and headed for the door. I wanted a look at the collection of Raven Hill yearbooks in the local history collection. While I was there, I could take a look at what we had on the manor's history. If there were any old architectural drawings, they'd be there or in the archives. The staff mailboxes were a good vantage point—I could see who was where and choose my moment. I wasn't ready to share my half-formed theories.

I arrived at the vestibule outside the director's office without encountering anyone. Helene was not at her desk.

I sorted the magazines into various slots as I reconnoitered. The lights near Circulation were on, and I could hear voices from the same direction. The back of the reading room was dark and quiet, only the natural light that came through the windows spilled out into the hallway. Perfect.

I slipped across the hall and paused in the rear entry to the reading room. The voices were clearer now. I craned my neck and spotted Helene with officers O'Donnell and Webber near Circulation. Helene and O'Donnell had their backs to me but Webber had a clear view up the center of the room and was dividing her attention between the conversation and regular scans of her surroundings.

Blast the woman.

The local history collection was in the far corner of the room. I eyed the distance and the arrangement of shelving units and spin racks and decided I could get there unnoticed if I was careful. The only wild card was the ancient wood floor. On some days it was sturdy and silent beneath the worn Oriental carpets covering it, and on others the tap of a toe or a dropped book would elicit a screech of protest. I'd have to risk it.

I flattened my hand against the door frame and slid into the room. I slithered along like the Grinch stealing Christmas, freezing in place at the squeak of a floorboard. I was so busy keeping an eye on Webber, I stubbed my toe on an abandoned book cart and swallowed a curse. This acting casual while sneaking around was no mean feat. I snagged a copy of *Vogue* as I went through periodicals, figuring I'd claim to be after some light reading if discovered. Another ninety seconds of cooperative floorboards and careful timing and I had achieved my objective.

Just under eight decades of Raven Hill High yearbooks were ordered by date, their colorful gold-stamped spines aligned precisely on the shelves. Beneath these were several bound volumes of the school paper. Running my finger along the row I did some quick math. Joanna was a few years younger than I, and I was pretty sure Vince was roughly the same age. I started in the mid-90's and hit pay dirt on my second try. There he was, beaky nose, prominent Adams-apple, and superior smirk. Vincent Goodhue, Senior Class Treasurer, lettered in cross-country and track. He listed as interests journalism and film, and his goals were "to run the New York City marathon and make award-winning documentaries."

Good for Vince. When I graduated high school, I wanted to get away from my mother, have a really good time, and make a whole lot of money. I had achieved my less lofty goals, at least for a while.

I flipped through the rest of the yearbook. No sign of Matthew Prentiss. Perhaps he was older than I thought. I didn't know Felicity's maiden name, but there was no senior portrait that could be her. I finally found her in a junior class photo. Felicity James, a slender blonde girl with glasses and a shy smile. I scanned the candid photos. Felicity and Vince appeared often, and more often than not they were together. Prom, club activities, hanging out—no matter the setting, the two were together. They were clearly a couple. According to Jilly, they were still pretty tight, in spite of being married to other people. The question was how tight?

The floor gave a protesting squeak.

"Find something interesting in there?" Officer Webber's voice came from behind my right shoulder.

I'd wanted to give the police a few more suspects. Time to throw somebody under the bus.

"Not really." I said, "It's just that I never realized Vince Goodhue and Felicity Prentiss were an item."

She raised her eyebrows. I felt a twinge of conscience. I'd always liked Felicity, but I'd liked Joanna more.

"In high school, I mean. Jill mentioned earlier that the Prentisses and the Goodhues were friendly, but that Vince and Felicity seemed especially," I paused, as if searching for the right word, "well, *close* you might say. But I guess it makes sense, given the two of them go way back."

I closed the yearbook and put it back on the shelf, leaving it sticking out slightly from the rest. I picked up my magazine.

"If you'll excuse me," I said.

Officer Webber nodded. I was sure she'd take the bait and look through the yearbooks. She was the thorough type. I'd wanted to snoop through them a little longer myself, but I'd leave them to Webber.

The yearbooks had given me an idea.

Chapter Six

~

Dinnertime found me at the door of my neighbor and landlord, Henri Martin. He had been a high school French teacher in Raven Hill for over thirty years, and was still teaching when Vince and Felicity were students. Though well into his eighties, his mind was still sharp, so he was my best and most discreet source of information.

"Bonjour!" I said when Henri answered my knock. Within minutes we exchanged greetings, I secured an invitation to dinner, and set off to walk Henri's French bulldog, Pierre. He had been "barking at shadows all day" according to Henri, and I was glad to give him some exercise in exchange for a good meal and conversation. People always stopped to greet Pierre, and I might have the opportunity to dig up a little more information.

Pierre hung a left out of the gate. He often wanted to investigate the woods at the end of the street in the hope of finding something smelly to roll in, but instead he turned to the path along the side of the house. Nose to the ground, he headed for the stairs to my apartment.

"Sorry, buddy, no sleepover tonight." I tugged gently on the leash, but the dog was insistent, planting his feet and sniffing at the stairs. I gave another tug and he turned his attention to the walk, led me to the gate, and then to the woods. He stopped, his little bat ears up and forward as he scented the air. The area before me was old growth, never farmed or developed. I sometimes thought I spotted a path through it, depending on the light or the season, but in this evening's twilight it looked dark and impenetrable. I was glad when Pierre turned and headed down the street, nose once again to the ground. I thought of the jogger who had lingered in the small turnaround at the end of the road, and wondered if Pierre had been barking at more than shadows that afternoon.

Our winding little road ended at Main Street. This is where Pierre and I usually turned around, but thus far we had encountered no one and I wasn't ready to give up on my intelligence gathering mission. We crossed to a small park. I lingered in the shadow of a monument and observed the action in Raven Hill's central business district. Pete's Pizza was doing a brisk business. The Java Joint wouldn't pick up until later, but just past it the Market on Main had a full parking lot. Nothing like food and gossip to bring out a crowd.

I turned my attention back to Pete's. The screen door slammed as someone came out, and a car pulled away from the curb. The outside lights illuminated the entry and the few parking spots beside the building, all full. Two people stood between the parked cars, their heads together. I couldn't hear their conversation, but something about their posture screamed tension. After a moment the taller of the two stepped back, looked skyward, and blew out an audible breath. The sharp profile was unmistakable: Vince. So, the bereaved widower was out picking up pizza. Well, the kids needed to be fed, but Pete's delivered, and Vince seemed more annoyed than upset. I heard the beep of a car door lock and another low murmur of conversation, ending with a forcefully delivered "Careful!"

Vince got in his car as his companion hurried to the sidewalk. I stood still, waiting until whoever it was hit the pool of light at the corner of the building.

Felicity Prentiss. She looked across the street before turning to go into the pizza parlor. Once the door to Pete's slammed behind her, I turned Pierre toward home. I glanced at the lighted windows of the stately old home long converted to offices. "Prentiss and Prentiss, Attorneys-at-Law," the sign in front read. Whatever Felicity was discussing with Vince, she didn't want her husband to know about it. Was the meeting planned or accidental? And if the two were in cahoots, wouldn't they be keeping a lower profile?

A fabulous aroma greeted me at Henri's. Pierre bolted for his supper dish as my host handed me a glass of wine.

"Sit and relax for a moment. All of this stress and worry—you are looking too thin."

I adored this man.

"We will have a nice meal, and of course a little sweet, and you will tell me everything." Henri turned to the stove. He was a marvelous cook, and there was always dessert. His family had a little shop—baked goods, sweets, and sundries—before the war had changed everything. He could have carried on the family business, but by the time he finished school and the reconstruction was underway, a pretty American nurse caught his eye and then his heart.

As we ate, I told Henri the whole story, from finding the body to my yearbook discovery. I left out Joanna's note, but was honest about my fear of being a suspect.

"I'm new here, and I found the body. With my husband having been killed, I'm afraid it looks bad, and I'm worried about my job."

"Villages run on rumor, and Madame Hunzeker is sensitive to reputation. I do not see how they could fire you, but things could get uncomfortable. Even if most did not believe ill of you, some would always wonder. You are right to worry."

"I know, but if the police had several suspects . . ." I trailed off.

Henri nodded, and thought for a moment.

"Is it not usually the husband in cases such as this?" he asked. "They will investigate Vincent, I am sure. But who else?"

"Felicity Prentiss? They go way back, and Jilly said they still seem awfully friendly."

"An affair, perhaps? They had an attachment once, it is true. For over a year they were inseparable. It ended after he went away to school, as these things do."

"Was she heartbroken?"

"She kept it very private, but she was hurt, I think. She did not have much confidence with boys. Felicity was pretty, but not the kind of pretty girls want to be at that age. The hair, the makeup, the clothes—she was not good at that. But she had a nice manner and she was very, very bright. I taught her for four years, Vincent as well, but she was the better student. They were an item, and he ended it, but I do not see her carrying a torch for all these years. Still, anything is possible in affairs of the heart."

"True." I related what I saw outside Pete's.

"In and of itself, it does not amount to much, but I have seen them once or twice lately, just as you said. More than a casual conversation. And from what Jill said, she has as well. So, maybe they wish to relive their youth? Or some other reason?"

Revenge. The desire for an "I'll make you sorry you dumped me" moment. Petty, but she wouldn't be the first.

"I guess it could be anything," I said. "They're not being very discreet, though, if they are up to something."

"Hiding in plain sight? But the tension you described, I have seen it, too. Lover's quarrel?"

"Or the stress of sneaking around, trying to act casual? It's possible Joanna, or even Matthew, had something going on that inspired Vince and Felicity to turn to each other."

"Joanna I did not know at all well. Matthew Prentiss . . ." He paused for a moment, pursing his lips, ". . . Matthew Prentiss has always been very careful, very concerned with doing the right thing. It was important to his family, I think. He was what you would call a real Boy Scout. It is important to him that people think well of him. I understand he has ambitions, political ambitions."

This was news.

"I hear things, you know, when Pierre and I are out and about."

The "Grumpy Old Men," Joanna had dubbed them. I thought they were more like the "Very Old Ladies" in a Gregor Demarkian mystery. The "Very Old Gentlemen" of Raven Hill didn't miss much. Singly or in small groups, they were always out taking the air, walking their dogs or lounging on the bench in the little park I had just visited. Cold weather drove them into the coffee shop or the library. I'd put money on the accuracy of Henri's information.

"He's been on the library board for a couple of years, hasn't he? That usually provides some positive press. He hasn't taken a stand on the idea of a new library building, so he's safe there, as long as he moves on before Anita forces the issue." I thought for a moment. "Mayor of Raven Hill or state legislature?"

"I have heard his name mentioned for both, and I understand he is receptive."

"Whichever it is, he would want to avoid a scandal. So would Felicity."

"And Joanna was your friend, your friend from your youth, and if she was killed, you would like justice for her."

"Yes." Henri's words conjured a memory, Joanna and I sharing a pizza and some cheap wine in our dorm, laughing and talking, all the world and all our lives before us.

"Yes," I said again, tamping down the wave of sadness the memory brought, and focusing on the cold fury that had fueled me since finding the note. "I want to know who killed her."

"Of course you do. But if it was not an accident . . ."

I gave him a look. It was no accident.

"If it was not an accident, you must be extremely careful. You are looking for a killer, perhaps a cold-blooded murderer. Such a creature is dangerous. Uncovering secrets is exciting, *oui*, but this is not a game. Cunning and subtlety are your weapons. Do you understand me, Greer?"

Henri's voice had grown harsh as he spoke, his accent more pronounced. The wiry little man seemed to vibrate with urgency. It was as if he had personal experience with hunting killers. He had been very young during the war, he once told me, too young to fight. "But I did my small part," he had said, "delivering messages, keeping my eyes open. A scrawny young boy on a bicycle sees and hears much, but is often overlooked." And his older brother had been in the Resistance.

"Greer!"

"I'll be careful, of course I will. I promise."

"*Bon*, good girl. I will give you what help I can. And now, dessert."

Henri's features relaxed, and he was once again the soft-spoken octogenarian I knew. As he rose to get the lemon tart, I wondered what it was exactly that Henri had done during the war.

I returned to my apartment replete with lemon tart, and with even more questions. The place was dark and cold. I should have left some lights on, I thought, turning on a couple of lamps and flicking on the gas fireplace. I felt a draft, a gust of cold, damp air, the kind I'd felt when I opened that door and found Joanna. The thought stopped me in my tracks. That draft had come from an open window, and I was sure everything was closed when I left this morning.

Pierre, barking at shadows, sniffing a path to my stairs.

I listened. There were no unusual sounds, no sense of another presence in my home. I rubbed my arms where I had goosebumps not entirely attributable to the cold. I was being paranoid. Must be. But there was the cold air again, coming from my left. The bathroom? Relief washed over me. I must have left the window open after I showered. I marched to the bathroom door and flicked on the light.

The window was closed.

But I could still feel the cold, and the dark length of my bathrobe swayed on its hook. "The Grim Reaper Robe" Danny had dubbed the long black hooded cashmere garment. I shivered. The linen closet door the hook was attached to was ajar, but the closet was too small for anyone to hide in. The wind sighed through the trees outside, the robe swung gently, and cold air touched my skin.

It *had* to be the window.

I bent to look more closely. The window was open, maybe three-quarters of an inch between sash and sill. The wood swelled when it was damp, making it difficult to close, but the morning had been sunny and crisp, and I was sure I had closed it all the way.

Almost sure. It never closed enough to lock, but I'd never worried about it, even though you could access it from a corner of my porch. Maybe it didn't close all the way this morning and I hadn't noticed. What else could it be?

Burglar? Crazy. But I shut the window and decided to ask Henri to fix it.

Within minutes I'd settled into my favorite overstuffed chair with a notepad, pen, and steaming mug. I turned to a fresh page and wrote across the top:

What Would Trixie Do?

Brainstorm with Honey Wheeler? Call a meeting of the Bob-Whites of the Glen? My friends were strewn from Manhattan to Hudson and wouldn't be any help. Other than Henri, I was only friendly with people from the library—my suspect pool. The officers of the Friends of the Library could undoubtedly provide information, but I didn't have an excuse to start calling them and asking questions. They were all in and out of the building quite a bit lately, hard at work on their fundraiser, but I couldn't insinuate myself into that too easily.

Or maybe I could. Every fundraiser needed door prizes or something to raffle. I had spent fifteen years working for an international cosmetics company. I grabbed my phone, scrolled through my contacts, and tapped the screen. It was answered on the second ring.

"Greer, honey, tell me you're coming home!"

"Sorry, Beau, I've decided I like it here. But you can always come visit."

"Visit? Raven's Breath?" Beau sounded horrified. In the background, someone burst into song.

"Greeeeeeen Acres is the place for me," warbled Beau's partner, Ben.

"Raven Hill," I said. "It's really quite charming. I was enjoying myself right up until the murder."

"Murder? Greer, what's going on?" The Green Acres theme cut off mid-word.

"Relax. I'm fine. But I need a favor."

I ran through the whole story for Beau, including Joanna's note and Anita's obvious desire to see the whole thing go away.

"So, you see, it's in my best interest to figure this out. I want attention off me. I want to know what was going on and what she wanted my help with."

"Because you didn't have time to help her, just like you didn't have the time to help Danny."

That stung. Beau wasn't playing around.

"Look, sweet pea, you don't need to do this." Beau's tone became a little kinder. "The police found Danny's killer, and they'll find this one."

I didn't kill your husband, lady, I swear it. He was alive when I left him.

"Don't go stirring up trouble because you feel guilty for no good reason." Beau's accent slid south, back to his roots in the Carolina Low Country, as it always did when he was tired or upset.

"It's not guilt; it's self-preservation. I'm not stirring up trouble. I just want to dig up a couple more suspects. We both know the police will take a long look at me and at her husband, but I'm sure they won't go much beyond that."

"Well, it usually is the husband or the wife, isn't it?"

"Yes, thank you, I am well aware of that. I am also aware of how the police do not look beyond the obvious until they have to."

I was paid to break into your place, sure. But I didn't kill your husband.

"I know, I was there. But this is different. Are you really a suspect?"

"I found her, so that puts me on the list. My alibi is not airtight. Besides, there's something rotten here, something beneath the surface. I can smell it."

"All the more reason to keep your nose out of it. Head down, mouth shut. You don't know what you might step in otherwise."

"I can't, Beau. She was my friend."

Beau let out a gusty sigh.

"Well, you're nothing if not loyal, Greer. I have reason to know. What kind of favor do you need?"

"Products, enough for a few gift baskets."

"So, you're going to bribe witnesses with age-defying youth scrum and some lipstick?"

"No, I need an excuse to chat up the rest of the Friends' officers about what Joanna was working on before she died. I'm going to tell them she had asked me about door prizes for the jumble sale."

"Jumble sale," he muttered, "door prizes. You ran away from home and landed in a Barbara Pym novel. Or maybe Agatha Christie. Tell me, will there be a fete?"

"October. Apple Festival, along with the annual book and bake sale. E-books are cutting into book donations, so they added the jumble sale. They'll raffle off the gift baskets. I'm sure they'll be a hit."

Another sigh. He wasn't happy, but he'd come through.

"You'll have it next week. I'll put Ben on it—he's better at this sort of thing. We'll tuck in some goodies for you, too."

"Thanks. You're the best. This will be a big help."

"Just be careful, Greer. Poking into other people's business can get you into trouble, even if that business has nothing to do with murder."

"Don't worry, I'll be discreet. Besides, how many deep, dark secrets can there be in a sleepy little village like Raven Hill?"

"Trust me on this one, city girl," Beau's tone became grim, "I was a gay boy in a small town in the South. People hide all kinds of things, and in a little place like that they've got more to lose if the neighbors see their dirty laundry. Everybody's got a secret, Greer. Everybody."

Chapter Seven

Friday morning, I was at work bright and early. I'd had another restless night. I hated to admit it, but Henri and Beau had unnerved me. I liked the girl detective game as an intellectual exercise, but I was a physical coward. I certainly stood my ground in the face of horrible bosses and backstabbing coworkers, but other than throwing a mean elbow on the subway I stayed away from the rough stuff. I tossed and turned, wondering if I *should* just leave it to the police. In the end I decided to carry on. Unearthing a killer didn't necessarily mean confronting one. I wanted this thing wrapped up fast. I wanted to go back to my peaceful new life and box up all the intrusive memories Joanna's murder had stirred up. Besides, she had been on a mission and I wanted to see it through. I wasn't going to fail her.

After giving my desk a quick scan to assure myself it was undisturbed, I headed for the kitchen. People got chatty around the coffee machine in the morning, and I wanted to know if there had been any developments.

Mary Alice and Jill were hanging up jackets and stowing their lunches in the fridge. Dory was putting an ice cube in a steaming cup of tea while she talked non-stop to David, an older gentleman who was a part-time clerk. His pained look implied she was regaling him with all her theories on Joanna's death. Anne Marie came in to confer with Jill as I poured my coffee. It was all hands on deck for the reopening—Helene being of the opinion that prurient curiosity would bring in a record number of patrons. I said as much to Mary Alice, who agreed, adding that our part-time reference librarian and cataloger would be in later as well. The more the merrier as far as I was concerned. I concurred with Miss Marple's method of always thinking the worst of people, because she was so often proved correct, and that tittle-tattle was true nine times out of ten.

I leaned against the counter and waited for a lull in the conversations going on around me. When Dory finally came up for air, I spoke.

"Any new developments? I'd love to hear this really was a freak accident, so things can get back to normal."

"Wouldn't we all," Mary Alice said.

"I heard the police spent a long time talking to Vince Goodhue yesterday," Dory said.

David shifted uncomfortably. He lived on the same street as the Goodhues, but I wasn't sure how close.

"Did you see them, David?" I asked, doing my best to sound sympathetic. "It must have been very disruptive. It's a quiet neighborhood, isn't it? Cul-de-sac?"

"More of a dead end actually. Older neighborhood you know, and the Goodhues live a bit farther down the road."

He stopped. David disliked gossip and never had an unkind word to say about anyone, but if he thought his little geography lesson was going to get him off the hook he was mistaken. We all stared at him expectantly. He sighed.

"Well, they were certainly around, but I don't know that I'd say they stayed a long time. Of course, Vince has been coming and going an awful lot, with the girls and his work on the *Haunted Albany* documentary. In and out at all hours of the night. I'm sure his parents will help with the children now. It's all so sad."

And with that he applied his attention to a breakfast bar he pulled from his pocket. We'd gotten all we were going to get.

"Of course, if you believe the papers," Dory said, her tone making it clear that she did not, "it was all an accident, and it was Joanna's fault for not being careful by the stairs. Well, you know who that came from. Anita, that's who."

"The lady doth protest too much, methinks," Mary Alice said.

She had a point. Anita feared more than bad press. She was afraid of a lawsuit. Blaming the victim might backfire, though. Joanna had done a lot for the library. An idea formed in my mind. It's all in the spin. The best move would be to honor Joanna's memory while downplaying how she died. I wanted to ask questions, and Anita wanted to control the story. I could use that. I ran through some options as I listened to the staff for a few more minutes. Once I ascertained there was nothing new to learn, I got some more coffee and left.

I checked the parking lot on my way back to the office. Helene was in, but there was no sign of Anita's car. I was sure she would be in today to gauge the public response to Joanna's death and to do damage control if necessary. It wasn't that Helene couldn't handle things, it was that Anita believed as chair of the board of trustees the buck stopped with her. I had to give her credit, though I was sure some of it was driven by her sincere belief that if she wanted something done right she needed to do it herself. Which could work to my advantage, but I needed to catch Helene and Anita at the same time to put my plan into action.

"It's easier to get forgiveness than permission." True, but I'd learned early in life that it was easier to get away with breaking the rules if you appeared to be following them. This not only allowed you to pursue your agenda under the radar, it also bought you the benefit of the doubt if you did get caught.

Anita, and presumably the rest of the board, wanted Joanna's death to be ruled accidental so the whole business would go quietly away. Based on the police activity and what I'd seen, it was no accident, and I was sure the board knew it, too. Still, they wanted to distance the library from the tragedy, and I wanted to stay on Anita's good side. So, if I wanted to ask a lot of questions I needed her permission, even if she didn't know exactly what she was agreeing to.

I wasn't on reference until the afternoon, so I could spend time on tasks that allowed me to keep an eye on who was coming and going. I didn't have long to wait. I heard Anita's voice ten minutes before the library was due to open. I waited a few minutes, grabbed some paperwork and headed toward the director's office.

Both Helene and Anita were there. I apologized for interrupting, explaining that I needed to drop off some things for Helene's signature.

"But as long as you're both here," I went on, "I had an idea I wanted to run by you."

I continued as though I was still forming the thoughts.

"I was thinking we should do something to honor all the work Joanna did for the library. Maybe a biography on the website, with some pictures and some of the video spots she did." Joanna had covered a few library events for local news segments, all of them with Anita's blessing.

"What a nice idea, Greer," Helene said.

"Of course we want to do something," said Anita. "But I thought we would wait and do something a bit more permanent."

Like a plaque or a tree or something equally lame and of no help to me, but I tilted my head and pretended to consider it.

"Well, yes," I said. "Perhaps something in the new library. Some part of the media center—but you've probably already thought of that."

Anita looked gratified. But I needed her to do something now, and she was still not convinced. If she said she wanted the staff to keep their distance, I'd be risking her wrath by nosing around.

"It's just that, well, we don't want people to think we don't appreciate everything she did." I paused, hoping I wasn't about to overplay my hand. "Or that we're trying to hide anything. Some people are always looking for a scandal."

Anita's eyes narrowed. I had struck a nerve.

"So, if we got out in front of it, it would look better. I know it sounds awful, but I can't get past my corporate spin control habit. And I *would* like to do something nice for Joanna."

I shrugged, adopting a rueful expression. My corporate background was one of the things Anita had liked about my resume, since in her opinion everything could benefit from a more businesslike approach.

"You make an excellent point, Greer," Anita said, drumming her fingers on Helene's desk.

"I'd be happy to handle the project," I said. "I worked with her on a few things recently. I'm sure I can put together a simple web page. Maybe we can even include a place where people can add their favorite memories of Joanna."

You never knew who or what that might turn up, and it would be nicer than those online obit guest books.

"Greer may be right," Helene said. "Vince has his hands full, and Joanna's family isn't from around here. It would be a lovely gesture, and politically I think it's a wise move."

"True," said Anita, still drumming. "I'd forgotten Joanna had no family here. And we certainly don't want that TV station she worked for to take charge and start sensationalizing the whole business."

Anita thought for a few more seconds, but I smelled victory. I would be able to nose around openly, and I'd have an excuse to talk to everyone who had contact with Joanna.

"It's settled then," Anita said, pulling out a pad and pen. "Greer will put together something for the website, and we'll have a memorial service on the manor grounds. A celebration of her life, we'll call it. That sounds positive, doesn't it?"

My jaw dropped.

"But Anita," Helene said, "the staff time, library operations—"

Anita cut her off.

"Don't worry, I'll put the Friends in charge of logistics, the board members will contribute time and money as needed, and I'm sure some of the local businesses will be happy to help with refreshments. I'll square everything with Vincent first," she added. "We don't want to seem intrusive."

And before you could say, "Let's put a bold face on it" Anita reached for the phone.

"Well," I said. "I guess I'll go get started."

Anita waved me out. Helene followed.

"Sorry," I said to her once we were out of earshot. "I didn't think . . ."

"It's all right, Greer. You were trying to do something nice, and though I wouldn't have approached it this way, Anita may be on to something. This gives everyone something more positive to focus on than the fact that a woman may have been murdered in our building."

But a woman had been murdered, and until I knew who did it, I had no intention of focusing on anything else.

Chapter Eight

The library was busy from the minute we opened. I could hear the hum of activity from my desk, and was grateful not to have to face all the curious villagers right away. Of course, I wasn't safe from staff and volunteers, all of whom wandered into the office to either commiserate or try for a firsthand account of the finding of the body. Since this group was familiar with the manor layout and Joanna's activities, I did a little discreet questioning in turn. All of them seemed genuinely distressed by events and sympathetic to the fact that I had tripped over a corpse, and of someone I knew at that. Several expressed the belief that they would have been promptly sick (I did get a little queasy), or possibly fainted (I never faint), or immediately panicked. I nearly had panicked, but for reasons I was not about to discuss. A couple had more contact with Joanna than I would have guessed, so I mentioned my web project and asked if I could call them later.

Around midday the stream of visitors slowed. I was reviewing a book order when Matthew Prentiss walked in.

My interactions with him were always informal and pleasant. Unlike those board members only seen at meetings, Matthew and his family were regular library users. Though Felicity spent more time in the building because of her volunteer work, her husband stopped in both on his own or with their two boys. I categorized him the way I did every other patron: by what he read. Matthew dabbled in naval adventures, but preferred biographies and was currently working his way through the robber barons. I decided to give him a closer look now that he was related to one of my murder suspects.

"Give me a second," I said, waving toward Jilly's chair. "I've been trying to get this done all morning."

He sat as I hit some buttons. Once I heard the printer whirring, I turned to face him. We began a version of the same conversation I'd had all morning, and I assessed our youngest board member.

Matthew Prentiss was that particular type of man whose success was based on having gone to the right schools and playing an acceptable game of golf. Their numbers are legion. Reasonably, but not excessively good looking, they are bright but not clever, well-dressed though never fashionable, and pleasant rather than charming. I had encountered several in my corporate life and found them to be manageable unless something or someone threatened their belief in their own superiority. Matthew was unlikely to encounter that here in Raven Hill, where his life-long residency and profession automatically provided some status. He appeared a genuinely nice, hardworking man, and if I needed someone to draw up a will or handle a real estate transaction, I'd hire him. If I wanted a real barracuda, I'd look elsewhere. Still, there was no way to know how he reacted to serious stress, and the desire to go into politics raised some questions. Possibly he wanted to "give back to the community." He would do well in local politics. Being a big fish in a small pond suited him, and he would take care his small pond was well looked after. Raven Hill could also be a stepping stone to higher office. I wasn't sure he could hack that, and I wasn't sure how far he'd go to protect his interests in either scenario.

I tuned back in to what Matthew was saying. He deviated slightly from the usual script.

"I hope this hasn't put you off Raven Hill," he was saying. "We would hate to see you go. Although it had to be horrible, finding Joanna. I understand you two were close."

Interesting. I thought he knew the story from my job interview.

"We were friendly. We worked on a few things together, and we knew each other in college. And I must confess," I flashed him a big smile, "we bonded over our outsider status. We used to joke about how long we would have to live here before people stopped referring to us as "new." I think I'm going to be the "new librarian" until the day I retire."

Matthew laughed.

"Seriously, people have been very nice, but I'll never be considered a real villager. Not like you." I paused. Then I added, "Or like Vince and Felicity."

Matthew's mouth tightened briefly at the linked names, and he sighed. I raised an eyebrow.

"Truthfully, I'm a little worried about Felicity. She's very upset. She's always been a worrier. I keep telling her it was probably an accident, but she's been jumpy ever since we found out. Felicity and Joanna were never close, but they'd been spending a lot of time together lately. I don't know . . ." He trailed off, and gave me a questioning look.

"They were working together quite a bit on the sale." I said. "So, I suppose it's only natural."

Matthew was quiet for a moment. I waited. Finally, he nodded.

"I guess you're right." He stood. "I'm glad to hear you're not thinking of leaving us. But you should consider some time off, maybe visit friends or something. I'm sure Helene would approve it, and I'd certainly weigh in on your side."

Helene might approve a little vacation, but Lt. O'Donnell wouldn't.

"Don't worry, I'll be fine," I said. "And I have no plans to resign. I couldn't possibly subject my replacement to a lifetime of being referred to as the '*New* new librarian.'"

It took him a second, but he got it. He laughed and said, "Glad to hear it. But remember, if anything comes up that concerns you, feel free to give me a call."

He headed out the door. I pondered his motives as I bolted my lunch. Real concern about his wife? Or his future career? Genuinely nice guy or a Boy Scout covering his ass?

Hard to say, and worth keeping an eye on.

*　　*　　*

Business was brisk in the reading room. That was both good and bad. It made the time go by faster but kept conversations with the curious brief. Mindful of Miss Marple and the importance of tittle-tattle, I wanted to see who might ask too many questions, or perhaps not enough. There was a steady stream of unfamiliar faces at Circ; apparently a number of village residents had suddenly recalled unpaid fines. Presiding over the cash register, Dory was in her element as she fielded questions. From what I could hear, she stuck to the board-approved message in terms of what she said, but implied a great deal more in how she said it.

Though books were still our stock in trade, Friday afternoon reference shifts ran heavily to movie questions as people looked for weekend entertainment. Today was no exception. Hardcore film buffs reserved new releases well in advance, but still arrived early in the afternoon to scan the shelves and quiz the librarian in case there was something they'd missed. The topography of the area made streaming services hit or miss, and many of our patrons had long been in the habit of stopping in to chat while they picked things up. I'd taken dozens of requests, dismantled a display, and excavated the overflowing book drop. While I had frustratingly little time to ask leading questions, I did have a reason to be all over the reading room. It let me keep an eye on the unfamiliar faces that were lingering, and there were a few.

There was no obvious police presence in the building. I'd bet Anita had squashed the idea of anyone in uniform, but was equally sure O'Donnell had one or more people on the property. It was a small force but I only recognized a few by sight, and they were usually in uniform. I was roaming around straightening and playing "spot the cop" when the first of the after-school crowd rolled in.

Jimmy and Joey Jovanoski were looking for a follow-up to *Thor*. They were a little too young for *Henry V,* even if it was the same director and followed the theme of the golden boy with problems. That brought me back to Matthew Prentiss and his concern about Felicity's nerves. A high-strung wife was not a political asset. I'd need to look into it. Felicity had been spending a lot of time with Joanna.

I led the boys on a hunt for *The Avengers* which was checked in but not on the shelf. We paused near one of the strangers I'd been keeping an eye on and compared our favorite characters from the movie.

"I like Loki best," I confessed. "He's not really bad, he's just misunderstood. It's the bad guys that make things more fun, don't you think?"

The stranger in question gave me a startled look. I smiled and waved the DVD. He adjusted his ball cap and looked back at his laptop.

Bingo. Plainclothes, I'd put money on it.

"Anything else?" I asked.

"No, thanks," said Jimmy.

"Yes," his older brother corrected him, "Mom said we have to get a book or no movies this weekend."

"Oh, right." Jimmy looked at me hopefully. "It can be a graphic novel. Do you have any about superheroes?"

"I think you have enough superheroes right there, but I have an idea. Go ask Mrs. Hutchinson to check in *Thor*, and Joey and I will go find a book."

I headed for the graphic novel section, Joey trailing along behind me.

"It's Joe, actually," said that young man, with all the dignity befitting one who would enter middle school in the fall, "and I like Loki, too."

"Good," I said, running my finger along the shelf until I found what I wanted, "then you'll like this."

I handed him *Trickster: Native American Tales*. He took it and flipped through, considering.

"Your mother will approve," I informed him. "Tell her I said it was really good."

It was a good book. A collaboration between Native American storytellers and graphic novel professionals, it would make both boys stretch a little, but they'd like it. I sent Joe off to check out, certain I'd made progress in my mission to cultivate a love of good books in my young patrons by whatever underhanded means necessary.

I worked my way back to the reference desk, straightening as I went and surveying my little kingdom. The rush was slowing. The number of unfamiliar faces was down to two, one being my friend in the baseball cap, and he was packing to go. It would get busy again in the half hour before we closed, but meanwhile I could look forward to a lull. My restless night was catching up to me.

The phone rang. Dory had someone at the Circ desk so I answered.

"Oh, Greer, I'm so glad it's you!"

I groaned. Agnes Jenner, one of our regular patrons. She was in her sixties, widowed, bright, bored, and fond of her cocktails, which she started in on around noon every day. At least once a week she called me looking for some obscure piece of information. She said she didn't use the Internet, but I thought she might just be lonely. Sometimes it was easy to find the answer for her, sometimes not. I hoped today it would be simple.

"How can I help you?" I asked.

"I need you to solve a mystery."

I'll add it to my list, right after "solve murder."

"What mystery is that?"

"Well, I was watching one of those DVDs you recommended. It was one of the new Marple episodes. There was an actress I'm sure I've seen in another one of those mysteries, but I can't put my finger on it. Now, what was her name? I wrote it down. Give me a second."

There was the sound of paper rustling. I drummed my fingers. Every British actor alive seemed to have done a turn in one of these mysteries, so without the correct name I'd be looking for a needle in a haystack.

"Polly Walker!" Agnes announced. "I knew I had it!"

"Let me check." The Internet Movie Database was perfect for this kind of question. I typed in the name and scanned the filmography.

At Bertram's Hotel," I said. "That's the episode you just watched, isn't it?"

"That's right, but I'd swear there's another one."

I looked further. Score one for Agnes. There *was* another one.

"*Peril at End House*. It's a *Poirot*. There's seventeen years between the two. She must look a lot different. You have a good eye, Agnes."

"People always said I had a photographic memory, and I guess I still do."

She also had a house on the only road leading to the manor, a window with a view of that road, and a habit of staying up late. The TV and bar were in the room with a view. I knew because I'd taken her books and videos after she had a knee replacement. She might have seen something unusual Tuesday night, and with luck she might remember it. I suddenly became much more invested in Agnes's reference needs.

"I'm glad you liked the videos. See? I told you there was life after Joan Hickson. I can find you some more, if you're through with those."

"That would be very nice, dear, but I'm afraid I won't be able to get in to pick them up right away."

"Is your knee still bothering you? I could drop them off on my way home. It's only been a couple months since your surgery, so you're still on my list of homebound patrons." It had been closer to three months but Agnes still complained of joint pain. She also didn't drive. Given her drinking, this was a blessing, but it did leave her stranded at times.

"Could you, Greer? I would appreciate it. All this rain has made me so achy."

"Sure. I'll check the new ones out to you and bring back the ones you're done with. Now, which ones haven't you seen?"

Agnes and I discussed some titles and I told her I'd see her in a few hours. Hopefully, she'd still be coherent. I collected her DVDs and returned to the desk. The library was quiet. In spite of the busyness of the day, its contented hum had not returned. The only sounds from the building itself were the tired sighs of old wood settling, and the irritated squeak of floorboards as a page pushed a heavy book cart through the room. I was tired and irritated, too.

I looked at the notes I'd scribbled while talking to Agnes. *Peril at End House* had something in common with *The Chinese Shawl*, the Patricia Wentworth novel I'd finished last night. A similar device, a colorful shawl, used differently by each author. Nothing was as it first seemed. The same was true of *At Bertram's Hotel*, where no one was who or what you thought you knew. Sort of like Raven Hill. My three suspects—Vince, Felicity, and Millicent—might be exactly what they seemed. Or not. Their motives were uncertain, especially Millicent's, and their whereabouts at the time of the murder were unknown. At least to me.

I glanced at the pile of videos, meeting the kindly yet shrewd gaze of Miss Marple. What would Jane do? She had a decidedly different M.O. than Trixie Belden. I leaned back in my chair. Miss Marple would wander around St. Mary Mead, or whatever little village or genteel hotel she found herself in, and exchange gossip with the locals, or park herself and her knitting bag in some public place, observing and eavesdropping. She could even play the dithery old lady card if she needed to. None of these options were open to me. I was neither dithery nor local. As a newcomer, I couldn't wander around town and start chatting with people I rarely spoke to.

I looked toward the Circ desk. Dory was local, and she gathered bits of information like a magpie collecting shiny objects, her bright eyes missing nothing and her ears attuned to any hint of scandal. She even had a knitting bag, which against all library protocol, had appeared on the chair next to her, a few bright skeins poking out the top. Dory often pushed boundaries like this. She figured if her work was done and there were no patrons to attend to, she might as well use her time productively. I drew the line at the curling iron, no matter how overdue she was for a perm, but I let the knitting slide. She was still able to keep an eye on things, and answer the phone, and indulging her on this won her cooperation elsewhere.

She saw me look over and glanced down. She must have had her needles just out of sight. She looked up again and I nodded toward the knitting bag, mouthing "pretty color." She smiled her thanks and turned her attention back to her work.

I studied Dory for a moment longer, trying to see her in the role of Raven Hill's Miss Marple. No. She had the yarn, but not the brains. What she did have was information, lots of it. And I had the brains.

I grabbed the stack of DVDs and headed over to Circ.

"What's that going to be when it's done?" I asked.

"Scarf. I'm trying to get a head start on the grandkids' Christmas gifts. Are those for Agnes Jenner?"

"Yes," I said, not surprised Dory had managed to listen to my conversation while carrying on one of her own. "She's still not completely recovered from her knee surgery."

"You're nice to do that, Greer. Most people ran out of patience with Agnes a long time ago."

"I run out of patience, too. But this *is* my job."

Dory sniffed. "Well, I must say you turned out to be much better than I expected when I heard our new librarian was from New York City. I thought you'd be real snooty, but you're not so bad. You do get impatient sometimes, but you don't talk down to people if they didn't go to college or if they maybe drink too much." Dory shot a scornful glance at the group photo of the board hanging above the Circ desk. Anita was front and center.

No love lost there. I could leverage that.

"Neither of my parents went to college, and my dad owns a pub. So, I'm used to dealing with the Agnes Jenners of the world."

"Still, not everyone takes the time to be kind. You fit in here better than I figured. Though you do still keep to yourself."

A note of disapproval crept into her voice. Even a hint of aloofness constituted a cardinal sin in Dory's eyes.

"It's easier to be kind than not." I had always found this to be true. I also always found it to be useful, as you never knew when you might need that kindness returned in some fashion. Like now.

"As for keeping to myself, I'm still trying to find my way around. It's a small community, and I don't want to give offense."

Dory considered this for a moment, and then nodded. "Well, I must say that's real thoughtful, Greer. It's what I'd call a delicate approach. Now if only Joanna Goodhue had thought like you, she might be alive today.

Which could mean Dory knew of something in particular Joanna had handled indelicately. Or it could be general disapproval of her approach. Either way, it gave me an opening.

"Joanna was really very nice, and certainly well-meaning, but I know she rubbed some people the wrong way. Do you think someone killed her over some village disagreement? You know absolutely everyone, Dory."

Dory looked at me over her knitting. It was a sympathetic look. She had caught the note of desperation in my voice, as the fear that I was out of my league floated to the surface. Like it or not, I needed whatever help she could give.

"I know you girls were friends, but you went about things differently. Joanna jumped right in with both feet. Take the new library building, for instance. As soon as Anita proposed it, Joanna was all over it. At the very first meeting, she managed to offend Millicent, the entire Historical Society, and about half the people in the room."

"Were you there?"

"Of course I was there. And I must say she made some good points. It was the way she made them that was the problem, if you know what I mean."

"Yes, I do know what you mean. But can you really see Millicent or someone from the Historical Society doing her in over it?"

I pointed out that the average age of the Historical Society membership was well over eighty, and unless we found out Joanna had been bashed over the head with a portable oxygen tank, I couldn't see it.

"Let's face it," I said, "I'm a much more likely suspect since I found the body."

Dory laughed. "I guess you're right. Millicent is pretty spry, but she has a problem with her shoulder. Arthritis, I think, or is it the rotator cuff? My cousin Angela had that, and she couldn't lift her arm to wash her own hair even. And as for you . . ." she gave her yarn a tug, ". . . I thought about it and I just don't believe it. You're not the type to sneak up on someone and bash them in the head."

I was momentarily gratified.

"No," she went on, "if you were going to kill someone, you'd be much more direct about it, or at least more elegant. I'm a good judge of character that way."

Indeed she was.

"Thanks for your vote of confidence, Dory." I *was* thankful. Dory would share her opinion far and wide. The police wouldn't drop me as a suspect until they had the killer, but Anita was more concerned with the court of public opinion.

"Anyway," Dory said, "I'd like to know what she was hit with, because I don't believe that shelf fell on her, not for a minute."

"I don't know. I didn't see anything obvious."

"Hmph. I haven't been able to find out anything about it. Sam O'Donnell is a little too closemouthed for my liking."

Most people were.

"If it's not related to one of Joanna's causes, do you think it could be, well, something of a more personal nature?" I wanted to see if she had heard any rumors about Vince and Felicity, but I didn't want to put any ideas in her head.

"Like an affair, you mean? You don't need to beat around the bush with me, Greer. There's plenty of that kind of thing that goes on even in a small town, though it's harder to pull off. Just look in some of the public parking lots after hours, and see whose car is there. Not people who lost their keys, I'm telling you. The smart ones will go into Albany, though, so it's less noticeable. Joanna and Vince both travelled around a lot for their work, too, so it's possible. Still tough to keep things like that quiet though, and I haven't heard anything of the sort about Joanna."

Welcome to Smallbany, where everybody knows your name. And who you're sleeping with.

"What about Vince?

Dory frowned.

"Now it seems like I heard something about him and Felicity Prentiss, but I can't remember where. Of course, the two of them used to go together back in high school. He used to come and pick her up from work. She was a library page, did you know that?"

I had not. So, Felicity likely knew every nook, cranny, and squeaky floorboard in the manor.

"And Vince?"

"He never worked here. He would come, do his homework, and drive Felicity home. He did hang around here a lot, poking into things, taking pictures. We used some of them for the library centennial celebration. Anyway, Felicity was a smart girl, what you'd call 'motivated' these days. It always surprised me . . ." Dory broke off as someone approached the desk.

"I'll help him," I said, moving to the computer and making polite chit-chat as I checked out a stack of gardening books.

"Garden Club plant sale next month!" Dory sang out as the man gathered his books. "Look for our fliers. You won't find better tomato plants anywhere. Heirloom varieties!"

The man smiled and promised to drop by the sale. Dory never missed a trick.

I gave the reading room a quick once over. Still virtually empty. Dory glanced toward our lone remaining Wi-Fi user.

"He's new," she said in a low voice.

"I checked in with him earlier. He says his Internet is out at home." I pitched my voice equally low.

"I don't recognize him. He's not from the village."

"We're a little out of the way, but he could live in that new development. Or he may have read about the murder and is curious."

"Long time to linger out of curiosity. I'll keep my eye on him. Now what was I saying?"

"Vince and Felicity. Felicity was a page."

"That's right. So was Matthew Prentiss, though a few years earlier. But anyway, I've seen Vince and Felicity around, but I can't say I had the sense something was going on there. Not something that would lead to murder. Felicity and Joanna had their heads together a lot lately, but they were working on the sale."

"Crimes of passion often don't make sense, but Vince is up a creek without Joanna in terms of their business. He would have been better off with a divorce."

"I don't know about that," Dory said. She motioned me closer and gave a quick look around. When she set down her knitting, I knew this was important. I pulled a chair over and started tidying the desk drawer.

"My cousin Angela, the one I mentioned, with the shoulder?" I nodded to show I remembered. "Well, Angela works at Schuyler Insurance, and she said the Goodhues had big insurance policies. They took them out when they started the business, and they recently increased them. Angela was there when they came in to sign all the papers. She said Joanna was joking that she'd cost more to replace, what with her job and the business and taking care of the kids, but Vince didn't think it was funny. So, you see," Dory gave me a conspiratorial look, "she might have been worth more to him dead than alive."

"When did this happen? Have you told the police?"

"Of course I told the police. I found out Tuesday night, the night Joanna died. We were out to dinner at that fancy new Italian place, Luigi's it's called, and there was a big table of people from Albany All News. They arrived right after we did. We recognized some of the newscasters. I mentioned that Joanna, our FOL President, worked there and that's when Angela told me about the insurance."

"Which people did you recognize?" Maybe this was work related after all.

"Shannon something-or-other, the one who does the weather in the morning, and one of the news guys, Ed Dexter. The girl was pretty, but I think Ed Dexter looks better on TV. He's awfully skinny. I prefer a man with a little more meat on his bones."

"Your Bill is a nice, solid guy." This was diplomacy. Bill Hutchinson was built like a tree stump.

Dory smiled and picked up her knitting.

"What time were you there?" I asked.

"Our reservation was for seven, and we were seated a little after. We left around nine.

"Were the All News people still there?"

"Most of them. They were still having dessert when we left. Ed Dexter and one other man left right after the main course. Probably doing the ten o'clock broadcast."

"Maybe," I said, mentally calculating the distance from Luigi's to the manor, and how long it would take to cover with no traffic.

Dory gave me a sharp look. "Do you think Joanna's murder has something to do with her work?"

"I don't know, but it makes as much sense as anything else we've come up with."

"Except the insurance policy."

"Except that. If you hear anything else, will you tell me? And the police of course. You need to be careful."

"Of course I'll tell you," Dory said, "and you do the same. Us snoops need to stick together." She smiled and patted my hand. I retrieved my stack of DVDs, looked pointedly at the knitting bag, and headed back to reference.

Us snoops indeed. That's girl detective, thank you very much. I dropped the videos on the desk and took a quick turn around the reading room. I stopped next to our mystery patron and let him know we closed at six. He looked up and thanked me. I'd definitely never seen him before. It wasn't that unusual to have strangers stop in, but right now everything seemed suspicious.

I was both wired and tired, not a good combination. I glanced at the clock and decided to do a quick walk-around in the building. I should have a good fifteen minutes before things got busy again, and the staff currently outnumbered the patrons. I let Dory know my plan and took off.

Using the back stairs, I went to the second floor. I worked my way through all the meeting rooms, checking for strays and making sure all the windows were closed and locked. The pages normally did this at the end of the day, but nothing was normal right now. I needed to feel in touch with the manor. Dory's question nagged at me as well. I wanted to know what Joanna had been hit with, too. Something at the scene, or something brought in and taken away again?

He hit his head on the way down, but he was hit with something else, too.

Something else.

Crime of opportunity, or premeditated? It would make a difference in the suspect list. I paused at the bottom of the stairway to the attic.

"I've checked everything, Greer, you don't have to go up."

I spun around. Millicent was coming toward me, keys in hand.

"Didn't mean to scare you," she said. "I thought you heard me locking up the archives."

"No," I said, falling in beside her as we walked toward the main staircase. "I was making sure the page hadn't missed anything. I always check, especially since there are no motion sensors up here. It may sound silly, but I don't want to lock anyone in."

Millicent gave a dry chuckle.

"It's not silly. It happened once. A college student working on a paper fell asleep in the community room. He didn't come to for hours. The whole place was dark and he was afraid to move. He called the police to get him out. That's what led to the alarm system and emergency lighting being updated. Before that, we only had something that went off if someone tried to open one of the doors."

"Why didn't they put sensors in the whole building?"

"The usual reason," Millicent said. "Budget. They had enough money for the main floor and the stairways. Any areas the public might be wandering."

We had come to the bottom of the stairs. Millicent paused and looked into the raven room. Apparently deciding all was in order, she said goodnight and walked out the front door. I didn't have time to go back to the attic and look for the murder weapon, so I waited until I could see

Millicent on the walk and stepped over the velvet rope into Horatio Ravenscroft's study.

I'd have loved to have a room just like it. The floor to ceiling bookshelves and small fireplace left just enough room for a desk and a couple of comfy chairs. It was a perfect room for a scholarly gentleman.

Or a librarian, even if she was a snoop rather than a scholarly lady. I thought of Harriet Vane in *Gaudy Night* dozing in her alma mater's library after spending nights patrolling for mysterious vandals. We had worse than vandals in the Raven Hill Library.

I looked at the raven. He looked back at me.

"Some goings-on in your manor," I said. "Any thoughts?"

He didn't answer. He never did. The only sound was the restless rustling of the trees outside the window.

"Well, you think about it. Maybe some of your friends saw something." I glanced out the window. As always, there were a few live ravens in sight.

"I'll keep at it then. It's personal, you see."

His eyes glittered in the shifting light, but he gave away nothing.

"Quoth the Raven, 'Nevermore.' Good night, my friend."

As I turned to step back over the rope I came face-to-face with Mr. Wi-Fi. Hoping he hadn't heard me talking to the raven, I gave him a pleasant smile.

"May I help you find something?" I used my best reference librarian voice.

"Men's room," he replied, shifting and looking over my shoulder.

"Other end of the hall."

"Oh, right, I guess I got turned around. Thanks." He looked into the raven room once more, nodded at me and walked down the hall.

What was he doing lurking in the hall anyway? He was a man in his fifties and he'd been here all day, so he'd certainly been to the restroom more than once. Was he following me? Looking for a place to hide? I'd have to make sure I saw him leave.

I watched him go into the men's room and then got back to work. I handed out a few more movies and a lot of new fiction. Mr. Wi-Fi returned to his computer. The rest of the crowd were regulars. I was starting another circuit of the reading room, when I spotted one of my favorite patrons curled up on the couch in the children's area. Sadie Barrett was eight years old, with a sunny smile and a great love of reading. With long slender arms and legs, honey-brown hair and hazel eyes, she had a fey quality that made me think of her as a bookish wood sprite.

I walked over and sat next to her. From here I had a good view of the room and the front part of the hall.

"How do you like the book?" I asked. I had recommended *The Mysterious Benedict Society* to her earlier in the week, and she seemed to be making good progress with it.

She beamed at me. "I really, really like it!" she said. "I just loved all the tests at the beginning. Do you know why?"

"Why?"

"Because in order to pass, you don't have to be really smart, or good at school, but you have to be . . ." She searched for the word, her face pinched in concentration.

"Clever?" I asked.

"Yes! Clever!" she said, her smile back in place. "And you know what else? You know what I think the most important question is?"

"What?"

Sadie flipped through the book. Finding the page she wanted, she handed it to me. "This one," she said, pointing.

"Are you brave?" I read. "You're right. That is an important question. Reynie gives a pretty honest answer, doesn't he?"

"I hope so," Sadie quoted. "It was brave of him to be so honest, wasn't it?"

"It was. Reynard is my favorite. I like the way he thinks."

"I like Mr. Benedict best. He reminds me of my dad."

I could see it. Rob Barrett was a highly respected botanist, but he did have a certain air of eccentricity about him.

"Did your dad bring you today?"

"No, my mom. She's over there talking to some lady about the new library." Sadie rolled her eyes.

"What's wrong with that?"

"I don't want a new library. I want this one."

"Why? The new one would be closer to school, and have more books and computers, and more room. Kids would have their own space."

"But the manor is special," Sadie said. "Coming here is like—like going to Hogwarts!"

I smiled at her. "How so?"

"Because it's big and old and fancy." She looked around and leaned closer. "There's a headless ghost, too, I've seen him. And the people in the pictures move. Sometimes they're in their frames, and sometimes they're not."

I raised my eyebrows and looked out into the main hall.

"Yes," she said, "those pictures." She lowered her voice to a whisper. "The people in them move, but only at night."

She leaned back and met my startled gaze with a solemn nod.

I knew she wasn't pulling my leg. She looked and sounded serious. What she was suggesting was crazy, but she clearly believed it, and Sadie was both sane and honest. She had seen something strange and unrecognizable. Something—someone—had committed murder in this building, perhaps a stranger, someone so far unrecognized in the light of day.

Had she seen the killer?

A chill spread from the marrow of my bones outward. I looked around, noting the few people who might be close enough to hear us.

"I've never seen that," I whispered back, "and I close a couple nights each week. Does it happen a lot?"

"I don't think it happens every night, because I've only seen it a couple of times. The headless ghost I've only seen twice. Maybe you just can't see them from your desk?" She looked down the room.

"Maybe not. When did you first notice the people in the pictures moving?"

She thought for a minute.

"Remember the big snowstorm? During February vacation?"

I nodded. She went on.

"It was that day when the library closed early, that I first saw the people in the pictures move. I thought my eyes were playing tricks, because of the lights flickering. But I've seen it since, so I know it really happens."

She looked anxious, not sure she'd be believed.

"Tell me about the ghost. Did it really look like Nearly Headless Nick?"

"Sort of. It didn't have a head at all that I could see, but it was sort of lumpy, like Nick when he lets his head go sideways. I only saw it twice, and it was dark."

"It's hard to get a good look at a ghost, from what I understand. When did you see it?"

"The first time was a couple of weeks ago, or maybe a month, but the second time was this week. I was here reading while my mom was at the jumble sale meeting, and she came to get me, but then she started to talking to someone like she always does. I was the only one still here, but Mrs. Quinn said I could stay while she counted the money."

"And that's when you saw the headless ghost out in the hall? Right after the library closed?"

"Not in the hall. Going up the big staircase by the raven room."

The only meeting related to the jumble sale had been the Friends meeting Tuesday night, which meant Sadie had seen someone go up the stairs after the building had closed and the outside doors were locked. Joanna had attended that meeting, gone up to the attic, and been killed, but I still didn't know what time. I also didn't know who else might have been around. From what Sadie said, a few people had lingered.

"You believe me, don't you Ms. Hogan?"

"Yes, I do."

She smiled in satisfaction. "Jake didn't believe me," she said, referring to her older brother. "He told me I dreamed it. He said people would laugh if I told."

"Well, lots of people don't believe in ghosts, and others are scared of them, so maybe you shouldn't tell anyone else."

Sadie may have seen a murderer, and the last thing I wanted was for the murderer to know it. I didn't want to scare her, either, but if she saw it again someone needed to check it out.

"Listen," I said, "I would really like to see the ghost. It could be an important part of the history of the manor, one we don't know about."

"Do you think one of the Ravenscrofts might have been beheaded?" Sadie asked, obviously thrilled at the thought.

"I don't know, but I'm certainly going to check. Meanwhile, if you see it again, tell me right away. If I'm not here, tell Mrs. Quinn, or Mrs. Hutchinson, or one of your parents. Tell them I said it was important, and they should call me. Stay with them until they do, okay?"

She nodded.

I looked around for Sadie's mother. She was still deep in conversation. Dory was busy at the Circ desk, but the children's area was deserted. I recognized everyone in sight, but I still didn't want to leave Sadie alone, and I'd spent more time talking to her than I'd intended.

"Would you mind helping me out until your mom is ready to go? You can help me pick out books to fill in the displays. We'll start with the picture books, okay?"

Sadie was delighted. She chattered about all the things she'd read as we worked our way through the stacks. When we got to the kids' mystery display, the first thing to catch my eye was a reissued *Trixie Belden and the Secret of the Mansion.*

Ironic, I thought, propping the book on an easel. I started out in Sleepyside, but ended up in Sleepy Hollow.

Chapter Nine

I was on the calendar for the Saturday reference shift, which was fine with me even though it made for a long week. My talk with Sadie had raised a lot of questions and made me fearful on her behalf. I wanted to compare notes with Mary Alice, and alert her to what Sadie had seen. Then I wanted to figure out what Sadie *could* have seen. After another restless night I had decided to rule out actual ghosts, though if I had the chance to haunt something, Raven Hill Manor would be at the top of my list.

When I arrived at 9:30, Mary Alice was already in. I went over to Circ to check in the DVDs I had picked up from Agnes Jenner. My visit with her had been a bust. She hadn't noticed anything unusual Tuesday night, but confessed she hadn't been paying attention. Agnes pointed out she would only register someone going by if it were quite late, since there was a fair amount of traffic on the road when the library was open. She vowed to keep a closer eye on things in the future, but I wasn't holding out much hope. It had been a long shot to begin with.

I told Mary Alice about my conversation with Sadie Barrett, and asked her what she remembered about Tuesday night.

"Sadie was here late," Mary Alice said. "Her mother and Darla Van Alstyne had their heads together over something on the table over there," she pointed to a spot between the two entrances to the reading room, "so I let her stay where she was. We were so busy that afternoon. I had a lot left to do before we closed."

"Who else was still around?"

"No one I could see. There was the usual clatter when the meeting ended, but I wasn't paying attention."

Mary Alice sighed.

"This business with Sadie worries me," she said. "I tend to think she dozed off, but if she didn't, she saw something very odd. It could have been one of the volunteers going upstairs carrying something, I guess, but I don't know."

"Remember, she saw it twice. The first time was about a month ago, so it could be unrelated to the murder. Which is probably what the police would say, if they believed her at all. I hate asking a kid to keep a secret, but I don't know who to trust. I don't want to draw attention to Sadie, and if the police talk to her it will get around."

"That's the horror of all this. Whoever killed Joanna is almost certainly someone we know. Still, I could have a quiet word with Sam. He's a smart man. He'll grasp all the implications."

"That would make me feel better, and I think it would be more credible coming from you. You've known him for a while."

"I'll call him at home. Keep it off the radar."

"Thank you. Now, do you remember where Sadie was sitting?"

"Beanbag chair. It's her favorite spot."

I walked over to the bright yellow beanbag chair. It got moved around a bit during the course of the day, but always remained in the same general location in the children's area. I plopped into it and looked toward the front entrance to the reading room to see what I could see. The answer was—not much. I was looking directly at the Story-Hour-in-a-Bag display. The colorful little backpacks hung from brass hooks on a repurposed hall tree. I slid lower and shifted to one side.

There. I could see the bottom half of staircase, framed by the bags above and the bench below. We hadn't turned on the hall lights yet, but the watery sunlight coming in above the front door pushed the shadows back just enough.

"About here?" I checked with Mary Alice.

"That's right, give or take half a foot. See anything?"

"Bottom half of the stairs and a little bit of the hall. The light would be different at night. It would be coming down the stairs rather than from the front. She would probably only have been able to see something in outline."

Mary Alice agreed.

"I turned off the entry lights as soon as we closed, but the stairway lights would still have been on, for what they're worth."

But the lights in the reading room were bright, which led to my biggest concern. Could whatever Sadie saw see her?

"I'll have to look tonight when we close. It's earlier than when we closed on Tuesday, but maybe I can get a better idea of what was visible."

The two of us went about the rest of our opening routine. I was on autopilot as I ran through all the possibilities of what Sadie might have seen. My initial presumption had been that it was a man, but that was because of the Nearly Headless Nick analogy. It could have been a woman. Sadie had been focused on the apparent "headlessness." How had she put it? Lumpy. Someone bundled up or hunched over? Someone who knew enough to avoid the back stairs, always in use by the staff and the Friends when a meeting ended or at closing time. The front door was locked promptly, and staff and volunteers exited through the back. Or perhaps it was someone not familiar enough with the building to know there *were* back stairs, someone who had hidden away and waited for the noise to die down before making a move through the front. That presumed a pre-arranged meeting, because someone who didn't know the manor wouldn't know where to find Joanna. Unless it was someone who pretended to leave and doubled back. I'd have to figure out who was where and when after the meeting in order to rule anyone out. Joanna wouldn't have turned her back to a stranger or to anyone threatening, but if it were someone she knew? How hard would it be to sneak up on someone at the top of the stairs? I remembered the squeaky floor-board. I needed to check the stairs as soon as I had a minute.

Anne Marie arrived a few minutes before we opened. We usually ran a skeleton crew on nights and weekends, but Helene had asked the intern to come in as backup. Good call—the place was mobbed again. Morbid curiosity had not abated. Again, it was a mix of library regulars, infrequent visitors, and strangers. I was busy for a couple of hours. Once things settled down to a few people browsing and using the computers, I decided it was time to do a little investigating. Telling Anne Marie I wanted an early lunch and to call my cell if she needed help, I let her fly solo at the reference desk and took off.

Once out of sight, I nipped up the back stairs to the second floor, pausing to peek into the hallway at the top. Deserted, just as I'd hoped. The door to the archives was propped open, though, which meant Millicent was in. Technically, the archives were only open on weekdays, but if someone wanted to do research and could only come on a Saturday, Millicent would often make an appointment to meet with them. Moving as quietly as I could, I crossed the hall and went up the next flight of stairs, firmly squashing all thoughts of headless ghosts and dead bodies.

I wasn't the only one who had decided to take a look around the crime scene. When I got to the landing, I found the attic door open and Vince Goodhue crouched at the bottom of the stairwell with a small flashlight. He obviously hadn't heard me coming, as he remained engrossed in his task, shining the light into every crevice on the stairs, and running his hands along the treads. If he was looking for something, it was obviously small and dark. I watched him for a moment longer and decided a direct approach was best.

"Looking for something?"

Vince jerked back and landed on his butt. He swore softly and twisted around to face me.

"Sorry." I did my best to sound contrite. "I thought you'd heard me coming."

"Obviously not." He grabbed the doorknob to pull himself up. He flicked his flashlight off and looked up the stairs. Blowing out a long breath he turned toward me. I didn't budge, leaving him no place to go on the small landing. Vince and I stared at each other for a few seconds. I said nothing. I'd stared down scarier people than Vince Goodhue. The police may have released the crime scene but this was not a public area. Vince was neither staff nor volunteer, and I wanted an explanation.

"Has anyone found a flash drive?" he asked.

"Not that I know of. Have you asked anyone at Circ to check the lost and found bin?"

He hesitated. "No."

"That might be a good place to start."

"Yes," he said and paused again.

I waited.

"You're right, Greer. But the reading room was crowded, and I didn't want to talk to anyone." He shrugged, not meeting my eyes.

"Ah, I see." Plausible, but he could have called, and he hadn't. Nice try.

"Well," I went on, "I can find out. What does it look like? Is it labeled or anything?"

"It should have a 'J' on it. It was Joanna's. I think she had it with her. I can't find it at home."

"And the police don't have it?"

He shifted around. "No."

I'd bet he hadn't asked. But I would, because I'm helpful like that, especially when a potential clue in no way leads to me. Still, if Joanna had the drive on her when she fell, it could still be here in some nook or cranny. Unlikely the police had missed it, but possible. Vince thought it was worth a look, and if he wanted it that badly, I wanted it more.

"I'm sorry," I said. "It's just awful that you had to come here and look for it. I can carry on the search if you want. Was there anything on it you need urgently? I have some time right now. I'm on my lunch break."

"A lot of details of our current project are on it. Joanna had mapped out the whole thing. I was working on specific segments. I need it badly to keep things moving."

I knew Joanna had helped Vince with running his company. It wouldn't surprise me if she did most of the detail work. He reluctantly accepted my offer of help, since I made it clear I wasn't going anywhere. If he thought I'd leave him here alone he was delusional. I had every intention of palming the drive if I got to it first. Besides, this might be the only chance I had to ask him a few questions.

"How are the girls?" I asked as we quartered the landing.

"I don't think they really comprehend it yet. They're staying with my parents. My mother said they cry sometimes and ask for her at bedtime, but the rest of the time they just act like kids."

A wave of sadness rolled over me, as I remembered there would be no courageous mommy reading bedtime stories about brave, clever little girls doing amazing things. I gave myself a mental shake.

"It's lucky they have grandparents so close. It would be harder if they were at home. They stay with your parents often, don't they? Weren't they there Tuesday night, because both you and Joanna were going to be out late?"

That last bit was a stab in the dark, but there had to be a reason Vince hadn't gone looking for his wife or at least a reason he could give the police.

"I was gone all night, filming downtown. Joanna was going to be organizing for the jumble sale and didn't know how late she'd be."

He was a little abrupt. I was sure he'd had to go over this with the police more than once. Since he was still a free man, his alibi must have held up. So far.

We searched a few more minutes before Vince said he was giving up. I told him I'd continue to look for it in the library and promised to let him know if I found it. Which I would, once I'd copied the contents, determined whether or not there was anything incriminating on it, and decided whether or not to hand it over to the police.

Once Vince left, I began at the bottom of the stairwell and worked my way up. I had no flashlight, so I had to feel my way along each step. Vince hadn't asked what I was doing here in the middle of a busy Saturday. That might be suspicious or it might not. He did have a lot on his mind. If anyone else appeared, I decided to tell them I was looking for my own flash drive which I thought I'd dropped the day I found Joanna's body. I didn't expect to see anyone, but I wouldn't put it past Officer Webber to turn up unexpectedly in the hope of finding someone up to no good. Or maybe I could use my own fictional missing flash drive to find out if the police had found one.

I hadn't found a flash drive or anything else unusual by the time I made it to the top of the stairs. I turned my attention to the shelves. Joanna had clearly been organizing for the sale. Neatly sorted board games and small toys filled the remaining shelves, whose gently rounded edges showed the scars of much use. I gave each an experimental tug. All gave slightly, but it would take a good yank to get them loose. Always possible the top one was an outlier, but I thought it more likely Joanna had grabbed for it as she fell, or someone pulled it down to make it look like that's what hit her.

Mindful of the time I'd been away from the reading room, I began to test the floorboards for squeaks while I studied the piles of stuff to the right of the shelves. Millicent had sequestered the original contents of the attic with some plastic barricade tape. The little needlepoint footstool I had noticed clearly belonged in another part of the attic, but it was likely Joanna or another one of the Friends had commandeered it so they could reach the higher shelves more easily. There were boxes and bags of everything from knickknacks to small appliances. I counted three bread makers, still in their original packaging, but nothing thus far that looked like a murder weapon. I didn't expect to find a bloodstained golf club the police had somehow missed, but some head wounds could kill you without the skin being broken, and she might have gotten that bloody gash tumbling down the stairs.

I turned the corner and found piles of used sports equipment. It was an embarrassment of riches in terms of blunt instruments. Baseball bats, an old croquet set, hockey sticks, and even a cricket bat were piled in no particular order. I'd registered this stuff on various trips through the attic, but had no idea how long each thing had been there. There was no way for me to know if something was missing. The Friends might have a record of who had donated what, but only if someone wanted a receipt for tax purposes. And if I had noticed all this stuff, someone planning a murder would have, too. Unless this was an unpremeditated, opportunistic crime, the killer had to know a weapon was at hand, or had to bring it, and roaming around the building at night with something large enough to mimic death by bookshelf would raise some eyebrows.

"Professor Plum in the library with a lead pipe," I muttered as I continued my journey through the attic. The floor, with the exception of the board I had discovered days ago, was surprisingly quiet. Someone could have sneaked up on

Joanna from either direction. I had made it to the other stairwell entrance when I heard the voices. If I hadn't been so attuned to any possible noise, I might have missed them.

The words were indistinct but the staccato rhythm and pitch screamed argument. I eased along the wall and peeked around the corner. I saw nothing but some light coming in through the partially open door at the bottom of the stairs. I held on to the doorjamb and leaned forward, unwilling to risk my floorboard luck running out and alerting the people below.

I heard a deep voice, the volume increasing each second until it became a frustrated shout.

"I've seen it! I know it's here, somewhere in all these books and letters!"

It was Vince. Could he be that upset about a missing flash drive, or was it something else?

He lowered his voice again, and said something I couldn't hear.

I barely recognized Millicent's voice as she responded in a low hiss, but I caught the phrase, "blackmail by any other name." Vince spoke again. This time I caught the name Joanna, but nothing else. The sound was fading—they were moving away from the door. I would have to get closer if I wanted to hear anything else. I shifted my feet carefully, and set one foot gently on the top step, keeping to the outside of the tread and still clinging to the doorknob with one hand. I still couldn't hear anything. I would have to go further.

I was feeling for the next step when the door at the bottom swung wide, flooding the lower steps with light. I sucked in a breath, conscious of how my white shirt would stand out in the darkness. If discovered, I could brazen it out, but given that I had just heard the word "blackmail," a long-standing motive for murder, I would rather not be discovered. I pulled my foot quickly back, now feeling instead for the top of the stairs. I found it and stepped up, careful not to move too suddenly and risk a noise. I kept my eyes on the lower landing, my urge to flee at war with my curiosity.

A hand appeared. Long-fingered and skeletal, its pale outline ended at a silver watch clasping a bony wrist. It moved slowly, feeling along the wall as if searching for something. I blinked at the weird apparition as it moved into the stairwell. A shadow fell on the landing, and as I watched, the inky darkness took on a grotesque, elongated human form. The shadow shifted, and with it the light, and I saw that the hand was not disembodied, but ended at the cuff of a black sweater. It was Millicent reaching in. I exhaled, but my relief was short-lived. She must be feeling for the light switch, and if she flicked it on and looked up, I was well and truly caught. Time to scram.

I eased back out of the stairwell, sliding along the wall until I was back where I started, with only my head peeking down. I reached up along the wall to steady myself as I turned. My hand brushed something. A small chime sounded. I froze for an instant, and then looked toward my right hand, now immobile. A short row of bells hung along the wall; their dull brass nearly invisible in the shadowy darkness. I heard a click, and the stairwell light came on.

I moved as quickly as I dared, trying to avoid knocking anything over. When I rounded the corner to the first half of the attic I paused and looked back. The light was still on and I was sure I heard footsteps, but that might have been my fevered imagination. I took off again, zigzagging around boxes and piles until I could grip the newel post and swing around and onto the stairs. I kept both hands on the stairwell walls to keep from falling, and when I got to the bottom, I pushed the door gently shut, keeping the knob turned until the door was in the frame to avoid the telltale click. It closed silently. All those years of sneaking around spying on my older sister had paid off.

I flew down the next flight of steps. Once again, I stopped short of the hallway and reconnoitered. Not empty as I'd hoped. There was a man standing at the opposite end studying the large leaded-glass window. He stepped back from it and looked up, and I took the opportunity to walk briskly across the hall to the stairs opposite. Once out of sight I was off again, covering the distance to the kitchen in record time. When I got there and shut the door behind me, I was panting and my heart was racing. I needed to get more exercise, perish the thought. Only so much of this was attributable to adrenaline. I took deep breaths as I made myself a cup of tea to take back to the reference desk, as was my usual habit. Time to act casual, and sort out what I'd learned.

Business remained steady, but slower than it had been that morning. People were still drifting in and out, pausing to gossip in the guise of expressing concern. I needed to get work done. I wanted all to be orderly and shipshape in my area of the library. I always did, but more so since finding Joanna. Like Caesar's wife, she who finds the body must be above reproach. No matter, I could multitask. By putting Anne Marie in charge and riding shotgun at the reference desk, I could give our intern some helpful experience, continue my weeding project, noodle through what I had overheard, and keep a sharp eye—and ear—on what was going on in the reading room. Piece of cake.

My stomach rumbled. Cake sounded good. It was that time of afternoon and I'd missed lunch. But I had a fresh cup of tea, a protein bar stuffed in my pocket, and access to a restroom, so I shouldn't complain. Kinsey Milhone often had it much worse.

I settled in at the desk with a scanner and pulled up the publisher websites I needed. Normally decisions on what to discard or update relied on circulation statistics, but the areas I was working on today needed a different approach. Our books on divorce and substance abuse tended to turn up in odd corners of the library or low-traffic areas of the stacks. Because we had no security system for our materials, they often left the library without benefit of check-out, only to reappear in the book drop after being returned anonymously in the dead of night. I couldn't blame people—it was a small town and these weren't topics anyone wanted gossiped about. No matter how much we tried to protect patron privacy, standing in the middle of a busy library waiting to check out an armload of books on addiction was bound to be noticed. I was glad so few were stolen. Still, it did mean I had to spend a little more time than usual evaluating wear and tear, and content and timeliness, as I couldn't trust the statistics.

I was flipping through a book on divorce in New York when I found a folded article. Tucked between the endpapers was a photocopy of the front page of the village paper dated thirty-five years ago. One headline was circled: "Local Child Drowns." I scanned the article, but didn't recognize any names. There were some notes penciled in the margin though, and I was sure I recognized the handwriting—Joanna's.

I glanced around. Other than a woman Anne Marie was helping, no one was nearby. I smoothed the photocopy and took a look at the things Joanna had scribbled in the margins. Most were a series of letters and numbers that seemed familiar but that I couldn't immediately interpret. There were a few words and phrases that didn't seem to relate to anything. I refolded the paper and slid it into my agenda. It would have to wait until I got home.

The photocopy had been in one of the books that had been sitting on my desk. I quickly flipped through the rest of that stack. Nothing. I knew Joanna had been at my desk sometime after I left on Tuesday night, because she had left me the note about the booklist. Had she been using the book and forgotten the article was there? I scanned the barcode—no recent check-outs. That didn't mean anything. If she was thinking about divorce, she wouldn't take the book home. She could easily stash it in the Friends' office and use it here. Maybe the rumors about Vince and Felicity were true, and she was studying her options. She could be doing research for a story or helping someone else.

She'd mentioned "other stuff going on" in her note, and that she trusted my discretion. She'd also said it was related to what we'd talked about. Little girls standing up for themselves? The connection was tenuous at best. It was also possible she had needed to slip the article out of sight quickly, and intended to retrieve it later. I needed to find out who had lingered after the meeting. Or come early, since I didn't know what time she had left the note.

At that moment Millicent stuck her head into the reading room. She looked around as though hunting for someone. I assumed a look of bland innocence and gave her a little wave. She had her handbag and was wearing a light jacket.

"Heading home?" I asked as she approached.

"Yes. I had a few people in doing genealogy research today. You know how long that can take."

"I do, and I have no patience for it. I'm so glad we have you, Millicent. You're better and faster at it than any librarian I know."

She gave me a genuine smile. Even in her seventies, Millicent was an uncommonly lovely woman. She had always seemed vaguely familiar to me, and I was sure she reminded me of an aging movie star. Of course, she was a native of Raven Hill and could be related to half the village. Hollywood or hometown, I couldn't figure out who it was she resembled.

"Well, dear, a passion for historical research is something in the blood, I think. No amount of schooling can compare."

There was a barely discernible edge to her voice on that last phrase. Technically, Millicent was neither a librarian nor an archivist, as she did not have an advanced degree. I'd heard Anita had been quick to point this out when she joined the board, but no one could top Millicent's knowledge. She was something of an institution here at the library, and so she was granted the title based on ability and experience. For once, Anita was silenced.

Millicent once again looked around the reading room.

"We've had a busy day," I said, "especially this morning."

"I thought as much. People have been roaming around upstairs. I don't like it. Not with everything that's been going on. I know we keep those rooms unlocked as a courtesy, but I don't think that's wise when there's hardly any staff in the building."

"I know. It's unnerving." I thought it unlikely Millicent had caught sight of me earlier, but decided on a pre-emptive strike, and figured I could kill two birds with one stone.

"Two or three times in the last two days I've found people wandering around in odd places, and it's made me wonder. Just before I went to lunch, I heard some man asking about the murder and the history of the manor. He spent a long time in the hall studying the antique windows. He even asked if there were any floorplans for the manor. I pointed him to Local History section, because I was helping someone else. I'm sure he went upstairs. I did run up and check later but I didn't see him. When we're busy in here it's hard to keep an eye on everything."

There. If she'd seen me, I'd given her a reasonable explanation, and if she'd seen the man in the upstairs hall, she had someone else to focus her suspicions on. And I'd worked in the question about floor plans.

"I saw him." she said. "But only from a distance. He didn't come into the archives to ask about plans or anything else. Just as well. There's nothing. The building has been added to so often they wouldn't be meaningful anyway. I'm sure you're doing your best, Greer. That's why I stopped by. I wanted to let you know I've checked all the windows upstairs and closed and locked whatever I could. You should only have to do a quick sweep when you close. The archives, of course, are already locked."

I thanked her and said goodnight. Too bad Millicent was on my suspect list. She was a walking encyclopedia of life in the village over the last sixty years. She'd be a great resource if she weren't a potential killer.

As the day drew to a close, I grew more and more anxious to get everybody out so I could try to figure out what Sadie had seen and if she had been visible to whomever was going up the stairs. I was also itching to get home and study the notes Joanna had made on that article. I was sure they were important. The usual late rush appeared, but at five o'clock sharp I sent the page to lock the doors and waded into the fray at Circ. When we had cleared everyone out, I sent the page home and turned to Anne Marie.

"Why don't you go ahead? It'll take me a little while to get organized, and it's been a long day." I caught Mary

Alice's eye and quickly glanced toward the yellow bean bag chair.

"Are you sure?" Anne Marie said. "I don't mind waiting. The place must get a little creepy when it's empty, especially at night."

Mary Alice gave a little snort.

"Greer is no Nervous Nellie, and neither am I. All of us are used to finding our way around the manor, even in the dark. Between the weather and the wiring, we lose power a couple of times a year."

"True," I said, "empty buildings don't bother me. Mary Alice still has a couple things to do, and if you put that cart back in the office I can finish in no time."

"If you're sure it's okay," Anne Marie said, looking out at the lengthening shadows, "I do have plans tonight."

"Off you go then. We're used to this—it's usually only two people to close."

Anne Marie took charge of the book cart and left. I organized reference while Mary Alice finished shutting down Circ. I went to the window and saw Anne Marie's tail lights as she exited the parking lot.

"She's gone," I said to Mary Alice.

She glanced at the clock.

"It's later than I thought, Greer. My sister-in-law is coming to dinner and I have to stop at the market. I can only stay a few minutes."

I thought I'd have Mary Alice play sidekick in my re-enactment. Now I'd be investigating on my own. A little zing of excitement shot through me.

"I don't think this can wait," I said. "If you could set the lights the way they were on Tuesday while I get my things from the office, it would be a big help. Then I'll only be a few minutes behind you."

She hesitated, but briefly.

"You're right, it shouldn't wait, and we've had everything locked up for a while. You should be fine. You drove today, didn't you? You won't be walking home? It looks like rain again."

"I have my car and I'll be quick. I have something to do tonight, too," I said, thinking of the photocopied article.

"All right."

By the time I collected my belongings, Mary Alice had adjusted all the lights and was headed for the door.

"Just like Tuesday night," she said, "and I'll call Sam when I get home."

I left my things at the Circ desk. There was a low rumble off in the distance. The predicted storm moved in quickly, and the light began to fade. Good. The darker it was in the hall, the better my chances of figuring out what Sadie could actually have seen. And if Sadie could have *been* seen. I looked at the motion sensor panel. According to the blinking lights, I was alone.

I'd been lying when I told Anne Marie I didn't mind being alone in an empty building. It wasn't that I didn't mind—I actually loved it and always had. As I stood alone in the middle of the large room, I felt the illicit thrill that comes with being somewhere you shouldn't be, at a time you shouldn't be there, for reasons of which no one would approve. One day I'd picked up a book by Lawrence Block and met Bernie Rhodenbarr, gentleman thief, and I knew I was not alone. I wasn't *The Burglar in the Library*, but I was the Girl Detective on the Prowl.

I walked into the hall and studied the portraits. The dead Ravenscrofts weren't a lively looking bunch, but Sadie had seen something that made her think they moved. I had just gone to the other side of the hall when something shifted in my peripheral vision. I turned and confronted a woman's pale face, a frock-coated man looming over her. I gasped and stepped back, and the image receded. A mirror. I went closer. It was old, this mirror, wavy glass in a heavy antique frame, the silvering dark at the edges. The face that looked back at me was distorted by the rippling surface. It was like looking at myself underwater. The gentleman in the frock coat seemed to move as well, disappearing from the frame depending on where I stood.

I walked up and down the hall. There were several mirrors in the same kind of ornate frames as the portraits. I had noticed them, but after my first few days never paid attention. Now I studied each one. No matter which mirror I looked in, there was a Ravenscroft looking over my shoulder. Charming. The hall had as many architectural oddities as the rest of the house, and the alcoves and odd protuberances had not been avoided by whoever had hung the portrait gallery. They seemed to have been used to make sure that the Ravenscrofts could keep an eye on any visitors. Or each other. Nothing would surprise me.

I went into the children's area and stood in a few different places. One of the big mirrors was visible from most of them, reflecting different portraits depending on where I stood. Anyone walking in the hall would move in and out of a frame holding a Ravenscroft reflection. So, would anyone standing still, waiting for a quiet moment to go up the stairs, believing themselves unseen. With the lights dim, or flickering, I could understand Sadie's theory. On to the headless ghost.

I moved to the beanbag chair and slid down until I could see the stairs. There was no light coming from the windows by the front door. The stairs and the small section of landing I could see were lit only by wall sconces and the chandelier in the main hall. Anyone on the stairs would be in shadow on the first few steps, and just a dark outline beyond that.

The windows rattled as I stood. Gusts from the gathering storm were becoming frequent, and I could see the agitated swaying of the trees as I walked into the main hall. I walked slowly up the stairs, counting eight steps until the light from the wall sconce fell on my face. I turned my head toward the reading room, but all I could see from here was a small portion of the children's area. I backed down the steps until I could see all the way in, spotting the bright yellow of the beanbag chair through the colorful Story Hour backpacks. The good news was I had to hunt for it, and I knew what I was looking for. It was unlikely Sadie had been spotted by whoever was going up the stairs.

I looked back over my shoulder and saw my own distorted shadow following me. Distorted but not headless. Looking left, I saw something similar but larger cast against the wall by the light from the chandelier. I tilted my head sideways. Not exactly headless but not lumpy either. I was convinced Sadie had seen someone, even if I couldn't replicate her description. I was also convinced she wouldn't have been able to tell if it was a man or a woman, which didn't do much to limit my suspect pool.

The wind was keening around the manor as I started back down the stairs. I stopped in my tracks when I heard a book fall.

The sound of a book thudding down on a hard surface is not an unusual one in a library, but it is unusual in a closed library. I stayed still. The sound did not repeat. There was no metallic clang of the book drop, no sound of a car pulling away. The noise had come from the empty reading room.

I grabbed my cell phone from my pocket. I clicked it on and brought up the dial pad as I strained to hear any other noise from the reading room. After another minute or two, I went down the stairs and crossed the hall. Pausing in the doorway, I scanned the length of the room in front. Nothing moved, and nothing seemed out of place.

I walked toward the Circ desk, looking down the aisles between the stacks as I went. The sense of being watched that I'd had on and off since my trip to the attic with Officer Webber crawled across the back of neck. *Turn around, don't turn around*, my mind whispered. A creak, and the trees moaning in the storm. Was that noise inside? Outside? I held my breath, listening. The wind slammed against the manor. I heard a whistling noise and another thud just ahead of me. I jumped.

Get a grip, Greer. There's no one here.

I walked toward the whistling noise, just to the right of the desk. One of the tall casement windows rattled. In front of it, two picture books lay face down on the deep wooden sill. I held up my hand and felt cold air moving. The window was locked but not properly shut. A slight warping of the frame allowed thin fingers of air to slide in. I pushed hard against the locking mechanism, and with a little groan it clicked into place. A trickle of air still came in around the edges, but that was true of every window in the place. It was part of Anita's argument for a new building—the lack of climate control wasn't good for the books. True, but I liked the fresh air and the smell of the seasons wafting through the place. The manor needed to breathe. It was all part of the charm. Though there had been a rough stretch this winter when I'd felt like Bob Cratchit shivering at the reference desk. I'd even bought a pair of fingerless gloves. Another gust set the panes rattling, and I decided I'd better check them all.

I'd finished the children's area when a flickering shadow caught my eye. I stepped back, looking through the shelves toward the main hall. The stacks were of uniform height, ending a foot above my head. The books on them were not, creating openings of various sizes, from peephole to window. I found a good vantage point, where I could see without being seen. With most of the lights off, the reading room was dim but comparable to the hall. I saw nothing moving. Directly across from me, the trees outside the raven room swayed in the wind, creating shifting bands of light and dark. Satisfied, I moved forward as another gust rattled the windows, leaving a silent stillness in its wake, a stillness broken by the soft click of a door latch sliding into place.

I froze, going cold right down to my bones even as my pulse kicked up. I sucked in air, whirled and sprinted to the Circ desk and the secondary alarm panel behind it. No lights flickered on the motion sensor except for the zone I was in. What I heard, or thought I heard, was close by—no one could have gotten out of range of the sensors in the few seconds it took me to cross the room, and I'd had a clear view of the front entryway and hall. I was alone.

Still. Even Bernie the Burglar knew when it was time for a quick exit. I had the information I needed—Sadie's presence was most likely unnoticed by whoever went up the stairs the night Joanna was killed.

I worked my way around the rest of the room, touching every lock and hyper alert to very sound. Each window and latch slid easily into place, as if the manor itself wished to speed me on my way. The wind keened as it wound around the building. Darkness fell, leaving me in a dimly lit cocoon.

I grabbed my things and decided to leave the remaining lights on until I got to the main panel by the rear exit. Keys in hand, I tested the front door. The inner fire doors were shut and locked, and through them I could see the dead bolt was shot on the original wood doors of the manor. The wind rattled and knocked, but the old wood held firm. I got to the back door and eyeballed the motion detector display once more. Nothing. I set the alarm and reached for the door.

The handle was pulled from my grasp and the door flung wide. I staggered. A cold wind whirled me around. I regained my balance and turned in time to see the door slam shut, rattling on its hinges as the wind swirled. I fought the currents of air long enough to check the lock, then turned toward the parking lot. Another gust of wind buffeted me from behind, pushing me along and tugging my hair loose. I ran. I made it to my car as the rain started.

I turned the ignition and shifted into drive. A warning light flashed into angry red life on the dash. I groaned. I drove a BMW so old it could have registered to vote, but it had been Danny's pride and joy. The car was still solid, but there was some kind of short in the electrical system and I never knew if the warnings were real or phantom. The last time I'd ignored one, the water pump had died in the middle of a busy road. I shifted back to park and waited to see if the light flickered back off.

I leaned back and studied the façade of the manor. Rain streaked the old stone walls. Shifting shadows danced across the slate roof. The scudding clouds lit the scene in shades of black and gray, like an old movie. The place would look foreboding to anyone who had not experienced its welcoming hum.

"It was a dark and stormy night." No, that didn't do it justice. As my eyes ranged over the craggy walls and shimmery windows of the manor, I remembered the best haunted house book ever written. *The Haunting of Hill House* by Shirley Jackson. It had scared me silly when I first read it, and some of the lines were with me still. The ending in particular. I paraphrased as I looked at the house, "*silence lay steadily against the wood and stone of Raven Hill Manor, and whatever walked there, walked alone.*"

But not tonight.

There was a face at the window.

I had not been alone, and whatever walked there had not registered on the motion sensors.

Chapter Ten

I blinked, hoping it was a trick of the light, but the face was still there. I was being watched. I stared back, grabbing for my phone. There was a flash, some movement to one side, and the figure pitched forward and dropped out of sight. I pictured Joanna tumbling down the stairs, lying in the dark. Had she been aware at any point during that long cold night?

I grabbed my keys and swung out of the car, dialing 911 before my feet hit the ground. I'm no hero, neither am I stupid. I was the last one out of the manor—if another body was found I was done for. I didn't want to be the next body, either, so I gave the emergency operator a play by play as I went. I fought the wind and rain all the way to the door, shoving my key in the lock. It wouldn't turn. I rattled the handle. No luck. The operator told me to stay outside.

"Someone's hurt. I'm the only one here!"

The lock gave a last protesting whine. The key turned. I yanked open the door and kicked down the stop. I left the alarm engaged and hit the panic code as well. I'd flipped every switch on the light panel and grabbed the heavy utility flashlight we kept on top of it when the alarm delay ran out. The entire building shrieked. Anyone up to no good would know they'd been busted.

I scanned the main hall and saw no one. I took the back stairs, the fastest route to where I'd seen the face at the window. I explained as much to the annoyed operator as I climbed.

I was on the second floor when the operator told me help was on the way. I let my phone drop to my side when I spotted the body—the unmoving, unnaturally still body—beneath the window.

"Damn it!" I said through clenched teeth. I looked up and down the hall before venturing out of the stairwell. No one else in sight, just the crumpled form on the floor. I had recognized him right away—Vince Goodhue. He was lying on his back, arms outflung and legs twisted sideways. His head was turned away. Scattered around him were miscellaneous items, as though he had turned out his pockets. Tissues, gum, change.

What the hell?

The operator squawked insistently, so I put my phone back to my ear as I knelt next to Vince.

"I've found someone hurt. I'm checking for a pulse."

Thankfully, I found one. Now that I was closer, I could see the slow rise and fall of his chest, and a lump at the base of his skull.

"He's alive," I told the operator. This should clear me as a suspect. I hoped.

"Please stay on the line." I sat back on my heels as the operator continued to do her thing, and I studied the scene in front of me. It looked like a mugging. Vince had been bashed from behind and then rolled. I replayed what I had seen from the car. The sudden drop when someone had surprised him from behind, less than a minute before I was out of the car and trying the door. Another minute until I was in and hitting switches, sixty seconds until the alarm sounded, maybe a minute and a half until I was upstairs. Not enough time for an amateur mugger to do a thorough search. But a search for what? The missing flash drive? Something else? Whatever it was, someone wanted it badly enough to knock Vince out to search for it. If it was that important, I wanted it, too.

The operator told me to remain where I was, the police would be there momentarily. I peeked over the windowsill. There were no flashing lights in view. I had a little time. I looked at Vince's unconscious form. It was a risk, but at least someone had started the job. I set down my phone.

"*Well begun is half done,*" I recited as I searched the rest of Vince's pockets. It was from my mother's standard repertoire of helpful sayings, not that she'd approve of how I was applying it. No matter. I wasn't interested in approval. I was interested in finding a killer.

I found nothing of interest except a bent business card. "Julia Wainwright, Esq." There was an Albany address and phone number below it. I flipped through Vince's wallet and examined his keychain. There was an extra ring attached to it, and on it was a key to the library. It must have been

Joanna's. As President of the Friends she would have a key to the building, and the key next to it was the make of car she drove. Another small ring was attached, but this was twisted open and held nothing. The missing drive?

A new set of sirens sounded outside. I grabbed my phone and scooted back, not standing until I was beyond the window. Someone killed the alarm. By the time Sam O'Donnell and a uniformed officer appeared on the landing, I was standing against the wall in full view, telling the operator the police were here. I hung up.

O'Donnell bent over Vince, performing the same quick check I had. The uniformed officer had been joined by another who had come up the front staircase. They worked their way down the hall, checking doors and examining unlocked rooms.

"His pulse is steady," I said. "I told the operator to send an ambulance."

"On their way," he said. "Anyone else here?"

"I don't know. When I saw someone at the window just drop out of sight I came straight here."

"We'll talk about that shortly." He stood to make way for the EMTs.

With brisk efficiency, Vince was examined and transferred to a stretcher. I wasn't sure, but he seemed to stir.

I turned back to O'Donnell. "We've got to stop meeting like this. If I'd known the citizens of Raven Hill were this blood-thirsty, I wouldn't have taken the job. Will he be all right?"

"I think so. We'll know shortly. Right now, I'm more interested in finding out what went on here tonight."

"I'm not sure."

"We'll begin at the beginning." O'Donnell pulled out his notebook. A uniformed officer interrupted. The archives were locked and needed to be searched. Did I have a key?

"There's one at the reference desk," I said. "I can get it for you."

O'Donnell nodded and we all trooped down the stairs. I sat at the desk, pulled an envelope marked "MISC" out of the drawer, and upended it on the blotter. I started fishing through the pile.

The young policeman looked in astonishment from the ratty brown envelope to the pile of keys to O'Donnell to me and back to the keys.

"What are all these for?" he said.

"The archives, public rooms, supply closets, staff areas, wardrobes that lead to Narnia, who knows? I haven't tried them all. Here you go. The big one is to the archives, and the smaller one should open every other door on that floor. There's a full set of building keys in the boiler room, so here's the key to that."

He took the three keys and looked at the pile on the desk.

"Shouldn't these be secured somewhere, ma'am?"

"It's a big building." I repeated what I'd been told when I'd asked the same thing my first day of work. "There's a lock box in the director's office, but she's not always here, so the most-used spares are kept in the drawer." I shrugged. "And, not my call."

The uniformed officer looked at O'Donnell, who waved him away. I put the remaining keys back in the envelope and was opening the drawer when O'Donnell stuck his hand out. I looked up. His spine was rigid and his lips pursed.

"You didn't know about these," I said, handing over the envelope, watching his face carefully. "Helene forgot— Helene! The alarm company! They call—"

"She's been informed of the situation. I'll speak to her later, and Ms. Hunzeker as well."

"Oh God, Anita." I dropped my head in my hands. "She'll have a fit."

"I'm sure I can handle it," he said, pocketing the envelope. "Now let's talk about today."

"From the time we closed?"

"From the time you opened. Don't leave anything out. I want to know everything that happened in this building today that you're aware of."

I went through the day. I had to fudge a little here and there to explain why I was in the attic on my lunch break, but I emphasized the number of strangers wandering the building and implied they made me nervous. He took notes and nodded a few times, but didn't say much. The only tricky part were the questions about the end of the day.

"Why were you here alone?" he asked.

"I hadn't planned to be but I wanted to check something, and everyone else had plans. I thought I'd only be a minute."

I had debated about this while relaying the day's events to O'Donnell. If Mary Alice had already called him, he might be waiting to see if I told him the truth. If she hadn't gotten to him yet, she would, which would only corroborate my story.

"There's a little girl, Sadie Barrett. She's here a lot. She saw something the night of the murder. But what she said didn't make a lot of sense. I wanted to see for myself. Come with me. I'll show you."

I walked him over to the beanbag chair, and ran through my conversations with Sadie and Mary Alice and my end-of-day experiment. He listened without interruption. I was gratified—what I was saying sounded farfetched even to me.

"Conclusions?" he asked.

"Sadie saw something. She saw it more than once, and if she saw it again, she would recognize it, even if she couldn't tell who or what it was. Whoever it was probably couldn't see her, but I can't be positive, and that scares me. And drawing attention to her scares me, too."

"Rightly so." He stepped into the hall, had a brief chat with a uniformed officer, and came back.

"Did you hear or see anything unusual while you were checking on what the kid saw?"

The whole place turned into a freaking fun house. But that wasn't right. It wasn't the manor itself that was the problem. *Whatever walked there.* I rubbed the back of my neck, reliving the feeling of being watched. But nothing on the sensors. I was starting to doubt myself. Not enough sleep. But Vince's presence proved I *hadn't* been alone.

"A couple of books fell over. I found a window not quite closed, and decided I better check them all. Then I thought

I heard a door close, somewhere close by, but I'd already checked. Everything was locked, and still locked when I left. And nothing registered on the motion sensors. I looked there first. No one could move that fast."

"Walk me through it."

I started with the window I found open and ended where I was standing when I heard the door. He turned in a circle and led me to the main hall and the glass fire doors.

"Everything look all right?"

I scanned both sets of doors, turned to answer him, stopped, and turned back.

"The crash bar." I reached toward it. O'Donnell put his arm between me and the door.

"Just tell me," he said.

"It's stuck. It wasn't before. It sticks just enough to keep from locking so we always check it and I know I did. Besides, this wasn't the right noise. The noise I heard was quieter."

I peered through the glass. The dead bolt was still shot.

"It had to be Vince," I said, looking around the hall and thinking through the events of the evening.

"Most likely. We'll ask him."

"If it wasn't Vince," I went on, "it was whoever hit him, and whoever it was had a key. No one went by me, so someone left this way, and either didn't know about the crash bar, or didn't take the time to check. But the deadbolt is locked."

He looked through the glass. He asked, in a tone devoid of all hope, "Do you know if there was an outside key, or a master key, in that envelope?"

"No outside or master in there. No need. Anyone who knew about the keys at the reference desk would already have a key to the building. I'm sure Helene could give you a list of those people if she hasn't already."

O'Donnell muttered something that sounded like "half the village," and asked me a few more questions. Five minutes later he sent me home, but accompanied by an officer since I'd had some car trouble.

Fine with me. This girl detective thing was wearing me out.

Chapter Eleven

～

It was Sunday morning and the cupboard was bare. My stomach was rumbling. By the time I had gotten home the night before, I'd had just enough energy to mix a medicinal martini and go to bed. The young officer who escorted me home had walked me upstairs, carefully examined my porch, and preceded me inside, turning on lights and having a general look-see. I didn't have the sense he was conducting an informal search, though O'Donnell might have told him to keep his eyes open for blunt instruments propped in corners. It seemed more like he was doing a general safety check. He didn't look under the bed, but he did ask if anything seemed out of place. When I told him everything seemed fine, he reminded me to get my car checked and left. I watched him hop into a patrol car that pulled up to the curb. I saw another, lights out, at the end of the street. Whether they were watching me because I was a suspect or the next potential victim I didn't know, but I was glad to have them handy.

I donned jeans and a sweater, did my best to disguise the dark circles under my eyes, and headed to the Java Joint. It was Raven Hill's answer to chain coffee bars, and a hub of Sunday morning activity. Like everything else in the village proper, it was locally owned and operated according to the whims of its owners, a couple of aging hippies who claimed they had come upstate on a pilgrimage to Woodstock and never left. Meadow baked and Jack roasted and brewed—the place always smelled delicious. The combination of good food and comfy, quirky décor meant the Java Joint was always hopping. Though most nights it was crammed full of the kind of college students who wore a great deal of black and fancied themselves poets, the morning crowd tended to be village residents who wanted breakfast and a look at an actual print newspaper. If there was any scuttlebutt about last night's events, I would hear it here first.

I settled in to an overstuffed chair with a good view of place. I thought longingly of the days—was it only last weekend?—when going out for coffee and the paper meant I would spend the morning drinking coffee and reading the paper. Instead, I prepared to gossip and eavesdrop on my neighbors. I'd had a brief conversation that morning with Helene, who was concerned and supportive, and another with Anita, who was clearly tempted to shoot the messenger for lack of a better target. I'd expected that, and immediately went on offense, gushing about how glad I was I had decided to stay and tidy up, because who knew what might have happened if I hadn't interrupted the attack? She grudgingly agreed, but warned me not to spend any more time alone anywhere in the manor "for safety's sake." I would have to step carefully at work.

After a few brief conversations with people I knew, and thirty minutes of careful listening to the chatter around me, it was clear that what had happened at the manor was not yet common knowledge. Saturday night sirens usually meant a traffic accident, so many villagers wouldn't have paid too much attention. I also had the sense Sam O'Donnell ran a tight ship, and anyone Anita informed would be strong-armed into silence. The library staff would have to be told, but that would be Monday. My guess was the official story would be that Vince got locked in accidently while looking for something he'd dropped, and somehow hit his head in the dark. Thin but until the police had some answers Anita would try to spin it.

Once I was sure there was no immediate intelligence to gather, I picked up the local paper and applied myself to a second mug of coffee. The warmth of the sun, the mundane sounds of voices and crockery, and the burble and hiss of the coffee makers lulled me into a state of relaxation. It was short-lived. Sensing movement across from me, I looked up to find Officer Jennie Webber, coffee in hand. It was a large to-go cup, but any hope she wouldn't be staying long disappeared as she said, "Mind if I join you?"

Like I could stop her. I shrugged.

She sat and adjusted her chair, shifting it enough to have a clear view of the entrance. She glanced over her shoulder once or twice, taking in the back of the Java Joint and the line at the register. She didn't like the blind spot behind her. I watched her over the edge of my mug. The whole process only took a few seconds. She picked up her coffee and looked at me.

"Got a good enough view of the door?" I asked.

"For now. Do you always sit with your back to a wall, Ms. Hogan?"

"Upon the advice of my Irish granny, whenever I can. This is the best seat in the house."

Kitty Hogan was a fount of wisdom. She'd followed the "always know your exits" portion of her fight-or-flight lecture with "and the more important question, Greer my love, is 'fight or fight dirty?' I'm sure you'll find that what the latter lacks in elegance, it makes up for in efficiency."

This didn't seem the time to share that little gem, though I suspected Officer Webber would appreciate it. She'd taken another quick look around at my "best seat in the house" remark and given a nod. Now she turned her attention back to me.

"I understand there was some more excitement at the library last night."

"I'm sure your boss filled you in. He was the first to arrive."

"I'd rather hear it from you."

I was under no obligation, but a little cooperation cost me nothing and might get me something in return.

"I set the alarm, locked up, and was pulling out of the lot when I saw movement in an upstairs window. I called

911 and went back in. I found Vince Goodhue in the second-floor hallway, unconscious. The EMTs arrived and carted him off to the hospital. I talked to Lt. O'Donnell and went home. That's it." I stopped, and added, "Vince had come to by the time he was taken to the hospital, so I presume he's fine."

"Treated and released. No signs of concussion, but he'll have a headache for a day or two." She sipped her coffee. "So, what do you think happened?"

"Well, I don't think he tripped and fell. Someone must have hit him, but I would've sworn there was no one else in the building when I set the alarm."

"Mr. Goodhue was there," she pointed out, "and you, of course. That doesn't leave a lot of options. Unless there was someone else, someone who managed to slip out without being seen. How likely is that, Ms. Hogan?"

"Unlikely, but not impossible." I flashed back to the unlocked door I'd found when I went back through the building with O'Donnell. Then I realized what she was implying.

"You can't honestly believe I bashed Vince?"

"You have to admit you have a habit of finding bodies. At least this one was still alive. Third time's the charm, I guess."

Bitch. She was trying to rattle me, hoping I'd let something slip. Nice try. Two could play at that game.

"Do you really think I killed Joanna Goodhue? Or my husband? I know you checked my story."

"I did. You're clear. The investigating officer confirmed your alibi, and said they'd made an arrest."

I didn't kill your husband, lady.

I silenced the voice in my head and gave her my best "so there" look.

"But he's also sure you weren't being totally straight with him. Some things didn't add up. He thought you felt guilty, but you were smart enough to keep your mouth shut. One smart cookie, he said. You didn't come clean, but you didn't kill your husband."

Bingo. My face got hot. Well, the best defense is a good offense. I looked her in the eye and smiled. "Everybody has a guilty secret, Officer Webber. What's yours?"

She blanched. A look that might have been panic flickered across her face and was gone in an instant. I'd scored a direct hit. I'd figured out she was willing to ignore protocol that day in the attic when she had decided to go it alone. Who knew what other bad habits she might have? We might have more in common than I thought.

"We're not talking about me, Ms. Hogan, we're talking about you."

"So we are. Since we've determined I didn't murder my husband, let's move on to Joanna Goodhue. I'm sure you've checked my alibi there."

The timetable on that was loose, but the police should have been able to verify my movements. I might have been able to pull off a quick trip to the manor attic to do someone in, but with the same problem everyone else had—being seen.

Webber said nothing, which I took as assent on the alibi check. I went on.

"And what's my motive?"

"None that I've found. But I'd put money on the fact you know something you're not telling."

"I've told you everything I know." Everything I knew was related. My wild guesses and the various bits of information I couldn't make fit were another story. Joanna's note, the whisper of blackmail, the feeling of being watched—all of it either led back to me or sounded crazy, and with Anita on the warpath I had to watch my step.

"If I think of anything else you might find helpful, I'll call you."

I picked up my dishes and stood.

"Chair's all yours. Have a nice day, Officer."

I left her in the Java Joint and mulled over what I'd learned. I pondered Jennie Webber while watching the hypnotic spin of the machines at the Suds-O-Matic. She had spent summers here as a kid, she'd said, but she had been in the Army for a while, and moved back for family reasons. Which could be anything, but was likely recent since I'd never seen her in the six months I lived here, and neither Dory nor Mary Alice had much to say about her. Everyone has a guilty secret, Beau said, and based on her response to my flippant remark, Officer Webber was no exception. But whatever it was, was it any use to me? Her standard operating procedure was along the lines of Mad Eye Moody in the Harry Potter books, "Constant vigilance!" Not surprising since she'd been in a war zone. She said little and missed less. My guess was she'd picked up plenty of information, both related to the case and random. Getting her to share was the snag.

Although—she had been willing to bend the rules before, and she had the air of an independent operator. The police traded for information when they needed to. I had watched it more than once in dark corners of my dad's pub when I should've been doing my homework. Sam O'Donnell, I thought, was playing a long game. He had not publicly ruled out the accident theory of Joanna's death, though it was clear he was not treating it as such. Some of those new faces popping up regularly at the library were undercover cops, I was sure, but borrowed from other jurisdictions so they wouldn't be recognized. They could gather information, but without much context. Jennie Webber had the context, but an official role that put people on their guard. No one wanted to reveal anything that put them in a bad light, even if it had nothing to do with the crime. People lied to the police all the time. The police were constrained by procedure.

I was a free agent.

While no one would be ruled out as a suspect until the actual killer was caught, O'Donnell had taken me at my word last night, so I wasn't at the top of their list. As long as I didn't break any laws or do anything to set Anita off, I would be left to my own devices. The constant police presence at the manor and Webber's habit of popping up were things I could work around and possibly use. People talked to me, and I had well-connected allies. I would take a page from the playbook of Sherlock Holmes.

It was time to activate the Raven Hill Irregulars.

*   *   *

Once back from the grocery store, I touched base with my little band of informants. Dory would be out all day, according to her husband, so I left a message. Mary Alice was home. She had spoken to Sam late the night before, and verified my story about Sadie and reasons for staying late. I filled her in on the latest developments and asked her to call if she heard anything new. Then I checked in with Henri. He had put out some feelers, but thus far had gotten nothing but some odd looks and promises from his acquaintances to let him know if they heard anything of interest. I told him what had happened the previous evening. He clucked over me, warning me to be more careful, and insisting I take Pierre while he went out to dinner with friends.

"He is a good little watchdog, if not exactly ferocious, and he will warn you if someone comes near to the house."

He had also had my window repaired, he told me, and I should let him know if it gave me any further trouble. The repairman had said there were a lot of scratches and dents in the wood, but he couldn't tell when they were made. The paint wasn't scratched, if that made me feel better. It didn't really, but I thanked him. At least it locked now, and I made sure it was before I hung up.

I'd volunteered to take Pierre right away, as he would work nicely into my plans. Before long the little dog and I had set out toward the village, the brisk air putting a spring in both our steps. I was planning to call on Agnes Jenner and see if she had followed through on her promise to keep a closer eye on the comings and goings on the road to the manor. I had a little box of tea biscuits, a brand I knew she liked, and figured I'd get an invitation to stay for a cup of tea and a cookie. I'd also timed my visit for the part of the day when she would be most lucid. Some drunks were more functional after a couple of drinks but before they were well and truly into their daily quota, and I knew from experience Agnes was one of them.

I was not disappointed. Agnes was glad to have company and eager to talk. She moved around her kitchen efficiently, putting the kettle on, setting out plates, even producing a dish of water for Pierre. She disappeared briefly into the living room, and came back with a large, dusty notebook of ledger paper.

"You'll want to have a look at this, I'm sure," she said, setting it in front of me and going to pour the tea.

I opened it and found the first page had been neatly gridded, with the day of the week at the top and time of day down the side. Each page had been divided in two, with half labeled "coming" and the other "going." Most blocks had a few things scribbled in them, some had a few notes and others question marks. She'd been tracking all the traffic on the road to the manor since the night I'd stopped by with the DVDs.

"Agnes, this is amazing. Watching all those detective shows has really paid off. I think you missed your calling."

She laughed but looked pleased.

"Well, I don't like what's going on, and I want to do what I can to help. Of course, I can't catch everything. I do doze off in front of the TV sometimes. Now, what were all those sirens about? I know you know because you left after they arrived."

She tapped at a square that held my name. She'd noted a name where she recognized the car, and a description when she didn't know the driver. While her handwriting got less precise as the day wore on, she'd done a good job of keeping track.

I gave her an abbreviated version of events, sticking to the facts and letting her draw her own conclusions. She turned to study her chart.

"Well, you and Vince are the only two who were still there well after five. Of course, he went up the road around lunch and came back soon after, but he went by again late in the day. I have matching entries for everyone else."

"His car wasn't in the lot. That's something I couldn't figure out. I thought he might have come on foot, though it's an awfully long walk, unless he'd left his car in the village. Are you sure you saw him come back?"

"Yes. I noted it because I was surprised. But he probably parked in the old lot, the one everyone used before the back entrance was opened. You can't see it at all well from the manor."

She was right. I'd forgotten about the old lot, as the locals called it. It was in front of the manor, off to one side and partially hidden by trees. You couldn't see it from the reading room. It was rarely used now, but Vince would have known about it and known his car would be hidden.

I studied the chart some more, but found nothing unusual. Agnes pointed out that she wouldn't have noticed anyone on foot or on a bicycle unless she happened to be looking out the window at the time. The cars she could hear coming. Patrol cars all looked alike to her, so unless she recognized the officer, she couldn't be sure if all of them had left. Still, she had done an impressive job. I was catching a glimpse of what Agnes had been before she started to drink.

We chatted a little while longer and then Pierre and I took our leave. Agnes vowed to continue her surveillance. I encouraged her. It clearly gave her a sense of purpose and could come in handy.

My next goal was to find out what, if anything, was going on at the manor. A continued police presence likely meant they were on to something. I knew I could get close enough to check without being seen, and I had the dog as an excuse. Still, I wanted to avoid any questions about "returning to the scene of the crime."

Clouds were forming over the Helderburgs, but I thought I'd have enough time. I heard voices as we rounded the curve, and spotted Sadie and her brothers playing on the footbridge.

"Whatcha doing?" I asked.

Jake answered as Sadie dropped to her knees to greet a bouncing, wagging Pierre.

"Studying currents, Ms. Hogan. Watch this."

He picked up a piece of broken branch from a pile at his feet and flung it hard upstream. It hit the water with a plop and bobbed back toward us, disappearing under the bridge. We turned and waited for it to emerge. It took longer than I would have thought, but then it popped out at an angle and shot downstream, bouncing energetically until it disappeared once again, right where the Ravens Kill curved out of sight into the woods.

"It always does that," said Nate, the middle Barrett child. "It goes under right there and you never see it come up."

Things that appeared and disappeared without rhyme or reason seemed to be the norm in Raven Hill, I thought, remembering the click of a door latch and the blank motion sensors.

"Some of them get stuck under the bridge," Sadie added, "like there's a beaver dam under there or something."

"There's no beaver dam," Nate said, rolling his eyes in the manner of older brothers everywhere. "The whole kill would be clogged up if there were."

Jake played diplomat.

"There *is* a little dam forming, but not from a beaver. It's from all the trees that came down this winter."

"Why does it sink there by the bend?" I asked him.

"It doesn't, at least not permanently. It only gets sucked under for a while, and washes up farther down. I've marked some with vegetable dyes and gone looking for them. This is going to be my science fair project."

Jake rattled on in a way that would make his academic father proud. I leaned over the footbridge as he made a point about the formation of rapids. The rail gave under my weight, and I pulled back.

Child drowns in Ravens Kill.

The muttering black water now seemed more ominous than academic.

"You guys need to be careful—" I started, but Pierre began to bark.

"Here comes Mr. Prentiss," Sadie said.

Matthew Prentiss was jogging toward us. He gave a friendly wave and slowed, jogging in place as he greeted us, the reflective tape on his running togs winking even on this cloudy day.

"Are you training for the Tri-City Triathlon?" Nate asked.

"Not this year. Too much going on."

He gave me a meaningful look and turned back to the kids.

"What brings all of you out on this cloudy day?"

"Science fair project," Jake answered. "I'm studying currents."

"Good luck with that. The currents have always been strange in the Ravens Kill."

The Barrett kids went back to their experiments and Matthew turned back to me.

"Your little buddy is with you a lot these days," he said, patting Pierre and receiving a curious sniff in return.

"Henri is out, and I can always use the exercise."

"Good stress reliever." Matthew glanced over at the kids, still busy tossing sticks. I kept an eye on the rickety rail.

"I'm glad to see you out and about, Greer," Matthew said in a low voice. "I heard what happened last night. I'm glad for Vince's sake that you went in, but I want you to be more careful. I cannot even begin to imagine what is going on."

He sounded both frustrated and mystified. He looked toward the manor.

"I'm told the police are done there. I'm going to check the locks and such on my way by. I need to get a handle on this one way or another," Matthew said.

He turned back to me.

"I want you to feel free to call me directly, any time, if you think there's something going on that I should know about. Even if it's just something that makes you nervous, or that seems strange. Please."

I nodded to show I understood. He took it as assent and gave my arm a pat as a low rumble sounded in the distance.

"That's my cue," Matthew said loudly. "I've still got some miles to cover."

He set off. I wondered if he intended to do more than check the locks. Though the police would have discouraged a solo visit to the manor by anyone, Matthew had a reasonable excuse—a board member's concern that the building was secured properly. If he had another, more sinister motive for visiting the old house, I couldn't fathom it, and I couldn't follow him without the risk of being seen. That invitation to call about anything unusual might be a desire to get a heads-up on any looming scandal that would impact his political career, or a genuine desire to get to the bottom of things. I was curious, though, and made a mental note to find out where Matthew Prentiss was both last night and the night of the murder. And the night after, I thought, remembering the jogger I'd heard. Matthew's office was down the street from my apartment. He could have decided to check on me, or check up on me. Or, it could have been a coincidence. I had no way of knowing, short of asking, and I didn't think that was wise.

Another rumble sounded, closer this time.

"You should get going, too," I said to the kids. "You'll get caught out in the storm."

"We'll be okay, Ms. Hogan," Sadie said. "We can cut through the woods. We know all the shortcuts and how to find the secret paths."

"How to find the secret paths?" I asked. "Are they different than the hiking trails and shortcuts?"

"Sometimes. You only find them when you think about where you need to go, and just look out of the corner of your eye."

I smiled at her. She was more of a wood sprite than I'd guessed. "I'll keep it in mind."

She gave Pierre a final pat and got on her red bike. Her brothers did the same. Amidst a chorus of goodbyes I watched them pedal away. Within seconds they had disappeared. I gave the rail of the footbridge one final shake. I needed to let Helene know, although I wasn't sure who was responsible. This wasn't technically manor property. I looked into the kill, thinking how mesmerizing the soft sounds and constant motion of the water were.

"*Come away, little lass, come away to the water,*" I sang the opening of a Maroon 5 song as I tossed a stick over the rail and watched it disappear.

Child drowns in Ravens Kill.

Thunder sounded again, and the wind picked up. I shivered and gave Pierre's leash a tug. We made it back to the carriage house as the first raindrops fell.

Chapter Twelve

I'd saved the photocopied article with Joanna's notes for when I'd have an uninterrupted stretch to work. I'd looked them over again that morning, and thought some of the odd notations were familiar. The answer was at the edge of my consciousness. Now that I'd had a day of fresh air and exercise, it was time to try again.

I popped some slice-and-bake cookies in the oven and assembled my laptop, notepad, and tote bag on the coffee table. As I pulled out the cookies, the doorbell rang. I opened it to find Pete Jr. of Pete's Pizza shaking water off his lanky frame.

"Hi, Ms. Hogan. Medium, extra pepperoni, still hot."

"Come in while I get my wallet." Pete was a nice kid who was working his way through community college. He spent most of his weekends at the family pizza shop, either behind the counter or delivering. Along with the Java Joint and the Market on Main, Pete's Pizza completed the Holy Trinity of information clearinghouses in Raven Hill, and young Pete liked to chat. He was a natural in the hospitality business. I was hoping he'd have some useful tidbits for me.

Pete had unpacked the pizza and was sniffing the air appreciatively when I came back.

"I hear you had some excitement up at the manor last night," he said as I settled up.

"How'd you know?" I asked, counting out a generous tip.

"My grandpop may be retired, but he's still got a police scanner and a cell phone He can't see too well, but there's nothing wrong with his hearing. He says staying in the loop keeps him sharp."

"Understandable." And useful. Having a police scanner made you privy to all kinds of interesting information, though not as much as it did before cell phones. A well-connected retired cop was good, too. I wondered if Pete's vision-impaired grandfather would have any interest in audiobooks. I'd follow up on that, but first the business at hand.

"So, you heard someone hit his head around closing?" I handed Pete a cookie.

"Mr. Goodhue," Pete said around a mouthful of chocolate chip, "but I heard he got bashed in the head and you found him. Did you see it happen?"

He was fishing, but so was I. I handed him another cookie.

"Only from outside, and I didn't see anyone else. But there were a lot of strangers in the manor all day. Apparently, Mr. Goodhue lost track of time. It's hard to check the whole building on weekends, and I guess if we missed him we could have missed someone else."

Pete shrugged. I'd have to give him something else.

"There was something odd, though."

Pete looked eager. He'd love to have some new info to bring home to his grandfather.

"When I found him, he sort of looked like he'd been mugged. Keys and stuff all around him. But he could've just dropped what he was holding. Maybe I lived in the city too long."

Pete's eyebrows shot up. This was news, at least to him.

"Anyway, I'm sure Mr. Goodhue can explain what happened."

Pete shook his head.

"He says he was there looking for something he dropped, and he didn't realize the time until he looked out and saw your car leaving. After that, he doesn't remember anything. Sam O'Donnell isn't buying his story, but that's the official version until he finds proof otherwise. At least, that's what Grandpop's friend on the force told him."

"What does your grandfather think?"

"He says it's too much like what happened to his wife. He doesn't believe in coincidence. He says if an accident is convenient for someone else, it probably wasn't an accident. But that's hard to prove. He was a really good police officer, my grandpop."

"It sounds that way. He must get bored now that he's retired. Would he be interested in audiobooks, do you think? There are some very good police procedurals I know of. Those would help keep him sharp, too, and I could arrange things through the library."

"That's nice of you, Ms. Hogan. I'll ask him. I've got to get back to the shop. You be careful."

"Thanks, I will. Drive safely."

In short order I was on the couch with my pizza, making notes between bites. The good news was that Vince's version of events matched mine, and placed me outside the library when he was hit. The bad news was everyone thought Vince was lying, and my little chat with Officer Webber made it clear she was still trying to shake something loose from me, even if she wasn't sure what that something was.

I tossed Pierre a last piece of pepperoni, wiped my greasy fingers and pulled out the photocopy I had found yesterday. Smoothing it carefully, I read the headline. "Local Child Drowns in Ravens Kill." The article was brief. One Carol Douglas, age six, had drowned in the kill after falling in and being pulled under by the current. The accident was witnessed by her brother and a friend, also minors. The little girl wandered out of her yard in search of her brother. Local children often played in the woods at the edge of the stream, but due to heavy snow and rain throughout the winter and early spring, the Ravens Kill was higher than usual, its rushing waters more treacherous. No negligence or foul play was suspected by local authorities.

And that was that. Thirty-five years ago, kids played outside on warm spring days, especially in small towns. Carol's parents were named but the two underage witnesses were not. There was not a lot of information here, but it was Joanna's starting point so I read it through again and moved on to her notes, hoping they would make more sense. Her handwriting was clear enough, though there were some smudges, but she'd used her own form of shorthand. Some of it was easy to make out. "Rep.?" near the byline clearly meant she wanted to track down the reporter. The name wasn't familiar so who knew if he was still around, but it shouldn't be hard to find out. "Alb Cty Deeds." A reference to property records. Most could be searched online through the County Clerk's website, but I wasn't sure how far back the digitized records went. Only to the eighties, was my guess, and everything before was still paper. Again, not hard to find out but I wasn't sure where she was going with it. I'd check. Real estate records told quite a story if you did enough digging.

I couldn't make sense of the next item. "Reno—lock—gaslighting?" The words were surrounded by squiggles, as though she'd been doodling as she thought. I couldn't relate them to anything. I'd have to leave them for now.

The next few notes were the ones that had been buzzing in my brain. Cryptic sets of letters and numbers. Code? Probably not. Some of the letter sequences seemed familiar. Acronyms? Abbreviations? I looked at the various strings of numbers. Some could be dates but others clearly weren't. If they were dates, only half would coincide with the drowning. Another would be from about ten years ago, and the rest seemed unrelated. I tried writing out each line, grouping the letters and numbers differently each time willing them to make sense. I was sure some were abbreviations and dates, others looked like Roman numerals.

Roman numerals.

A visual of the local paper flashed into my mind.

I launched myself off the couch, crossed the room in a single bound, and dove into the recycling bin by the door. I found a rumpled copy of the latest issue of "Helderberg Highlights" and studied the masthead. There it was— volume, issue, date.

Score!

I did my fist-pump-one-skate victory dance and went back to my laptop. At the state library website, I went to the New York State Newspapers and scrolled the list of titles for Albany County. I matched most of Joanna's abbreviations to newspapers, most small, local, and out of print. The numbers were either dates or volumes and issues. The *Times Union* was still around, as was the *New Holland Republic*, but the rest had either consolidated or simply folded. Thanks to grant money and a zeal for preservation, many were now on microfilm. But which, if any, were online?

I could search the Albany *Times Union* back to the mid-eighties, beyond that I'd need to go to microfilm. The dates I needed from the smaller papers weren't digitized, so that meant microfilm as well, and microfilm meant a trip downtown. I'd made an appointment at Albany All News for the next morning, ostensibly to gather information for Joanna's memorial. I couldn't miss it, and didn't know how long I'd be there. If I hit pay dirt with some of my questions, it could be a while. Either way, I doubted I'd have time to get to the state library and do the necessary research and still make it back for my afternoon reference shift. The state library closed at five, so unless I could finagle some time off on Tuesday I was out of luck. I did know someone in reference there, though. She'd be able to find what I was after, and if she wasn't too busy she might turn it around quickly. I organized my list of newspapers and dates and e-mailed it to her, saying I was helping a friend with some research. I asked her to respond to my personal e-mail and let me know when she thought she could get to it. I made a separate list of the dates Joanna had noted for the village paper. Those would be in the archives, and I could check there as soon as I could get in without Millicent around. That was as much as I could do for now.

I stretched my cramped hands and checked the time. It was later than I thought—much later. Normally Henri would be home by now, or I would have heard from him. I checked my phone. No texts, no messages. Very unlike Henri. I sent him a message asking for his ETA.

I waited a few minutes and tried again. He said he'd gotten some odd looks when he asked questions. Could he have asked the wrong thing of the wrong person? We didn't know what we were dealing with, or who.

I stared at my phone, willing a message to pop up. Maybe he'd gotten home and I hadn't noticed, and he was waiting for me to bring Pierre downstairs. I called the dog and leashed him up—it was time for his last outing anyway.

There was no sign of Henri. Pierre sniffed around the front garden for a few minutes, did his business, and headed for the door to Henri's apartment, where he sat and whined.

I was trying the door handle when my phone beeped. Henri. He apologized, dinner involved much wine, would I like to keep Pierre for the night?

I agreed, and carried the little dog upstairs, where he promptly went to sleep. I was too wound up. Ignoring the fact that my octogenarian landlord had a more active social life than I did, I tucked in with Hercule Poirot. Maybe my own "little gray cells" would be inspired by his company.

Chapter Thirteen

I was at Albany All News by nine the next morning. The PR manager met me in the lobby. She looked harassed but was pleasant enough. Handing me Joanna's official work biography, she said she had a few fires to put out and left me in the charge of an intern. Fine with me. While gathering information for Joanna's memorial page was the official reason for my visit, I wanted to see what else I could unearth. Workplace gossip might yield some new angles, and Joanna's co-workers were more likely to open up if there were no management types around.

I explained the memorial plans to the small group that had agreed to help me. Most had worked with Joanna for many years and seemed genuinely fond of her and upset by her death. They knew Vince as well, but the response to him was lukewarm. The consensus was that Joanna was both talented and hardworking, Vince considerably less so.

"That's why I don't buy the idea that he killed her," said a man who had introduced himself as John. "He couldn't run that documentary business of his without her. He likes to think of himself as a 'big picture' guy, but as far as I could tell it meant he didn't like to do the grunt work. Joanna was like the Energizer Bunny with an amazing head for detail."

"I don't know what the police think. It's all so unbelievable," I said. "The talk in the village is that maybe she was working on a story that upset someone, or she angered someone in the course of her work. You know, that sort of thing."

I didn't have a clear idea of what Joanna did on a day-to-day basis, but I was hoping to get some kind of reaction. If there was friction with a co-worker or someone she came into contact with in the course of her job, someone would know, but all I got were non-committal noises. The only exception was the intern, Grace, who looked up quickly at my question, glanced at the others, and went back to studying her fingernails.

With no information forthcoming, I handed out my card and invited people to send any anecdotes or photos they thought should be included on the memorial webpage. All promised to do so. I thanked them and turned to Grace as they left.

"I know you must be busy, but there is one other thing I'm supposed to follow up on. Joanna was working on several projects for the library, and we can't find the files. Would it be all right if I took a quick peek at her desk to see if they're there? Some of it was pretty important for our fundraisers."

There was enough truth in this to give me cover if any questions were asked. I was after anything related to the notes she'd made on the article. If she wanted to keep something under the village radar, her office would be the best place to work on it.

"I don't see why not," Grace said. "The police have already been through it. They took her computer, and her husband was here looking for a flash drive. I'll probably be the one cleaning out her office anyway. I worked with her a lot."

She turned and headed down a hallway. I fell into step beside her.

"I don't think the police or Vince would be interested in what I'm looking for," I said, mentally crossing my fingers behind my back. "I know Vince was looking for a drive. Did he find it?"

"Nope, and he wasn't very nice about it. He went through her desk last week. I got put in charge of him, too. He's called twice since to see if it's turned up. Guy sounds desperate."

"I appreciate your help. I'm sure a small station like this can't function without interns."

"Depends on who you ask."

There was a definite tone to that. I'd need to follow up, but the set of her jaw suggested a delicate approach was required.

We arrived at the end of the corridor and Grace flicked on a light. I looked into what appeared to be a tarted up broom closet. There was barely room for a small desk, two file cabinets, and a visitor chair.

"Wow," I said, "television is so glamorous."

Grace laughed. "And high-paying," she added.

"Free labor? I did that in grad school."

"I get school credit if I complete a certain number of hours. And I get minimum wage, which is more than most of my friends."

"I'm sure you earn every penny." I looked at the jumble of papers and files on the desk.

"I'll help you," Grace said. "What are you looking for?"

"Anything that says Raven Hill or library I guess. I'm not sure how she'd label it."

Truthfully, I *wasn't* sure. I'd have to try to snag anything that looked even remotely related. If the mysterious flash drive had been here Vince would have it, so that was out, and who knew what the police had taken.

Well, Grace might.

"Did the police take anything other than the computer?"

"Not that I saw, but I wasn't in here. Some blonde woman was here for a while. She talked to HR before and after, but that's all I know."

We sorted and stacked methodically, chatting about internships and Grace's career plans. We found nothing related to the village or the library. I had written off the search from a detecting standpoint when Grace spoke.

"You know," she said, affecting a casual tone, "there *was* someone who really didn't like Joanna. I'm not saying he'd kill her or anything, but, you know, since you asked."

She stopped sorting and looked at me.

"You never know what's important," I said. "People do crazy things sometimes."

"Especially when they're high, and think they're important enough to get away with it."

The tone I'd heard earlier was back. Grace's hands were clenched around the files she was holding.

"What happened?" I asked, keeping my voice low.

Grace looked out the door. Assured there was no one around, she leaned forward. "Ed Dexter, the anchor, you know?"

I nodded. He was one of the people Dory had seen at Luigi's the night of the murder.

"Well, he's got a pretty pricey cocaine habit. Bad and getting worse. I'd say most of his paycheck is going up his nose. Nothing you'd notice on air, yet, but starting to affect production. People cover for him—he's really popular with the viewers. They don't know what a scumbag he is. But Joanna had finally had it. She threatened to get him fired."

Grace let her breath out in a whoosh. It sounded like she'd wanted to get that off her chest for a while. But she hadn't. Why?

"What was the last straw for Joanna?" I asked.

"It was a couple of things, I think. He started to use at work, for one, and he'd get a little free with his hands. And he was really mean to one of the other interns," she added quickly. "He made fun of Nick behind his back but where he could hear, you know what I mean? Nick's nice but kind of goofy looking, and he stammers when he's nervous."

A faint blush was creeping up Grace's neck. I could guess who Dexter was harassing. Joanna would have gone through the roof. She was not the type to tolerate abuse of power in any fashion.

"Did you tell the police?"

She shook her head.

"No one asked me anything, and there was always someone from the station around."

"And you didn't want to cause trouble because you need the internship."

"It's only another month, and I'll have done all my hours."

Welcome to the working world.

"Joanna might have told someone in HR," I said.

Grace shook her head.

"It was right before she died. She and Dexter had a big blowout late Monday, and she wasn't here on Tuesday."

And on Wednesday she was dead. But this was one mission of Joanna's I knew I could complete.

"The police need to know. They'll want to talk to both you and Nick." I considered Mary Alice's trust in O'Donnell's discretion, and Webber's ability to give away nothing by either word or expression. The kids might feel better talking to a woman.

"You know the blond woman who was here?" I asked Grace. She nodded. "I've talked to both her and her boss. I'm sure they can look into this, and let the station know what was going on without letting on it came from you. Other people saw it happening, right?"

"Lots of people."

"All right. I'll tell Officer Webber to get in touch with you. I'll say you were helping me look for a file about the library fundraiser and you told me you heard Joanna and Dexter having a fight, but you weren't sure anyone else knew. Will that work?"

"Okay. I'll talk to Nick, too," she said and wrote down her number. "I should go," she said, "but if I find anything I'll call you. I have your card."

"Thanks, Grace. You've been a big help. Hang in there."

As I stood in the lobby fishing for my car keys, Ed Dexter walked in, takeout coffee in one hand and cell phone in the other. Dory was right—he was positively scrawny.

Pretending to be engrossed in hunting through my tote bag, I drifted into his path.

"Oops, sorry!" I said as I narrowly avoided impact. I widened my eyes. "Oooh, aren't you Ed Dexter?"

He dropped his phone into his jacket pocket and stuck out his hand, flashing a megawatt smile.

"At your service."

"I'm SO glad I bumped into you," I said, doing my best to sound breathless with excitement. "You were one of the people I most wanted to meet while I was here."

"Then I'm the one who's glad. It's always great to meet a fan. I'd be nowhere without you."

A rehearsed line, but he delivered it well.

"Oh, that's so kind of you to say. I don't want to take advantage, but I was wondering—"

"No problem," he cut in, gesturing at the receptionist, who dutifully produced a glossy photo and a Sharpie.

"Um, Greer, thank you. But I was also wondering if you could answer a couple of questions for some research I'm doing. It will only take a minute."

"I have a few minutes. Who do you work for? Local paper? Radio? Rival station?" He wiggled his eyebrows. "I have to warn you—I can't comment on any rumors you might have heard about me moving to a major network!"

He gave another big smile and a conspiratorial wink.

"Oh, no," I protested, giggling, "I'm hardly cut out for television."

I was making myself sick.

"Not true," he said, "you've got the right look and even women your age do well in smaller markets."

The pompous twit undoubtedly considered that a flirty compliment. Fervently hoping he'd choke to death on his pricey veneers, I plowed on.

"You flatter me, Mr. Dexter. I'm here on behalf of a community organization. The Village of Raven Hill. You've heard of it?"

"Heard it's nice. Never been there. And requests for appearances or interviews go through my agent."

His interest had plummeted now that he realized I was not a source of the kind of publicity that would further his career. He looked at his watch.

"We're putting together a webpage to honor one of your co-workers, and it wouldn't be complete without a contribution from you."

I had a mental image of Joanna making a gagging motion.

"I'm sure you've heard about the death of Joanna Goodhue?" I asked.

Dexter looked taken aback for an instant, but rearranged his face into an attitude of deep sorrow.

"Of course. Such a tragedy. A terrible accident, I understand."

Interesting that he went straight to the accident theory. What had Pete's grandfather said? *When an accident is too convenient for someone else, it's no accident.* And from what Grace told me, Joanna's death was very convenient for Ed Dexter.

"Something like that," I said, and explained about the memorial page.

Dexter was bouncing on the balls of his feet, his eyes going repeatedly to the lobby exit.

"Why don't I e-mail you something? Tomorrow?"

"That would be fine, thank you." I handed him my card. He pocketed it and bolted down the hall.

When I started my car the warning light flashed again, and the engine made a funny noise. I hoped it remained a funny noise, and not an expensive noise. I let it run for a few minutes, and used the time to call Officer Webber. I told her about my conversation with Grace and her fears about rocking the boat. I stuck to the story I'd told Grace I'd give to the police, and suggested that some careful nosing around might unearth more witnesses to the harassment, if not the fight between Dexter and Joanna. She listened to the whole story, verified a few details, told me she'd speak to Grace and Nick at school, and be discreet around the TV station. She thanked me for calling, and told me to get in touch immediately if I came across anything else. It had a strong undertone of "and keep your nose out of a police investigation" but the words were gracious enough.

Nothing untoward had happened to my car engine while I was on the phone, so I headed back to Raven Hill. I turned onto Main Street and heard the noise again. Mentally checking my bank balance, I veered off Main onto the little side road leading to Darryl Brothers Import Motor Works.

Lawrence, the eldest brother, waved at me from the garage bay. Joanna and I had had a running joke about the brothers, riffing on the old Newhart show. I could hear her voice in my head, intoning *"Hi, I'm Larry, and this is my brother Darryl, and this is my other brother Darryl."* It would have been awful and snobbish if she hadn't shared the joke with them. As it was, she'd blurted it out the first time she brought her car in, and they'd responded by refusing to admit the two younger brothers had any name other than Darryl. A guessing game commenced, with Joanna putting forth a new set of names whenever she came in. The last pair was "Erasmus and Cornelius." The Darryls remained steadfast in their denial. She was relieved they all had a sense of humor. A good mechanic was hard to find. I felt a stab of melancholy that the game had come to an end.

I handed my key to Lawrence and told him what was going on. He promised to call me later and offered a lift to the manor. One of the things I missed most about the city was being able to walk everywhere, and it was a nice day, so I declined. I decided to treat myself to lunch at the Java Joint before the horrifying reality of the car repair bill hit. It would give me a chance to check in with Jack and Meadow, and see what news had come through their doors. They'd both been too busy to talk the previous morning.

Joni Mitchell greeted me with the refrain from "Coyote" when I walked in the café door. The album cover to *Hejira* was propped behind the glass by the register, though I knew Jack used what he called an iThing to do the Java Joint's music— no top 40 radio for his customers. It was late for breakfast and early for lunch, so I had the place to myself. Jack and Meadow were at a big table in the back going through piles of receipts. They waved me over. Meadow wasted no time.

"WHAT is going on up at the manor?"

Jack got me some coffee and I filled them in. I gave them a firsthand account of what was public knowledge. They likely knew most of it, and were equally likely to have picked up additional information from their customers. I did mention I'd heard there was bad blood between Joanna and Ed Dexter, glossing over how I'd come by the information.

"Well, now, that *is* interesting," Meadow said. "He was here just the other night."

"Dory said she saw him at that new Italian place on Tuesday," I said, "but he left early on. He told me he's never been to Raven Hill."

"Then he's lying. He was here in the café." Meadow turned to Jack. "You remember—I pointed him out."

"Hmph," Jack said. "I think so. Skinny, twitchy guy? Hung out by the window. Seemed to be waiting for someone."

"That's right. Ordered a large dark roast and a sugar cookie. Didn't think he needed either the caffeine or the sugar—he was practically vibrating as it was. It was a slow night with all the rain, so I kept my eye on him. He looked familiar, but I knew he wasn't a regular. Took me a little while to figure out where I knew him from. He looks better on TV. A car pulled up outside and he got in. That's the last I saw of him."

"When was this?" I asked.

"Sometime between eight-thirty and nine on Tuesday."

The same night Dory had seen him—this time much closer to the manor.

"Are you sure it was Tuesday?"

"I'm sure, because Jack had to inventory the beans for an order on Wednesday."

"Besides," Jack said, "we usually get a little rush when the Friends of the Library meeting ends, so I was trying to get the inventory done early. But we didn't have the usual crowd, just a couple of people."

"The meeting ran late," I said, trying to remember if Mary Alice had told me the exact time she had locked up.

"Who did come in?" I asked.

"Felicity Prentiss was here early on, with that woman with the pixie haircut. The one who always orders the decaf soy latte." Meadow uttered the last bit with an air of "why bother?" and Jack nodded.

"Lawyer," he said. "Julie? Something like that."

"Julia Wainwright?" I remembered the bent business card in Vince's pocket.

"That's it. Later a few of the other ladies came in."

They rattled off names, occasionally checking details with each other. A couple of kids who lived in the village and went to local colleges were in and out as well.

"But not Joanna?" I asked. If I could place Joanna and Dexter here at the same time on the night of the murder, I might have the thing solved.

Meadow shook her head.

"I didn't see her at all."

It was a long shot. There was still a slim chance Joanna had run into Ed Dexter, but it was more likely she had gone into the manor late afternoon on Tuesday and never left. It was possible they'd arranged a meeting, but that would be tough to prove without a witness.

"Didn't anyone see anything?" Meadow asked. "I know the place is big, but someone who didn't belong there late at night would be noticed."

Her statement hung in the air for a moment, and she sighed.

"I know. Joanna was probably killed by someone she knew. Someone we know. It's awful."

I decided to take a chance.

"You know, someone did think they saw a headless ghost in the main hall."

Jack's coffee cup hit the table with a thump.

"Headless?"

"Like Nearly Headless Nick in Harry Potter."

"Huh. I thought it looked more like Quasimodo."

"I beg your pardon?"

"The Hunchback of Notre Dame. Victor Hugo," Jack said, "Quasimodo's his name."

"Yes, yes, I know Quasimodo, but—"

"You'd better explain, Jack, or she'll think you're crazy," Meadow said.

"There's not much to tell," Jack said. "A couple of nights this spring I've seen something. Something strange. At first I thought I imagined it, but it kept happening."

"What kept happening?"

"Well, we've had some really slow nights lately, because of the weather. So, I'd close early, turn off the lights, and play some music. Put my feet up and relax with a—a drink," he said, not meeting my eyes.

"Of course. I like to unwind with a martini myself."

Meadow looked bemused. I had often suspected the "joint" in the café name had more than one meaning, given the hippie antecedents of the proprietors.

"Anyway," Jack continued, "a couple of times I saw something go by. It was just a shadowy outline. It looked like a really tall person, but with nothing where the head should be. Just rounded and lumpy on top. That's why I said Quasimodo. But it moved gracefully, not like a hunchback. Of course, it didn't glide like a ghost either."

"When did you see it?" Sadie had seen her ghost twice, the last time on the night Joanna died.

"The last time was about a week or two ago. I can't remember exactly."

"But you'd seen it before?"

"More than once. Maybe two or three times. That's why I finally told Meadow. I was beginning to think I was losing it."

"I don't think you're crazy, but I don't know what it means, or if it's connected. Will you call me if you see it again?"

"Sure," Jack said.

I gave him my number and ordered a big enough lunch to leave leftovers. We talked some more about the murder as I ate. According to Meadow and Jack, everyone who came in had a theory, each more farfetched than the last. I listened to them all, sifting through them for the nuggets of truth that had sparked them. There was still a small group that refused to suspect one of their neighbors of being a killer, and put it down to an accident or a nameless, faceless stranger. None of them mentioned a headless stranger. A subset of this lot was for a new, more centrally located library with up-to-date security. The balance muttered darkly that Anita was behind it all, that she had convinced Joanna to go along with a staged accident to make the case for a new building, and the stunt had gone horribly wrong. According to Meadow, at least one of the conspiracy theorists had flatly stated that Joanna wasn't supposed to be there after the meeting, that she had changed her schedule, and this supported the put-up job idea. I thought the anti-Anita scenario was way off base, but the bit about the schedule change interested me. Meadow wasn't sure who said it, but thought it was one of the volunteers working on the sale. I'd have to try to track down the source.

Among those who believed it was murder, the love triangle theory was popular, though no one could agree on the main players. Others were convinced money had to be at the bottom of things. Large life insurance policies were mentioned, but Jack and Meadow figured it was standard speculation. Wills and inheritances were mentioned as well, with a couple of the older village residents exchanging knowing glances as they discussed decades-old rumors of disappearing codicils and family scandals. That had potential, given what I'd overheard between Vince and Millicent, but I'd need more details. Meadow gave me a couple of names. One was a regular library user, so that helped, and Henri and the Very Old Gentlemen might shed some additional light.

There had also been some speculation that Joanna was involved in some kind of story for Albany News that had gotten her in trouble. The fact that she was no longer a reporter didn't seem to matter. All people knew was that if she worked for the news station she would come into contact with unsavory characters. If you counted Ed Dexter, she had, but I knew that wasn't what anybody meant.

"Were you here when a little girl drowned in the Ravens Kill?" I asked. "It would have been nearly 35 years ago."

"That was before we moved to the village, though not long before," Meadow said. "I remember hearing about it, though. Not in a lot of detail, though it seems like there was something—"

"We were the first long-haired freaky people in town," Jack said with a smile. "People didn't exactly confide in us."

"Do you think it's important?" asked Meadow.

"I have no idea what's important. It's just something someone asked me about. Thanks for all your help."

Jack got me a bag for my leftovers. I mulled over my theories as I walked to work. I had a few "almost, not quite" scenarios, but not one that hung together in every element. With a few minutes to spare before my shift, I sat on my favorite bench outside the manor. I was immediately joined by one of the resident ravens. He cocked his head and looked at me expectantly.

"No crumbs today," I said.

He ruffed his feathers, looking like he was shrugging in response to my statement.

"So, who do you think did it?"

He kept a steady gaze on me.

Headless ghosts and hunchbacks. Harassment, addiction. Disappearing wills. Insurance policies. *Local Child Drowns in Ravens Kill.* "Blackmail by any other name." Old scandals. "Don't you think this all looks a bit staged?" A put-up job gone wrong. *"I didn't kill your husband, lady."*

The thoughts swirled around. The word cloud hung there, some phrases large and bold scattered through it. A sense of calm, certainty settled over me as I sorted and parsed, ignoring reason and letting my instincts loose.

"It isn't the obvious, is it? The answer lies in all the small, strange details."

The raven bobbed his head. He gave me a long look, and made a soft noise in his throat. He shook out his wings and flew off, disappearing into the woods at the edge of the Kill.

Chapter Fourteen

After a steady but quiet reference shift, I settled in at my desk to continue my work on Joanna's memorial page. My friend at the state library had said she'd get me the articles soon, possibly late in the day. Dory caught me early and told me she had some news, but in a dramatic stage whisper said it had to wait until we could speak privately. I couldn't go through the old village papers in the archives while Millicent was around. I was left with no alternative but to do my actual job all afternoon. I put aside my growing frustration and tried to do justice to my friend's memory.

The building grew quiet as dinnertime approached, the sound of voices and footsteps receding. The hum of hard drives and servers provided white noise but couldn't muffle the weary groans of the manor settling itself for the night. It seemed whenever I moved, the floor gave an irritable creak, the walls around my cubicle whined, or the radiator sighed.

"Leave me alone, I'm trying," I muttered.

My moderate web design skills required I give my full attention to the task at hand, and for a while I was able to keep at bay the waves of melancholy that rose as I looked at pictures of Joanna at various library events through the years. I came across a more recent photo, one taken the previous fall for the newsletter. In it, Joanna and I stood in the main hall, laughing, a benevolent Horatio Ravenscroft gazing down from his portrait above us. The President of the Friends of the Library welcoming the new librarian. Right as the picture was taken, Joanna told me she'd chosen the spot because old Horatio was the least constipated looking of all the Ravenscrofts. It was the kind of irreverent humor we both loved, and as we burst out laughing. I felt immediately at home.

"Shit!"

The hissed oath was accompanied by the slithering sound of papers hitting the floor on the opposite side of my cubicle wall. I jumped in my seat, then went still, listening. The sound of a file drawer sliding was followed by another muffled curse and a thump. Someone was in the FOL office, and trying—unsuccessfully—to be quiet about it.

I slid out of my chair and around the corner. The office door, usually closed and locked, was ajar. I peeked through and saw Felicity Prentiss crouched on the floor, surrounded by file folders whose contents were strewn all around her. Unusual, but not alarming. I stepped into the doorway.

"Need a hand?"

Felicity gasped and rocked back on her heels.

"Oh, it's you, Greer. I didn't realize anyone was still in the office. No, I'm fine, thanks. I don't want to keep you."

She quickly pulled everything into a stack, avoiding my eyes. I glanced at the file cabinet. The top drawer was pulled open and nearly emptied. It was labeled "Meeting Notes" and from what I could see scattered on the floor, that's what it was. But Felicity was nervous.

"Oh, no problem!" I beamed at her. "I was about to break for dinner."

I stepped around her and started gathering the files she hadn't gotten to. I saw Joanna's handwriting among others, amid printed meeting minutes, but everything I touched seemed legitimately Friends related. Felicity hesitated, then began sorting and stacking.

"Were you looking for anything in particular? I'll see if I come across it."

"Some of Joanna's notes," she said. "We've divided up her projects so we can keep things moving. We'll have to appoint an interim President, I guess."

"Why don't you do it? If you have time, that is. Dory told me the other day how glad she was you were in charge of the hospitality committee."

"Really?" Felicity's face brightened.

"Yep. Dory tells me that you are not only the most organized person she knows, but that you make the most amazing artichoke squares. She's hoping some will appear for the jumble sale refreshment table."

Felicity rolled her eyes.

"Great. Artichoke squares. For this, I went to Wellesley."

She looked down, all the brightness of the previous moment fading.

"She meant it kindly," I said, "and being organized is key. Managing volunteers is like herding cats. And any number of people have told me how smart you are. You'd be a wonderful President. You should think about it."

"Thank you, Greer. It's nice of you to say. I will think about it."

Felicity set down her stack of files. She paused, and turned her head toward me. I sensed some internal struggle. She gave an almost imperceptible shake of her head and turned back to the files.

"There we go," she said. "I don't want to keep you from your dinner. I'll take those."

She wanted me gone. I handed over the files and mentioned the door prizes and Joanna's fictional request. Saying she didn't know anything about it, she gave me the name and number of the volunteer she thought handled that sort of thing and said goodbye. I took the hint. I heard the office door close as I rounded the corner. Whatever Felicity was doing, she didn't want to be observed.

What was she looking for? And what was it she almost told me? I would swear she was about to confide something. Did she know or suspect something about Joanna's death, or was she trying to search out and destroy evidence of her own complicity? She was in the Java Joint talking to Julia Wainwright after the meeting. The timing would be tight, but she could have killed Joanna between the meeting and coffee. Organized for sure, and a cool customer to pull it off. But possible.

When I returned from my break Felicity was gone. I did a quick scout around the main floor. Other than the staff and a few people in the reading room, I was the only one around. I tried the door of the FOL office—locked. In most places, this would be a real impediment, but this was Raven Hill. I hunted around the area outside the office. Underneath a calendar, thumb-tacked to a bulletin board, I found a key.

Bingo. I returned the key to its hiding place and slipped into the Friends' office. Starting with the file cabinet Felicity had been rummaging in, I made a thorough search of the place. I hunted for stray flash drives, anything related to the article I found, or anything that looked out of place, period. I gave careful scrutiny to any notes with Joanna's handwriting on them, but when I was done, I had found nothing more interesting than a plastic case labeled "In Case of Emergency" stuffed with an assortment of fun size candy bars. I started to close it, but recalled that the last time I stayed past five I'd ended up here half the night. I pocketed a couple of Snickers.

You never know.

I locked the office and checked the clock. I had an hour to go before the library closed and I couldn't face going back to the memorial page. There was nothing in my e-mail from my friend at the state library. I'd seen Millicent leave earlier, so now was the time to go through the bound volumes of the village paper and check all the dates Joanna had noted. I retrieved the spare archive key from the reference desk and slipped up the back stairs.

I stopped at the top of the landing and eased around the corner. There were voices coming from the community room.

"Damn coyote will be the death of me!"

Matthew Prentiss, using his best gruff and hearty "Hale-fellow-well-met" voice. It certainly carried. I heard the phrase "nearly into the Ravens Kill" and other voices chimed in. "Bears are awake" and "have to be so careful." This was followed by a more strident, "you'll all agree we need more signs and better lights."

Anita. No doubt this was one of her numerous committee meetings. She was adopting a "Keep Calm and Carry On" philosophy. The last thing I wanted to do was explain myself to Anita, and I had no legitimate reason to be snooping around in the archives. I would have to postpone my search.

Dory was still busy at Circ when I returned the key, but she wiggled her eyebrows and looked pointedly at the clock. I'd have to wait until she was done. Back at my desk I found an e-mail from my friend. She couldn't scan the articles, but had managed hard copies of most. She could get the rest of them done and into the intersystem mail tomorrow.

That meant I wouldn't get them until Wednesday at the earliest. I had no reference shift tomorrow but no car either, unless the Darryls worked a minor miracle. Even if I could finagle a few hours off at the last minute, I didn't have anyone to drive me. The memorial for Joanna was planned for Wednesday, though no one knew yet when her actual funeral would be. By Thursday, the articles should have arrived.

Dory stuck her head in the office.

"Oh, good, you're still here. I was just going to turn off the lights."

"I'm almost done. I'll get the lights."

"I saw your car at Darryl Brothers when I went to the post office. I'll give you a lift to the end of your street and we can fill each other in. The reading room is empty. I'll be done in jiff."

She was true to her word. I settled into the cushy passenger seat of Dory's enormous Cadillac, marveling that she could see over the steering wheel, and she was off and running.

"Anita said she'd close the building after her meeting. If you ask me, she wants to hide the evidence if another body turns up!"

Dory cackled at her own wit. I had to smile—her theory was not farfetched. She went on.

"Well, I guess you know Joanna's body was released early today. Pagliaro's Funeral Home is handling everything. They always do such a nice job. Dignified. And they made my cousin Gladys look ten years younger than the day she died. I think it's the way they do the hair."

Dory paused and gave her own springy perm a pat. She went on, "I understand Joanna's service is private. Graveside, and just the family. I'm sure the police will be around. Sam O'Donnell will be discreet though. Everyone else is being encouraged to attend the memorial at the manor. I wasn't too sure about that at first. Thought Anita was up to something. But still, I think it'll be nice, and easier on

Vince and the girls. Refreshments afterward. I'm sure there will be a real nice turnout."

Dory paused for breath.

"I was surprised by the memorial idea, too," I said, "but I think it will be all right. Joanna devoted so much time to the library."

"That she did," Dory said. She gave me a sympathetic look. "You'll miss her, I'm sure. Do you have any better idea who killed her? Any new clues?"

I filled her in on the gossip I'd gotten from the Java Joint. I didn't mention anything about Ed Dexter or the notes I'd found. Dory was a talker and I was afraid she'd give the wrong person the idea she knew more than she did. She was interested in all the various theories, though she'd heard most of them already. I told her the people Joanna worked with couldn't see Vince killing her, because they didn't think he could manage without her.

"Well, normally I'd agree with them, but there's the insurance. And didn't I tell you David saw Vince coming back to his house Tuesday night and then leaving again? I thought Vince said he was out all night working, but I remembered David said he was always coming and going, so I asked him some more questions. He told the police, but Vince is still a free man, and someone did attack him."

She hadn't told me. As she said, Vince was still a free man, but it did look more like he had the opportunity. It still felt too obvious, and too unlikely.

"We need to watch our step with our snooping, Greer. We don't want anyone hitting us over the head. Here you are. Be careful."

Dory deposited me at the end of my street and, with a jaunty wave, she drove off. True to my word, I remained alert during the short walk to my apartment, encountering nothing but the familiar, comforting noises of the night.

Chapter Fifteen

~

Since I had no reference shift Tuesday, I was determined to get a look at the back issues of the village paper. Though slim, there was always a chance Joanna's flash drive was still undiscovered and somewhere in the building. I'd thought of a few more places to check and times when a search of those places wouldn't be noticed. The newspapers were my main objective, though. Fortunately, Millicent was a firm believer in the great British tradition of elevenses, so I lurked near the hall at the appropriate time. As soon as I saw her head for the kitchen, I shot upstairs and into the archives. I had, at best, twenty minutes.

I had modified my list of the dates I needed by interspersing some other random dates and references. I was able to locate the first article easily. It didn't have much more information than the one I had, but it did include both the name and partial address of the child who drowned. The street name wasn't familiar to me, but the area was full of old dead ends that once led to farms and houses no longer in existence. This was no doubt why Joanna had planned to search property records. The more closely I followed her plan, the more likely I was to figure out what she was after, or what she had found, so I would take a look at those property records as well.

I moved on to the next volume and flipped through it to find the correct date. The issue was missing. I checked the date again and ran through the whole volume. The date sequence was consistent, and the note Joanna had made would fit into it. The issue was simply gone, with no insert in the volume to show something was missing.

I checked my notes to verify the next date and flipped through the bound volume to the appropriate spot. Nothing. The date sequence was again correct with one issue gone. I took the volume and moved into better light. Holding it flat, I ran my hand down the intersection of pages where the missing issue should be. I felt loose threads and bits of paper and dried glue stuck to my fingers. I tilted the book and squinted at the binding. It was intact, and old enough to be original, so it hadn't been broken and repaired with the issue lost in the process. The issue I wanted had been deliberately cut out and stolen. These things were hard to unbind—I'd seen it done in a preservation workshop—but making off with a few pages required only a sharp knife and a steady hand. If you were going to do as neat a job as this, it also required time. Something I was quickly running out of.

I quickly shelved the volume and pulled down the next. A fast scan showed it to be intact, which would have been great if it held any of the issues I needed. Ditto the next one. There was only one more at the end of the shelf. I pulled it down and heard a little clink. Standing on tiptoe, I swept my hand along the back of the shelf. I felt nothing but smooth wood, and then my fingers closed on something plastic. I was holding a small, dusty flash drive with the initial "J" painted on it in purple glitter nail polish.

I shoved it in my pocket. A glance toward the door reassured me that no one had witnessed my discovery. The placement of the drive was likely not random. I flipped through the last volume. Nothing seemed relevant, and the dates didn't match anything on the list. I pictured Joanna's probable movements in my mind's eye, watching her find something of interest and put down whatever was in her hand as she took something off the shelf and moved to better light. I went back to the previous volume and took another look. The only thing even remotely related was a long article on the late Horatio Ravenscroft and his many contributions to the village, most notably the gift of the manor to be used as a library.

Missing codicils and family scandals. Blackmail by any other name.

There was a noise in the hallway. I was sliding the volume back into place when Millicent appeared in the doorway.

"Hello, Greer. Were you looking for me?"

"I had a question from someone doing historical research, but it was simple. I managed. I'm getting much more familiar with the collection."

"I'm glad to hear it," she said, gliding to her desk. "Was there anything else?"

"Not at the moment, though I know Vince Goodhue was looking for something rather specific. I offered to help him, but he headed off to find you. Has he stopped by?"

One sharply indrawn breath and a tightening of her grip on her pen were the only tells.

"He's been in and out. Did he happen to say what he was looking for?"

"He's working on something for the Historical Society, and he said it was related. I think Joanna had been handling the research, but, well . . ."

I trailed off.

"Yes," she said, "of course. Well, I'm sure he'll be back."

I agreed and took my leave.

The flash drive was burning a hole in my pocket, but I couldn't risk looking at it until I was at home. I had planned to spend the afternoon finishing the memorial page, but I wanted to check something first. Back at my desk, I pulled up the catalog and checked the entries for the village paper. If anyone had noticed those missing issues, their absence would be noted on the record. I found no notes to that effect. I stared at the screen and drummed my fingers on my desk, frustrated by the fact that I had no way of knowing when they'd been taken. Had they been there when Joanna started poking around? I sensed it was important for me to know how much she knew. My guess was they were gone before she got there, but I couldn't be sure.

My mind wandered to one of my favorite mysteries, *Gaudy Night*. Sayers' plot had hinged on a historical document, stolen but not destroyed. But those were scholars,

Oxford dons and graduates, as was the author. The papers I was looking for were almost certainly destroyed. While nothing was as awful as the murder of my friend, the defacing of those volumes and the destruction of those issues was infuriating. Someone had taken an X-acto knife and sliced away at the history of Raven Hill. It was a violation of all that the library and archives stood for, a point of pride in this little community, of something that was important to Joanna. Something that was important to me.

I wanted to take an X-acto knife to the heart of the faceless killer. Such arrogance. This was the final insult.

I jumped up from my desk. I needed to check on the rest of the library, reassure myself, and burn off some angry energy. I moved swiftly, up and down the stairs, in and out of the reading room, noting who was where and what they were doing. I ran my hand along walls and banisters. The manor's happy hum had not returned, but the mourning silence had been replaced by a sullen buzzing, like bees whose hive has been disturbed. I ended my tour where I always did. The raven room was cool and silent. I breathed it in. A cold calm settled over me. I looked up at the bright-eyed beast on the mantel.

"You know what happened in the archives?"

The air around me seemed to shift. The raven's feathers trembled ever so slightly. I detected the faint scent of cherry-tinged pipe smoke.

"Unacceptable. But I'm on it. It's time to take the gloves off."

With that promise I bid him adieu.

*　*　*

As soon as I got home, I popped Joanna's flash drive into my computer and scrolled through the files. It was mostly work related, both her work and the projects she worked on with Vince. A file labeled "FEL" caught my eye. I figured it was a typo for "FOL" and would contain library-related documents. I opened it and found only one item. It was a list of names, addresses, websites, and strings of numbers in varying lengths and formats. Some of the names I recognized from the articles I'd found, others I knew as library patrons, and a few didn't ring a bell at all. The addresses and websites would be easy enough to research, but I would have to work on the numbers. Some could be dates; others were too long.

I copied the contents of the entire drive onto my computer, renamed it, and buried it deep in some subfiles. Then I copied all of that onto a blank drive of my own. You can never be too paranoid where technology is concerned. For the sake of thoroughness—Poirot would be proud—I opened and scrolled through every file on the drive. There was little of interest. I could see why Vince was desperate to get his hands on it—every detail of every project was mapped out and annotated. All Joanna's work, I was sure. The only thing that caught my eye was in the "Haunted Albany" file. That was the current project. The file contained a subfolder called "Unused/Unverified" that contained a short entry on the manor. The names of two long-dead Ravenscrofts appeared first. One was the amateur astronomer who had added the roof deck off the attic, the other I knew nothing about. There was a note to find original building plans, and a couple possible locations. There were two other lines: "Horatio research Poe" and "Orig. Deed and Will/Trust."

I thought of the comments Jack and Meadow had mentioned. The two might be connected, or they might be a dead end. I had no way to go any further with it. Any related information would be paper based or lodged in the mind of Millicent. I remembered the overheard fight. What had Vince said? "I know it's here somewhere, in all these books and papers." Something like that. The plans, which Millicent said didn't exist? The will? Horatio's research? It didn't look like Joanna had gotten very far with it, whatever it was, and I wasn't sure how it related. How many mysteries could one girl detective be expected to solve at once? I would have to leave it for now, and work on things I had a shot at finding easily. I went back to the "FEL" file. Being an old-fashioned kind of girl detective, I printed out the lone document. Nothing helps my little gray cells more than putting pencil to paper.

I started with what was simple—the names I recognized. I already knew who Julia Wainwright was and what she did, but I checked her firm's website anyway. Julia specialized in trusts and estates, but her firm handled most standard civil law issues, predominantly family and small business. According to her bio, Julia enjoyed hiking, was an avid reader, and did pro bono work for her local library. I could find out about that through casual conversation or the FOL meeting minutes.

The next name was Susan Douglas, with the letters DOB/DOD next to it. Susan Douglas was the name of the mother of the young drowning victim, Carol. Douglas was a common enough name, but it would be too much of a coincidence if it weren't the same woman. DOB/DOD likely meant "date of birth" and "date of death." No idea why they were important, but I could get them through the Social Security Death Index in one of the genealogy data-bases. No remote access, so I made a note and moved on.

"Quinn, MD" was next. Mary Alice's husband was a doctor, though he had retired a few years earlier. "Salvatore Cosmopoulos" was no one I knew, though I had a feeling I should. Most of the other names were familiar; I guessed they were library patrons. I did a web search on all of them, noting ages and addresses and whether or not they were on social media. At first glance I found nothing in common among them. I'd delve deeper if I had to but I wanted to keep working through the list. Social networks were a rabbit warren of information, most of which was meaningless unless you were looking for something specific.

"James Family Trust—deets." James was Felicity's maiden name. Next on the list was "Douglas wills? Ask G." Beneath that were two strings of numbers of equal length. There was a line break both above and below these four items, as though Joanna had grouped them deliberately.

The trust might be where Julia Wainwright came in. She was too young to have been involved in any will made by Susan Douglas, but her firm might have handled it.

Unlikely they would share the information even if they had. The "Ask G." bothered me. Maybe this is what Joanna was referring to in her last note to me—digging up the details of a decades old will. But why me?

Probated wills were a matter of public record, but to my knowledge not available online the way deeds and mortgages were. If you wanted a look, you had to snoop the old-fashioned way—in person. A quick web search told me where. Surrogate's Court was in downtown Albany. Not a trip Joanna had recently made, I thought, and not one I could make until I had my car. Though any large bequests would have made the local paper, and would have to be recorded in official records, so we were back to Millicent or downtown. Though it would be easier for me to go through the archives or see what the Historical Society had than it would have been for Joanna. I could always make up a genealogy request, even if it required a fake e-mail address.

There was one other way of finding out how someone had disposed of their assets, particularly in a small town. Gossip was not as accurate in the details, but included underlying motivations in a way court documents did not. This would be tricky. Not the kind of questions I could ask, as there was no reason I should have any knowledge of the Douglas family. Dory and Mary Alice might know something, or know someone who did. They could come up with a reasonable excuse for asking, but if this had any bearing on the murder it could put them in danger. Henri was a possibility but would also be at risk. I would have to tread carefully here.

By midnight, my body was stiff and aching, my eyes watered, and I was barely getting a glimmer of what Joanna was after. She was researching two different deaths, Carol Douglas and Susan Douglas. Almost certainly mother and daughter, they'd died decades apart, one in a tragic accident and the other apparently of old age. Some of the websites and addresses were either thrown in at random or had some connection I couldn't follow. Random facts teased at the edges of my tired mind. I stared at the printout and my notes, willing something to click. All I got was a vague sense of unease. All in the small details. But which ones?

I needed a Pensieve. Albus Dumbledore's office was out of reach, and I doubted I'd find one in Horatio Ravenscroft's study. Perhaps if I closed my eyes and tapped my mechanical pencil against my temple? Crazy. Did I have a better idea?

I leaned back and closed my eyes. I tapped the eraser end against my head, and waited for inspiration.

"I know it's here somewhere." Ravens flying over the Kill. The Purloined Letter. "Don't you think this looks a little staged?" The Chinese Shawl. Headless ghost. Child drowns. "We know all the secret paths." Artichoke squares. Keys. Pizza.

I was aware of a gnawing in my stomach. I scribbled down everything that had come to mind, and shut down my computer. I had a snack and got ready for bed, convinced I'd be sound asleep in minutes and that everything would make more sense in the morning. I stared at the ceiling, seeing fantastic swirling shapes in the dark, my sense of unease growing. It was all in the small details. Secret paths, parallel paths, all leading to the same place, a dark, cold place.

I sat up in bed and listened. The only sounds were usual ones—the murmur of the sleeping trees as the breeze disturbed their rest, the rustle of leaves as predator and prey went about their business, a series of faint warning yips in the distance.

Coyote.

I padded through the darkness to the kitchen. Returning to my desk, I folded my notes around Joanna's flash drive and tucked them into a snack-sized Ziploc bag. The drive with the copied file went into the middle of a purse pack of tissues, which went into a second bag. I found some cough drops, tucked them in with the tissues, and pushed it all to the bottom of my tote. I returned to bed, checked the charge on my cell phone, and put the first baggy under it. Tomorrow, both would go in my pocket.

From now on, the evidence went where I went.

Chapter Sixteen

The weather cooperated for the memorial, which went smoothly. Anita welcomed everyone and made a few remarks about a life well-lived, and invited people to share their fond remembrances of Joanna on our special page on the library website. The rest of the board worked the crowd, the Friends provided refreshments, and Helene took charge of Joanna's parents, who looked shell-shocked. Jilly had arranged some quiet activities for whatever children were in attendance, and the rest of us took turns monitoring the reading room. It would have been a lovely spring gathering, were we not there to memorialize a murder victim while wondering which of our friends or neighbors had killed her.

I was glad of the chance to move around. I'd decided to take a page from Officer Webber's playbook. I would find an opportunity to talk to everyone I considered a suspect, no matter how farfetched a suspect they were, and try to shake something loose. Risky, but after another sleepless night, frustrated by my lack of progress, I decided it was worth it. I didn't want any of my friends asking questions that would tip off a killer, and the police didn't seem to be getting anywhere.

I wandered over to my favorite bench. Situated between the manor and the lawn, it was screened by budding forsythia, but still offered a good view of the proceedings. I watched the kids gathered nearby, some coloring at the picnic tables, others blowing soap bubbles. In the manner of children, they had quickly forgotten to be somber, and were taking full advantage of being sprung from school and allowed to play while their parents were distracted. Sophie and Olivia were among them. I watched Joanna's two little girls, alternately caught up in the moment, playing with their friends on a warm spring day, and suddenly stopping, remembering they were sad, and why, and probably feeling bad that, just for a little while, they had forgotten their grief. I wished with all my heart they could understand that their mother would wish them only joy. Feeling bad about not feeling bad was something I understood all too well. Joanna's murder had made it clear I still had ghosts to lay to rest, but first I'd do my part toward closure for Sophie and Olivia. I only hoped it didn't mean revealing their father as a killer.

I shifted on my perch and turned my attention to the large expanse of lawn that sloped from the manor to the woods lining the Ravens Kill, seeking my prey. I had five suspects and I knew they were all here somewhere. The lawn was crowded with people—many of them in black, forming groups and then scattering, homing in on the refreshment table and wheeling away, expressing condolences and exchanging gossip. Unanswered questions created an undercurrent of tension and excitement. They looked like crows who had stumbled upon a feast, wary of any danger attached to this sudden largesse, but unwilling to pass it by. Ravens tended to work alone, but crows were social. They formed a group. What was that called?

A murder. It was a murder.

"I beg your pardon?"

I turned to see a startled Matthew Prentiss behind me. I had spoken aloud; a bad habit I had when lost in thought.

"Crows," I said. "A group of crows is called a murder. I was trying to remember."

He gave me an odd look. I gestured to the group on the lawn.

"They reminded me of birds, everyone flitting around. Like crows."

"Not ravens?" he said.

I shook my head.

"Ravens are larger, and don't travel in groups from what I understand. But I've read that all corvids mourn their dead."

"They all look alike to me," Matthew stared at the gathering around the refreshment table. After a moment he turned away. "I'll leave you to your birdwatching, Greer, and go make sure there are no ruffled feathers that need smoothing there in the crowd, or flock, or whatever."

He gave me a thin smile and left.

Odd. Matthew seemed grim. I had expected somber yet reassuring. Perhaps the mention of murder had thrown him off his game?

"Murder," I muttered, turning my attention back to the gathering.

Shadows crisscrossed the patch of sunlight in front of me. The manor ravens were on the move. One by one, they glided across the lawn and took up posts in the trees that fringed the property. It was rare to see so many at once. And what was that called?

"Unkindness," I said, "an unkindness of ravens."

Rubbing my chilled arms, I rose from the bench and took a last look at the scene below me.

"Unkindness and murder," I whispered.

Enough. I moved swiftly toward my first victim.

"Vince, I'm so glad I spotted you. I only have a minute, but I found something I'm sure you'll be interested in."

He was standing with Felicity. She had arrived as I approached. Perfect. They both turned to me, curiosity writ large on their faces. Vince's expression held an underlying tension. Felicity seemed hesitant, almost afraid. Interesting, but I had to be quick.

"I didn't want to mention it before," I had expressed my formal condolences earlier, to Vince and Joanna's parents together, "but I thought you should know. Joanna left me a note early last week. I just found it. She wanted my help with some research. She gave me a few details but not much. I haven't been able to make sense of it, but I thought you might. It was all very odd."

I paused, watching their faces. Felicity shot one quick sideways glance at Vince, then went still. Vince frowned.

"I'd have to see—" he began.

"That's what I thought, and of course now is not the time. Any luck with the flash drive, by the way? No? Well, I have some ideas. I'll see what I can do. We'll have to talk but now I've got to run. I'm supposed to touch base with some people before they leave. Be in touch!"

I dove into an opening in the crowd. I worked my way across the lawn, exchanging pleasantries with various villagers, my eye on the prize that was Ed Dexter. I was surprised he had come and didn't expect he'd stay long. I was so focused on my quarry, I didn't see Anita until she was right in front of me.

"Oh, hello," I said, keeping my eye on Dexter over her shoulder. "Lovely event. Such a good idea. It's going well, don't you think?"

She looked pleased. "Thank you, Greer. We've got a good turnout, and it's a beautiful day. A much better picture to leave people with."

"Oh, yes," I said. Anita was feeling chatty, and Dexter was moving toward the parking lot.

"The memorial page is very nice, Greer. You found some lovely pictures."

"Thank you. We've had some nice anecdotes contributed, too. Though I was hoping for more from the *All News* people. I think I see some of them—"

"Those people." Anita sniffed. "They want to offer a reward for information leading to an arrest! Can you believe it? I made it clear they would make no such announcement today. Not only is there no proof of wrongdoing, it would be insensitive to mention it here. Now I hope I don't see it on the evening news."

I thought she had her priorities out of order, and was indulging in some wishful thinking, but I told her I agreed. Ed Dexter was getting closer to the edge of the lawn. Fortunately, he was always willing to stop and talk to a fan, but I had to get away from Anita if I wanted to catch him.

"That would be dreadful. You know, I hit it off rather well with a few of them while I was at the station. Perhaps I could have a word? Mention the family's feelings? Oh, I see one of them now. Don't worry, Anita, I'm on it!"

I dashed away, careened around a few clumps of people, and skidded to a halt a few feet behind Ed Dexter. I called out.

"Mr. Dexter! Hello! So glad I caught you! It's Greer Hogan. We met the other day?"

I got the practiced smile again, though not the same wattage as before.

"Of course. I hope you got my e-mail?"

"Yes, thank you, this morning. It will be on the website today."

He'd sent a brief paragraph praising Joanna's concern for others and her high professional standards. He used the word "stickler." I was pretty sure he didn't have any sense of irony and had come up with whatever he could on short notice, but his choices had been interesting.

"I'm so glad you could make it today. And I understand this is your second visit? A few people saw you having coffee on Main Street the other night. So exciting to have a celebrity in our midst."

He looked genuinely confused for a minute, then briefly panicked before his usual smooth mask slipped back into place.

"Ah, yes, I'd forgotten. Thursday night. Met a friend. Charming little place. And of course, I wouldn't miss an event to honor a co-worker. Everyone at the station is distressed."

Lying about the night he was here. I let it go.

"Actually, that's why I wanted to talk to you. We've heard there will be a reward offered, and the announcement could come any time. Given the circumstances, don't you think that would be a little awkward for you?"

He narrowed his eyes.

"I'm afraid I don't follow, Ms. Hogan."

"Oh, I'm sorry, I thought you knew. The police haven't given a cause of death yet, and it would be so distressing for the family if anything else were implied and it turned out to have been a tragic accident all along. Not to mention how it would look for the *All News* team. Or if it did turn out she was killed, and it was somehow related to her work. I'm sure you understand."

"I get your point. It's not up to me, but I'll mention all this to the station manager. I'm sure it can wait a day or two."

"Thank you. No one wants any unnecessary bad publicity."

He gave a nod and left.

I reported back to Anita, who agreed I'd done the best I could, and headed to the refreshment table. The adrenaline from my suspect hunt was wearing off and my sleepless night was catching up to me, and I had yet to tackle Millicent. I loaded up on whatever sweets were left and grabbed a big cup of coffee. Felicity's fabled artichoke squares were nowhere in sight, and neither was Felicity. All of Joanna's immediate family had gone. Things were winding down.

Back at my desk I checked all the traps I'd left for anyone who might be inclined to search it while I was elsewhere. Nothing had been touched. I left them in place. I'd locked my bag in a file cabinet and tucked the key into my pocket, the same pocket that held my little baggie of evidence. They would stay where they were until it was time to go home. I'd be where the action was.

Back in the reading room I found Officer Webber, neatly turned out in a navy skirt suit. Even with her long blond hair released from its usual tidy bun and a pale pink blouse peeking out from under her jacket, she still managed to look like she was in uniform. She was inside the entry in a shallow alcove that housed a narrow tapestry. I watched her study the room's occupants. She either hadn't spotted me or didn't want to speak to me. Too bad. She might let slip some new information if I caught her off guard. She was still focused on her surveillance when I reached her side.

"Hello," I said. "You look very nice."

She looked at me, surprise etching her features. "Thank you. I attended the service this morning."

"Hmm, I thought that was just family. Part of the investigation, I guess. Anything new there?"

"We were there to ensure privacy for the family."

"Uh-huh."

She shot me a look. "Anything new here?" she countered.

I followed her glance around the reading room.

"More strangers than usual. Not surprising, with the memorial—"

I stopped. I'd spotted a familiar profile. It looked like the man I'd seen in the upper hall the day Vince was hit in the head. I leaned past Webber to get a better look but he'd turned his back.

"Thank you for putting me in touch with Grace," she said, shifting into my line of sight. "She was very helpful. It was useful information and I appreciate your calling me."

For Jennie Webber, this was positively loquacious. Perhaps I could affect an exchange of information.

"Have you spoken to Dexter yet?"

She gave me a sidelong look. I waited. She shook her head.

"I wasn't able to get to Grace until late yesterday."

"Did you know he was in the area on the night Joanna was killed?"

"We haven't released cause of death."

I snorted.

"But yes," she went on, "we know. Dinner with colleagues. He left early. Said he wasn't feeling well and went home. I suppose he just happened to mention that to you in passing?"

"Dory saw him, and she mentioned it to me. When I told him where I was from, he said he'd never been to Raven Hill."

"The restaurant is in the next town."

"I know, but he was at the Java Joint after he left dinner. Meadow recognized him. Why lie if he isn't hiding something?"

She gave me a considering look. "It could be anything. Remember, he allegedly has a drug problem. You need to be careful. You're not a cop."

"No, I'm not. I'm a librarian, so people talk to me who wouldn't talk to you. They think I'm nicer."

I gave her a winning smile. She pursed her lips and looked skyward. Probably counting to ten.

"Anyway," I said, "I got information you didn't."

"That's true."

At last, the girl detective gets some credit.

"But," she added, "you're not a professional, and this is a murder investigation. You're just as likely to screw things up as help. Don't stick your nose in."

She'd confirmed it was murder. I smiled.

"I'm already in. No matter what anyone says, I'm either still a suspect or was. And Joanna was my friend."

Her expression softened. "I'm aware of all that. I'm sorry for your loss, and though I shouldn't comment on an ongoing investigation, I can tell you you're not too high on the suspect list at this point."

How very reassuring.

"Look, Ms. Hogan, you've been helpful. I don't care what secrets you're keeping as long as they have nothing to do with this case. But if you come across anything, anything at all you think is related I want you to call me immediately. You have my cell number. Program it, and use it."

I was on the verge of behaving like a law-abiding citizen and handing over the flash drive when we were surrounded by a sudden influx of people. Now was not the time.

"They must have run out of food," I muttered as the mob flowed past.

Officer Webber actually smiled. Matthew Prentiss came bounding in, his mood clearly much improved. He saw us standing together in the alcove and gave us a big grin.

"Snow White and Rose Red," he said, and with a jaunty wave disappeared into the crowd around the New Book display.

"Did he just call us princesses?" Webber sounded appalled.

A derisive snort came from my right. Our heads swiveled in unison. It was Mick Johnson, a regular patron. Whatever he saw in our faces, thirty years as a Marine told him it was time to take cover. He dove into the stacks. I turned back to Webber.

"It's a fairy tale. Grimm, I think."

"Aren't they all?"

Was she making a joke? Hard to tell—she'd gone back to scanning the room, her usual inscrutable expression firmly in place. Jilly called my name and waved me over. I waved back.

"I have to go help out."

She nodded, never taking her eyes off the crowd.

"Remember what I told you," she said, her voice pitched low. "Be careful, and call me. You're not Nancy Drew."

No, I thought, *I'm Trixie.*

Chapter Seventeen

I was in and out of the reading room the rest of the day. The crowd never thinned out. The fact that the police had given out so little information left lingering questions. I thought people were hoping for some kind of resolution with the memorial service, but it was not forthcoming. Many of those who had been at the service lingered, and those that hadn't, came after school or work to see what they'd missed. I saw our regular patrons and a good number of those who usually only appeared during fine forgiveness week. The place was busy but edgy. Even the air started to seem oppressive, as if a miasma of fear and suspicion was thickening the atmosphere. Sprinkled into the mix were new faces, the strangers I'd mentioned to Jennie Webber. These I kept my eye on. I thought I spotted the man who had overheard me talking to the stuffed raven, but he disappeared too fast for me to be sure.

The younger man I'd pegged as one of O'Donnell's plants was there most of the day, hunched over his laptop. I was reasonably sure he was the man I'd seen in the upstairs hallway the day Vince was knocked out, but I'd seen that man standing up, from behind, and mostly in outline because of the light. If my little friend in the baseball cap would abandon his fantasy sports drafts and move around, I would be able to tell. I'd ruled out the nameless, faceless stranger theory along with the ghosts, but it would be nice to be sure.

Finally, I had my chance. He was packing his belongings just as a young woman in bicycle gear paused near the shelves in front of him. I nipped over.

"May I help you find something?" I said, positioning myself at an angle that allowed a good view of both of them. I looked at the book the young woman was holding.

"Romantic suspense fan?"

I heard a strangled cough from behind me. The young woman blushed. I shot a look at the laptop guy, who was wearing a faint smirk. He turned and headed toward the door. I watched him for a minute, until I was sure he was the man I'd seen. I turned back to my patron, and found her studying the reading room with the same detached professionalism I'd seen from Officer Webber. I glanced at the retreating cop and back to the woman next to me. Shift change? Protecting us, keeping an eye on us, or both?

I asked her a few questions and recommended some books, giving her an armful topped off with some Jayne Ann Krentz. *White Lies* and *Smoke in Mirrors* were two of my favorites, and seemed particularly appropriate in the circumstances. She settled into a chair in the periodicals section, one that gave her a good view of the room. I was impressed that O'Donnell had managed to find a plant who had a library card.

I'd gone back to straightening when a rumble of thunder sounded and a strong breeze set things fluttering and tumbling all over the room. All the windows were open to take advantage of the rare sunny day, but the air blowing in now was warm and humid, and dark clouds were rolling in. Jilly was at reference. We decided to shut the place up. She was still helping patrons, so I corralled the page and we got to work.

I cranked windows, wondering why I ever thought librarianship was a desk job. I'd built more upper body strength working at the manor than I ever had working out at a gym. An ominous grumble sounded in the near distance, catching the attention of the crowd. The tension ratcheted up as people gathered themselves and moved toward Circulation, all the while keeping one eye on the approaching storm. I finished my half of the room and made for the hall, knowing Millicent was on her own upstairs. This would be my best chance to catch her alone without being obvious. A crash of thunder sent me sprinting up the stairs with a newfound appreciation for Anita's insistence on a library with up to date HVAC.

I was still going full tilt when I reached the top and swung around the corner. Only a quick grab at the newel post kept me from careening into Millicent.

"Whoops!" I skidded to a halt.

Millicent gave me a discreet once over, and I was conscious of a stray lock of hair sticking to my sweaty face, and the fact that my tailored skirt had twisted and hiked as I ran up the stairs. The woman never had so much as an eyelash out of place. She always managed to make me feel as though my slip was showing, even when I wasn't wearing one.

"I came to help with the windows before the rain starts," I said.

Millicent glanced toward the front of the building, where the sky was considerably darker. I quickly tugged at my hem and tucked the errant strand of hair behind my ear. Millicent returned her attention to me.

"Thank you, Greer. I was going to see if someone was available. My shoulder has been acting up lately."

"Perhaps it's the weather. It's been so damp. Has it been bothering you for long? Of course, all the recent events—it's been tense, hasn't it?"

I trailed off. I didn't want to imply she'd hurt her shoulder while wielding a blunt instrument, but she might have. I was sure she was right-handed, and I was curious about which shoulder pained her.

"It's been bothering me off and on all spring. Age and damp, my dear. But the recent tension hasn't helped. It's the uncertainty that's the worst."

"I agree. So much suspicion. I've heard more wild rumors than I can count—love affairs, family scandals, missing documents, professional rivalries, life insurance policies—like a soap opera crossed with an episode of *Mystery!*"

"Really?" Millicent looked shocked. I wondered which of my little gambits she'd follow up.

"How odd," she said, a frown creasing her brow. "Was Joanna perhaps working on something, shall we say— questionable—before she died? Some stones are better left unturned, after all."

Millicent was looking at me with a peculiar intensity. What unturned stones concerned her?

"I really couldn't say." I opted for vague in the hope of eliciting a more specific question.

Millicent narrowed her eyes but said nothing. Thunder rolled, and I caught a flash of lightning out of the corner of my eye. Stray wisps of my hair moved of their own volition; their action mirrored by the questing ends of Millicent's perfect silver bob. My damp skin tingled and crawled. The air was becoming electric.

"Do you know of something—questionable?" I asked.

Her mouth thinned. A damp wind sighed through the hall.

"I thought she might have asked you for help with some research. She asked me, but never got too specific. Did she come to you?"

Nothing ventured, nothing gained.

"I'm afraid not, Greer. How unfortunate. We might have been able to shed some light on this. You really have no idea?"

I paused, as though deciding what to say. She watched me closely. After a moment I shook my head.

"Nothing that makes any sense. Some vague references to things I should find here in the manor, an old newspaper article, but nothing hangs together. I suppose I should hand it all over to the police."

"And they have no theory? I saw you talking to the Webber girl, the police officer. I though perhaps she might have mentioned something."

"She's tight-lipped, and I don't think she has a very high opinion of the investigative skills of librarians."

"It's dangerous to underestimate people. One never knows what they're truly capable of."

The wind swept through the hall again, colder this time. Outside the trees began to toss. Goosebumps rose on my arms.

"Well, truthfully, this is not the kind of research I ever thought I'd be doing. Motives for murder isn't covered in library school."

Millicent gave a dry chuckle. "I'm sure it isn't, dear. I've worked at the manor my whole life and never expected to be involved in anything so sordid. I would have been happy to continue my father's work."

She sounded wistful. I looked at her and wondered what that was, and what I would be doing at her age. What I would feel I had left undone. A wisp of melancholy uncurled in my middle.

"Your father—" I was interrupted by a roof-rattling peal of thunder.

"Uh-oh. I better get busy," I said, raising my voice to be heard.

"I'll do what I can, Greer," Millicent said as I turned to the opposite end of the hallway.

I heard hard rain assault the manor. Then a wordless, startled cry. Millicent. I spun around.

She was standing at the window, half-turned toward me, wiping her face.

"Millicent?"

"I'm fine. Just the cold rain."

A thunderclap burst around us. Lightning tore the air outside over and over. The manor shook beneath my feet. The lights dimmed, flickered, and died. Millicent reached up to grasp the window. She used her left hand, her right resting on the sill. Another flash of lightning outlined the skeletal frame beneath her elegant blouse, and cast death head's shadows on her face.

There was a great disturbance around Raven Hill Manor, and I wanted nothing more than to cower in some safe spot until it had passed. I stood rooted as the building groaned and the emergency lights spilled small, sickly pools of yellow at the edges of the hall. The wind shifted and, once again, I heard rain beat at the manor, this time behind me.

"Go!" Millicent ordered, waving a bony hand toward the back of the hall.

Drawing a deep breath, I forced myself to turn my back to her and face the seething shadows lurking between me and the far end of the hall. The air swirled around me as all the open windows created cross drafts that plucked at my hair and clothing. The frenzied motion of the trees outside allowed shifting streams of gray light into the rooms along the hall. It was like being underwater, with a host of things that never saw the sun moving beyond my line of sight.

Suddenly and desperately, I wanted to go home. Back to the city, where I knew what was what, where I belonged. Back to a place where Danny and Joanna were still alive, where this sucking sadness and fatigue did not exist.

A door slammed shut beside me. I shivered in the chilling air and stuck to the center of the hall as I moved forward.

"Only the wind," I told myself. Just another storm in a season of violent storms, the inland version of a nor'-easter, according to Jake Barrett.

The currents have always been strange in the Ravens Kill.

More thunder. I kept my eyes fixed on a small picture at the end of the hall, an oil some long-dead artist had done of the manor ravens.

Unkindness and Murder.

I heard my own whispered voice in my head, and pictured the scene on the lawn. The manor gave another anguished groan. The lights flared to life and quickly died. I paused, waiting for my eyes to adjust.

Be careful, be careful, Greer.

So many warnings. So much unexplained.

You're not a cop. Not your job. Just walk away.

I had walked away before. It wasn't so hard, and I was so very tired.

The wind howled. Another door slammed. I jumped.

"Are you brave?"

The line from the book came back to me. The most important question, Sadie Barrett and I agreed.

"Are you brave?"

The images raced through my mind. Henri and Pierre, my gatekeepers. A sleepy Sadie spying a headless ghost. Jack and the loping hunchback. The loathsome Ed Dexter. Vince and Millicent, a frightened Felicity. Neighbors casting suspicious glances at one another. My neighbors.

Joanna, cold and dead at my feet.

Nevermore. No matter who or what it took.

"Are you brave?"

"I hope so," I said, setting off down the hall.

The wind rose to a scream. Doors slammed bang-bang-bang hard on my heels. The emergency lights flickered and faded.

"I hope so," I whispered and stepped into the darkness.

Chapter Eighteen

The storm subsided around dinner time, leaving behind a trail of debris and a creeping fog. The manor's electricity was quickly restored. None of the trees or big limbs the storm brought down hit the building. The only one of our power lines affected was quickly repaired. The road and the banks of the Ravens Kill were littered with branches, but the house seemed to exist within its own protective bubble.

Much of the afternoon staff never made it in, stuck on the opposite side of downed trees or power lines. The remaining staff put the place to rights and drifted out as the weather eased. I was glad of the early close—it was one of my nights to stay and I was exhausted. The one part-timer who made it in managed to finish most of the closing before a phone call summoned her to pick up a stranded child whose planned carpool had been disrupted by the storm. It wasn't until I had set the alarm and reached the parking lot that I remembered I had no car.

I'd gotten a message mid-afternoon from the Darryls—they needed to order a part but promised to have my car ready by Friday. In all the excitement I'd forgotten. Now I was stranded.

I debated calling Henri. He still drove, though rarely at night, and the patchy fog would be problematic for him. He'd be my last resort. I ran through all the people I knew who might be able to come and get me. The ones who were closest were on my suspect list, and the rest lived far enough out of the village that I could walk home by the time they arrived. I didn't fancy spending the next twenty minutes alone on the manor grounds, and I had no desire to go back inside and wait. I'd cast plenty of bait that morning, secure in the knowledge that I had a bright and busy afternoon in which to reel in any takers. But now it was full dark, and I was uneasy. I wanted to get away.

I scrolled through my contact list, hesitating at Jennie Webber's number. She'd warned me to be careful and not do anything stupid, and wandering around the manor grounds at night would undoubtedly qualify as stupid. Besides, the weight of the flash drive was heavy in my pocket.

"What the hell." I hit the button. A tendril of mist wound around my ankles. "*The fog comes on little cat feet*," I muttered as I waited. I heard a click. Voicemail.

I waited a minute and tried again, the manor moaning and settling behind me and the wind sighing in the trees. Voicemail again. There was never a cop around when you needed one. Finally, I dialed the Java Joint. If Jack or Meadow weren't available, there might be someone there who wouldn't mind giving me a lift home.

The rapid busy signal put an end to that plan. Their line was down. I tried the Darryls, always good for a lift if they had your car. Same result. All of Main Street must be out of order. I set off on foot. I was a brisk five-minute walk to Agnes Jenner's house, and from there it was a short walk to Main. If anything seemed off, I could bang on Agnes's door. At this point, any action was preferable to lingering.

I moved quickly down the drive and along the road, avoiding the footbridge and staying on the one meant for car traffic. I paused and looked over to the side, curious as to how much the water had risen from the rain, but the angry bubbling that had caught my attention was obscured by a blanket of swirling fog. It was like looking into a giant witch's cauldron. What would the Brothers Grimm do next?

"Get a grip, Greer." I rolled my eyes at my vivid imagination, but I moved on at a good speed nonetheless, keeping a firm grip on my cell phone. I slowed as I crested the hill on the other side of the stream. A couple hundred yards of moonlit darkness, punctuated by drifting fog, stretched between me and the streetlamp near Agnes Jenner's driveway. Woods lined the road on either side. I moved to the middle of the street, where I had more light and could see anything that entered the empty space around me, a habit learned long ago in the city. I continued to walk, in and out of the fog, listening to the night sounds of birds and animals going about their business. They remarked on my passing with an occasional silence or quick chitter, then went back to what they were doing. I was reassured by their lack of concern—if there was something out here with me, some human predator, the woods would be still.

I gave a sigh of relief when I reached the streetlamp. I could hear cars in the distance and see lights in Agnes's windows. The only remaining obstacle between me and civilization was a large patch of undulating fog at the foot of the Jenner driveway. I marched forward at a steady pace, only slowing when the fog wrapped itself around me, muting sound and limiting my vision. Still, I kept moving. I was following the reflective line at the edge of the road and congratulating myself on maintaining my "Keep Calm and Carry On" attitude when a noise stopped me cold.

The muffled cough came again, about three feet ahead of where I stood. I froze, straining to see through the swirling fog. The atmosphere shifted. A breeze whispered through the treetops. The whirl of air created a clearing in the mist, and I found myself staring into a pair of amber eyes.

"Hello, there," I said.

The big red fox stood facing me, ears flicking and gaze steady, clearly on alert but not aggressive. I kept still. His ears flicked again, rotating back and then forward. I tilted my head, listening, and heard nothing but a car engine at the end of the road.

The fox barked again, the sound clearer with no fog between us. The engine noise grew closer. With one last warning yip the fox launched himself past me, seeming to pull the fog behind him like a cloak. It swirled around me as I stepped back, startled and off balance. Bright head-lights flashed, every drop of moisture in the air became a dazzling prism. I stumbled back again, squinting against the glare, my foot squelching into the sodden verge.

I stopped and considered flagging down the driver. In seconds I realized the car was headed straight for me. I turned in the direction the fox had taken and dove off the road, rolling down the slope until I fetched up against a tree stump. Tires squealed and I smelled burned rubber. The car roared off.

I was shaking and gasping when I heard my phone buzz. I could see it blink to life a few feet away. I crawled toward it and made a grab. On the second try I managed to thumb it on.

"This is Webber," I heard. "What's going on?"

"I think someone just tried to kill me."

Chapter Nineteen

"Seven minutes!" Officer Jennie Webber banged the steering wheel of the unmarked police car, in which I was receiving the much sought after ride home.

"You couldn't wait seven minutes for me to call you back?" she accelerated through a yellow light on Main and turned toward my apartment.

"People who hang out alone at the manor after dark tend to come to a bad end, remember? And you weren't the only one I called."

I sniffed, feeling soggy, sorry for myself, and annoyed. I was being scolded for nearly being the next victim of a killer the police had failed to apprehend. Granted, I had set a trap with myself as bait, but I had not expected it to be quite so successful. And while I'd withheld evidence, I'd had every intention of handing it over earlier that day.

"That's fair," Webber said, easing the car to a stop. She drummed her fingers against the wheel for a moment, brow furrowed.

"That shouldn't have happened, and it's not going to happen again. Wait here."

She pulled the keys from the ignition and hopped out, locking the car behind her. I huddled into the seat, pulling the jacket she had given me more closely around myself. The blanket provided by the EMTs was soaked by the time they were satisfied I was not concussed and in no need of a trip to the ER. Jennie Webber had assumed responsibility for me, handed me her coat, and bundled me into her car.

I watched the beam from her flashlight bounce around as she did a circuit of the house. Pierre barked, and lights went on briefly in Henri's apartment. She went up the stairs to my place, where she did a thorough check of the porch. She returned to the car and grabbed my bag from the back.

"Let's go. Everything seems fine. But I want you to take a good look around when we get upstairs. If anything seems out of place or not quite right, you tell me."

Worked for me. I wanted to get somewhere safe and hand over the evidence, and I'd decided Officer Webber was my best bet. She was twitchy and ever-vigilant, but she wasn't easily fazed and she'd proven willing to bend the rules. After I'd dragged myself up the stairs and assured her that everything was as I left it, she took my keys, unlocked the door, and we repeated the drill inside. The place was its usual degree of untidy—stacks of books here and there, a pair of shoes by the door, and the hamper of clean laundry in the bedroom. Not great, but not bad. I could tell that nothing was disturbed, but I doubted anyone else could.

"It's fine. Everything is just as I left it. I'm not what you'd call a neat freak."

"No judgement. I'm not either."

I doubted that, but it was nice of her to say.

"You should be okay here for the rest of the night. We'll have someone in an unmarked car on the street in a couple of minutes. You're not going anywhere alone until we catch whoever killed Joanna Goodhue."

"I'd rather you stayed. I found something. And I've heard things, things that don't make a lot of sense, but I think they're important."

"I can call O'Donnell—"

"No. I'll talk to you."

She looked surprised, and a little suspicious.

"While you've been watching me, Officer Webber, I've been watching you. Sam O'Donnell outranks you, and is more inclined to take me at my word, but he's from Raven Hill. We're not. What I think is going on? I think you'll get it. I don't know that he will."

She didn't look entirely convinced, but she pulled out her phone.

"Give me a minute," she said and stepped onto the porch.

I used the time to fill the kettle and put it on. By the time she came back I'd decided on my approach.

"I'll stay," she said, "but if I feel I need to call Lt. O'Donnell in, I will."

"Fine. Take a look at this. I'm freezing, I need to take a hot shower and change."

I dropped the baggy of evidence on the kitchen table and headed to the bathroom. I needed a few minutes to figure out how to finesse the details of my story. I leaned on the vanity, let out a big sigh, and looked in the mirror.

The Hag of the Dribble looked back.

"Gah." I turned my back on the apparition and peeled off my wet clothes. Within a minute I was in the shower, sudsing and lathering and hoping the hot water pounding on my head would help me order my thoughts. By the time I emerged, I had my story straight. I needed to gloss over some of the timing, but otherwise I was giving her the truth.

Officer Webber was sitting at my little kitchen table, frowning over the evidence. The kettle was rattling on its burner, emitting little puffs of steam. I rummaged in the pantry for what I needed.

"Tea?" I called over my shoulder.

A brief pause. Perhaps breaking bread with a former suspect was not covered in the police academy.

"Sure, thanks," she replied.

I set a tin of Irish Breakfast on the counter, and added a jar of honey and a bottle of Jameson's. I was pulling mugs from the cabinet when I saw her eye the whiskey.

"Irish cough syrup," I said, as I set the tea to steep.

"Do you have a cold?"

"No, but I've had a chill." I coughed. "See? I think I'm coming down with something."

She rolled her eyes but her lips twitched.

"Cream? Honey? Whiskey?" I waved the Jameson's at her.

"Straight."

"The whiskey?"

"The *tea*."

I set it in front of her and turned back to the counter. After a few sips of my own doctored tea, my nerves settled.

"We need to talk about all this, Ms. Hogan."

"Call me Greer. I think it's time we dispensed with the formalities. Fire away."

I took another swallow of my tea and pulled out a frying pan.

"This flash drive, Joanna Goodhue's?"

"Yes."

"And you came across this how?"

This was the tricky part. I stuck my head in the fridge and pulled out eggs and butter.

"I found it in the archives this afternoon."

"You just happened to find it?"

"I was looking for something else at the time."

Silence.

I looked over. She raised an eyebrow.

"Really," I said. "Did you look at the sheet of paper that was wrapped around it?"

"Yes."

"And?"

She smoothed out the notes and studied it while I whisked eggs and made toast. She didn't say anything until I set the plates on the table and sat across from her.

"A girl's gotta keep her strength up," I said. "I've never been one of those women who are too delicate to eat a bite after a shock."

"Neither have I."

"So, what do you think?" I waved my fork at the notes.

"I have no idea what any of this means."

I was impressed she admitted it.

"Neither did I at first."

"But you do now?"

"I think so, but it took me a while. I found the paper a couple of days ago, tucked in a book. I kept it because I recognized the handwriting. I wasn't sure it meant anything, but look."

I turned the paper so we could both see, and explained the letter and number sequences.

"I was looking for some of these issues today. I pulled out a bound volume and found the drive. More interesting is what I didn't find. These issues are missing. They've been cut out of the binding."

"And there's no way to tell when, since the books would still be there, right where they're supposed to be. Unless someone went looking for these specific issues, no one would know they were gone."

"Right," I said.

"Do you think Joanna Goodhue could have taken them?"

"I don't see why, because she could have copied them anytime. That's what she did with the ones she found. Remember—she had a key to the building and knew where the other keys were kept. No, I think they were gone when she got there."

"And a lot of other people have keys, or know where they're kept. So, Joanna either dropped the drive, or hid it."

"I assumed she set it down and forgot it," I said, trying to picture the scene.

"Maybe. Tell me again exactly how you found this."

"It was folded into a book. I was weeding nonfiction—legal and business—deciding what to keep, toss, or update. I always flip through before I scan the barcode. People use all kinds of things as bookmarks and forget about them. This sheet was tucked into a book about divorce law."

"Hmm," Jennie said, "and you pulled it off the shelf?"

"No. It was on my desk, or on a cart next to my desk. I had pulled several the day before but hadn't gotten through all of them."

"This was one you pulled?"

"I'm not sure. It was relatively new but hadn't been checked out recently. It went back on the shelf."

"So, Mrs. Goodhue could have checked it out in the past, put this paper in, and forgotten about it, which seems unlikely, or she deliberately left it where she knew you would find it."

Jennie sat tapping her pencil against her notebook.

"There's another possibility," I said. "She might have been looking something up in that particular book, and didn't want to be seen putting it back, or wanted to put it somewhere it wouldn't be noticed. But then why leave the notes?"

"Because she was afraid, and wanted to leave the evidence where it wouldn't be obvious, but where she could find it again. Or where someone else would."

"You think she knew she was in danger?"

"I don't know, but from what I've learned, she was an organized, intelligent woman. She was an investigative reporter once, wasn't she?"

I nodded.

"Then I think this was deliberate. We don't know how long she was alone in the building, or if she knew someone else was there. It was risky, but if she had to move fast, not a bad plan. And it worked. Someone she trusted found the evidence."

Someone she trusted, and someone she'd asked for help. Just like Danny.

I slumped back in my chair. Had Joanna known she was being stalked? Had Danny? No. They wouldn't have left themselves vulnerable, alone. But they both knew something was wrong, something dangerous. Had either of them seen the blow coming?

I rubbed my eyes. This was not a productive line of thought.

There's a real problem here. I'm going to be late.

One of the last messages I had gotten from Danny. I'd been annoyed.

I need your help.

Both of them. I'd put them off. Other things to do.

I kept my eyes shut and concentrated on my breathing. I heard Jennie shift in her chair.

"What's the matter, Greer?"

I opened my eyes. I looked at the face now a foot from my own and made a decision. She was not just some small-town cop. She'd been around. I trusted her to the extent that I trusted anyone in Raven Hill, and I needed her to trust me. What Sadie and Jack had seen sounded crazy, but I was sure it was important and I needed her to believe me. I couldn't follow up on everything myself. Joanna had been smart enough to leave a trail. I would do the same. There were some secrets I was tired of keeping.

Chapter Twenty

~

"Do you trust me?" I asked Jennie.

She sat back in her chair and considered me.

"To a point," she said, "but you haven't been completely honest from the start. I still think you're hiding something important."

"I am, but it's not about Joanna's death. It's something important to me. I know I was twitchy and not forthcoming but that was more about the habit of hiding things. Do you know what I mean?"

Her mouth tightened and she drew back slightly. But she nodded. My conclusion after our conversation in the Java Joint was correct. The woman had secrets of her own. If that's what allowed her to withhold judgement and listen, fine.

"It's about the night my husband was killed," I said, then stopped. Where to begin? I tried again.

"You've read the reports, I assume. From the police in New York?"

"I talked to the investigating officer. He sent copies."

I filed that away for future reference. I might need a look at those.

"So, you know I didn't have anything to do with Danny's murder?"

"You were out of it almost immediately. Your cab driver picked you up past the time of death, and except for a brief time at the hotel you were within sight of a lot of people."

"Yes, it was a real crush, that gathering, and Danny was supposed to be with me."

Running late. Meet you there. The first text. I was still in my office.

She nodded. She knew this.

"Well, it's that 'brief time' that's the issue."

It had been an unseasonably hot night for early spring in Manhattan. I'd been loosening up my more conservative office look, and was stripping off my pantyhose when the first text came. I was annoyed. I had debated attending this event, and finally let Danny talk me into it. Just drinks with his business school cohort. A few of them were attending some meeting in the conference room of a trendy hotel, and would adjourn to the equally trendy bar afterward to meet the rest of the gang. Those inclined would find a suitably pretentious restaurant for a late dinner. I wasn't interested in the agenda, potential IPO or not, but I was interested in the attendees. I figured I would arrive with my husband, say my hellos, and plead a headache if I wanted out. Now I would be making an entrance alone. I took a long look in the mirror before heading downtown. Not the carefree college student I'd once been, but not so bad. Not that it mattered, I told myself. These were Danny's business school friends. I spritzed on some of my company's newest fragrance and left. The second text came as I reached the subway.

Dealing with that problem I told you about. Still at office. Leaving soon.

"Danny had something going on at work. There was some problem he'd found. It really bothered him, but he couldn't make sense of it. We were going to meet some of his friends from his MBA program. I think he wanted to talk it over with them. But it got more urgent. He wanted to tell me about it that morning, but we didn't have time. *I* didn't have time."

Jennie sat and listened. I felt my way along.

"So, I figured we'd all talk about it over drinks. But he kept texting that he was stuck at work because of this issue."

"You knew all these people? The ones you were meeting?"

"Some of them."

"But you don't have any idea what the problem was?" she asked.

I shook my head. Knowing Danny, the problem could have been anything from a sudden drop in revenues to someone's expense account not adding up. At first I thought it was the latter. Now I wasn't so sure.

"It was complex enough and sensitive enough, that he wanted to talk about it in person. To a couple of his business school buddies, one in particular. And to me."

She raised an eyebrow.

"I know. I told him I didn't know enough about his business; I didn't see how I could help. He said that was why, because I would make crazy connections that he couldn't see, because I didn't know what I should be seeing. Do you know what I mean?"

"It's why I'm on this case, instead of a more senior officer, and why Sam has let you run loose with no more than an occasional warning. Because we're inside enough to know the players, but outside enough to see them clearly. No expectations. Go on. How does this relate to the time you were MIA?"

This was the tough part.

"Danny had a mentor, through his MBA program and after. A man named Ian Cameron. They worked together on a few things. Ian was brilliant, creative. Danny could do anything with numbers, but he was methodical, very attached to details. They made a good team. Ian would make the leap of faith, and Danny would anchor it in a balance sheet."

Find Ian. Have him call me ASAP. Still here. Use cell.

The third text. I was three drinks into the night and angry. I'd already found Ian once.

"Hello, gorgeous. What a lovely surprise."

"Ian. Hello, yourself. I was invited, you know."

"You've been invited before. You've never appeared. Where's Dan?"

"Hung up at work. Hopefully on his way. He wants to talk to you."

"I know. He left a couple of messages during the presentation. I hope he gets here soon. I have a plane to catch."

"Don't you always? So sorry we won't get to catch up over dinner. I hear you got divorced. Again. I'll ping Dan. We'll find you when he gets here."

His eyes hadn't left me once. The bastard.

"I guess you could say Ian Cameron was my first love," I told Jennie. "Dan introduced us."

Danny, who I'd known my whole life. I'd been his prom date, flattered at the attention from an older boy. We'd gone out once or twice, and then he'd moved on to college and college girls. Like Vince and Felicity. But I hadn't been heartbroken. I dated a few boys with varying degrees of seriousness after starting at NYU. Danny and I remained friends, ending up at some of the same parties when he came back to the city for his MBA. He got into the habit of dropping by when he was at my end of town. We'd have coffee at one of the village cafes and discuss the latest news from our neighborhood. He was always good for some homework help if I was having any trouble with something business related. The fact that he was taking a semester abroad at the same time I was taking an advanced statistics course is what led to Ian.

"Dan asked Ian to check in with me. We had coffee and talked business statistics. Then we had coffee again and talked for hours. That led to dinner and drinks, and soon to a red-hot love affair. It ended badly."

I was wild about Ian. He claimed to be wild about me. We had a great spring. I'd just been offered a job by the company I'd interned with when Ian delivered the blow. He was taking a job in Silicon Valley, a start-up with a lot of potential. He was sure I could find something to do out there, if I wanted to come. I had a vision of myself relegated to the role of "the girlfriend" and eventually "the wife" and said no thanks. He wasn't as heartbroken as I'd hoped.

"So, Ian went for the brass ring, and I went for the sure thing." The job where they already knew me and liked me. The city I loved. And eventually, the boy from the neighborhood. And for a long time, it worked. I hadn't seen Ian since he left.

The last text came a few minutes later.

Just leaving. Meet you at home. Ian?!?

I'll find him. Pick up dinner.

Ten minutes later I found him. I stepped into the deserted conference room and waited for my eyes to adjust to the dim light. Ian spoke out of the darkness.

"Looking for me?"

He was packing up the presentation, his standard gin and tonic on the table. He walked over, standing a little too close. He'd had more than one drink.

"Dan can't make it. He wants you to call," I said.

"I just tried him. Direct to voicemail."

"He must be on the subway."

"What's it about? This problem?" he asked.

"Confidential."

Ian reached over and closed the door.

"No. I mean I don't know, I can't tell you anything."

He frowned and took a deep breath. He glanced away. Then back.

"You've changed your perfume, Greer."

"It's been fifteen years. I've changed a lot of things."

"But you're still so pretty."

He moved closer. I stood my ground. I could see the faint lines around his blue eyes, the slight silvering of his red hair. He was still handsome. He brushed my hair away from my face. I turned my head. I felt his lips on my neck, the worn denim of his jeans against my bare knee, and the cool conference table behind me.

"Haven't you ever thought about it, Greer? If we were both free?"

Sixty blocks uptown, someone was murdering my husband.

"So, there you have it," I said to Jennie, "my dirty little secret. The only time I've ever cheated, and Danny dies."

"A kiss? A conversation? Not exactly cheating."

"It felt like it. It was—emotional infidelity? I don't know. I'd thought about it. Was thinking about it. And then when I got home—"

"You didn't make it happen, Greer. It was coincidence. Bad luck."

"I know. It's just—I know. Danny was supposed to be there. I never went to these things."

"Why did you go this time?"

There was no judgement in her voice, only curiosity.

"I wanted to see him. To see if he was sorry he dumped me all those years ago. To make him sorry. It was ego, pure and simple."

"It's never simple. There's always something more."

"I don't know. Anger, boredom, too many drinks."

"Or fear, uncertainty, too many drinks. The usual suspects," she said. She sighed. "Alcohol and ex-boyfriends. Never a good thing."

That last bit was delivered with real feeling. I raised my eyebrows. She looked at her notes.

So much for an exchange of girlish confidences.

"It wasn't your fault your husband died," she said. "It could have been you, if you got home first, or even both of you, if the guy was high or desperate."

I shook my head. That didn't feel right.

She shrugged.

"I can see why you wanted to keep it quiet, though," she went on, "and why you felt so bad. It could've looked worse than it was to some people.

"Yes. I felt terrible, I still do. At the time, I worked for some very conservative people. But they're nothing compared to a small-town library board of trustees. When I found Joanna's body all I could think about was keeping my secrets. I wanted to deflect attention. Just like when I found Danny."

"And now?"

"Now I think there's a whole lot more to all of this than I ever realized. I wish I'd paid more attention."

"Hindsight but I agree with you."

She fanned out the papers once more and shook her head.

"There must be a connection between all these things she was looking into and her death, but I can't see how it all links."

"Neither can I, but I requested copies of all the articles listed. They're coming from the state library. They should be here tomorrow."

"Call me as soon as you get them. Any way to make sure no one else sees them arrive?"

"I get stuff from other libraries all the time. It won't get a second look. Circ just hands the stuff off to me."

"Good."

"There are some other things, odd things, but I think they're important."

I told her about my conversation with Sadie, and that Jack had seen a similar apparition, both of them more than once. I told her about every overheard conversation, pointed question, and mysterious noise. I told her everything I could think of, no matter how strange. I was relieved when she took it all seriously.

"Some of that is odd, but it doesn't mean it isn't real, or important."

"So, you believe us?"

"I believe all of you saw and heard these things that made you take notice. I believe in instinct. If something sets off an alarm bell in your head, you need to pay attention. Instinct is what keeps you alive."

Her tone was grim. I thought about her time in Iraq. I believed in instinct, too, but my life had never been on the line. Until now.

Jennie seemed to be lost in thought. She rubbed her arms and I saw goosebumps.

"I'm sorry. I forgot you're sitting here in damp clothes. Come with me."

"I'm okay. It was just a little rain."

I stood and headed to the bedroom, calling over my shoulder, "If you're planning on staying all night, or what's left of it, you'll put on dry clothes. We can hang yours by the radiator to dry."

God, I sounded like my mother. But Jennie had fished me out of ditch and sat here listening to me, so I was going to make sure she was comfortable.

By the time she arrived in the bedroom, I had pulled a clean white tee and a blue cashmere hoodie out of my dresser. I tossed them to her and rummaged through my basket of clean laundry. When I turned back to her, she was holding the shirt and sweater to her nose. She caught my eye and flushed. It was a glimpse of a younger, less assured Jennie Webber.

"They *are* clean," I said.

"I know. It's just that I got a whiff of something—I don't know. They smell like—like you look."

"How's that?"

She shrugged. "Sophisticated. Expensive."

"Ah." I handed her a pair of fleece sweats, then moved to my vanity and picked through a basket of cosmetic samples. She reached past me and pointed.

"That's beautiful," she said.

I glanced at the intricate Venetian carnival mask hanging from the mirror over my cosmetics.

"Thanks. It was a gift from a friend. So were these, but they're more suited to you."

I handed her a little bag of cleansers, toners, and moisturizers. Based on her expression, it was more skin care product than she'd ever used in her life. I plucked a dainty bottle off the vanity.

"Go ahead, I get that stuff by the barrel. And take this, too." I handed over the little atomizer. "It smells like you look. Outdoorsy. On me it smells like someone just cut the grass."

All my adrenaline faded. I was as tired as I had ever been in my life. I washed the dishes while she changed. I was pulling out blankets when she came out of the bathroom.

"The afghan and the chair will be fine. I don't sleep much. Thanks for all this stuff."

She was no longer holding the bag as though it might explode. I took that as a good sign, and began my own nighttime ritual of potions and lotions. After giving her some hangers for her wet clothes, I tucked in. It was strange having someone else in my apartment, and I lay wakeful, listening to her moving around, checking locks and looking out windows.

I finally dozed. I found myself in a surreal landscape of twisting fog, where I raced down an endless corridor of doors swinging open and shut, pursued by thudding footsteps while skeletal hands plucked at my clothing. A coyote yipped, unseen. Danny and Joanna stood at the end of the hall, he in a suit, holding an envelope, she in her bright blue

Raven Hill hoodie, a red fox between them, never getting any closer no matter how hard I ran. A raven swooped at me out the darkness, cawing "Nevermore!" and I jerked sideways into swirling darkness. I came awake with a gasp, my heart pounding. The dream image faded, leaving only my husband and my friend. They disintegrated into mist, and I was left with only the night around me.

I sat up and listened, relieved to hear only the usual calming night sounds.

It's a message, whispered a voice in my head, *it's the answer*.

I replayed the dream, but found no answer. If I let it go, maybe it would come.

There was a faint light coming from the living room. Jennie Webber keeping watch. I shifted slightly, angling so I could see the tri-fold vanity mirror, positioned so that no matter where I was in the room I could see out into the rest of the apartment. Jennie was visible in the dim light of a small lamp. She'd slid my reading chair close to the window. She held a pad, larger than the little notebook she always carried, and was moving a pencil with swift, sure strokes across the page. She stopped as something caught her attention outside, her head tilt reminding me of the ravens, who always seemed to be listening to something beyond my hearing.

Satisfied, she relaxed back in her chair. She put down her pencil and stretched, pushing her hair off her face. As she finished, she sniffed her wrist, and rubbed the back of her hand along her cheek. With a little shrug, she adjusted the afghan, rubbed each hand down the opposite arm, and picked up her notebook. Getting in touch with her inner expensive girl, I thought.

I spied a few minutes more, knowing that if Jennie looked toward the mirror in the dark bedroom, she would see nothing but shifting shadows.

Chapter
Twenty-One

⁓

Jennie dropped me at the Java Joint mid-morning, warning me repeatedly not to wander off alone. As if. The goal was to always be in sight of a crowd or a police officer until whoever killed Joanna was caught. Whatever I knew, it was apparently too much for the murderer's comfort. Jennie assured me the police were making progress but I had a niggling suspicion that waiting for someone to take another whack at me was a key part of their strategy.

Promising to pick me up in time for my afternoon shift, Jennie headed off for a change of clothes and a hunt for the files relating to the two deaths Joanna was researching. Glumly stating that anything useful was probably buried in storage, she left with an enormous cup of coffee and a bag of goodies to bribe the department's tech wizard into dropping everything and devoting himself to the flash drive.

I settled in with my own jolt of caffeine and a large breakfast. While I was anxious to get back to the investigation, I had to admit it was pleasant to be somewhere sunny and bright, full of nice, normal people who seemed more interested in pastries than homicidal mania. My respite was brief. Felicity came in, attired in exercise gear and looking pale and tense. Apparently, her morning yoga class had not had the desired calming effect. She caught my eye as she got in line, and I gave a little wave. Within minutes she was at my side, gesturing at the empty chair across from me. I nodded. The minute she landed in the chair she erupted into speech.

"Greer, I heard you were in an accident. I'm so sorry! Are you all right? What happened? Did you see who hit you?"

Felicity's hands on her coffee cup were white to the knuckle, and she was chewing on her lower lip as she waited for me to answer. I decided keeping her off balance was my best bet.

"Someone tried to kill me. It was no accident."

She gasped, then got hold of herself and took a sip of her coffee.

"How can you be sure? Did you see who did it?"

There was that question again. Did she know who it was, or was she afraid to find out?

"Someone drove straight at me on a deserted road, so yes, I'm sure it was deliberate, and no, I don't know who it was. I didn't get a good look. It was foggy."

"It was foggy," she repeated, "yes, very foggy. It's possible that whoever it was didn't see you."

Who was she trying to convince? I shook my head.

"Well, are you all right?" she asked.

"No permanent damage, just some bumps and bruises," I said. My clothes were another story. My carefully preserved designer basics were ruined. Not as important as me being in one piece, but still. Another thing the killer had to answer for.

"I'm glad, very glad to hear that."

She fidgeted some more. Once again, she seemed on the verge of asking me something. I waited.

"Do you think," she said, "that maybe someone was just trying to scare you? Because of Joanna?"

"You mean because of what I know about her death? Or what she was looking into right before it?"

"Yes," she said, and leaned closer and whispered, "do you know? Do you know anything she found out?"

"I've found some notes, and some articles." Then I leaned toward her. We were nose to nose across the table.

"You've lived here all your life, Felicity. What can you tell me about Carol Douglas?"

Felicity grew even more pale.

"That poor little girl. It was so awful. He never talks about it. If it weren't for Vince—"

She broke off.

"Vince never talks about it?" I prompted.

"No, Matthew. Carol was his sister, well, half-sister, you know. No, how would you know? He found her there, in the water. The two of them did, Vince and Matthew. Playing in the woods. Such a beautiful, sunny day. But the water in the kill was high, and so cold."

She rubbed her arms, staring past me.

"Her poor mother. She never got over it. It's too awful even to think about. If only I could be sure."

She paused again. Sure of what?

"Joanna knew this whole story?"

Felicity snapped back to the present.

"Not all of it, I don't think. I don't think that's what got her killed. No."

"Then what did, Felicity?"

"I don't know," she said, now sounding more frustrated than frightened. "I can't be sure of anything. Listen, Greer, you need to be careful. Do the police know all of this?"

"I've given them everything I've found."

"Good. Let them deal with it."

"Oh, I am, believe me," I said. I didn't think Felicity was the killer, but she was wound tight about something, so putting it about that I was well out of things was to my advantage.

"Good," she said again, adding, "maybe you should take some time off. Get away for a bit. I'm taking the kids to the lake house tomorrow. My sister's there now. We're opening it early in case it needs any repairs from all the snow. Why don't you join us?"

A cabin deep in the woods at a lakeside Adirondack retreat that would still be deserted this early in the season? This was the stuff of which horror movies were made. Whether or not Felicity was a murder suspect, I thought not.

"I'm afraid I can't get away from work on such short notice. We've been so busy. But it's kind of you to offer."

"Oh, I see," she said. She scribbled something on a napkin and pushed it across the table.

"Here's my cell if you change your mind. Or if something new comes up. You'll call me, won't you?"

She sounded anxious again.

"Of course."

She looked around the room, and with one more "Be careful, Greer," she was gone.

I was mulling over my conversation with Felicity when Meadow appeared. She'd heard about the events of the previous evening.

"How're you holding up?" she said, taking Felicity's place across the table.

I filled her in on my bruises, aches, ruined outfit, and general frustration. When I wound down, she waved Jack over.

"I think we have some new information, for what it's worth," she said.

As Jack arrived with the coffeepot, Meadow told me she'd seen a "whole flock of headless ghosts" running down Main Street the day before. She'd done a double take and gone to the window for a closer look. It was the high school track team, caught out in the rain when the storm hit.

"They had their hoods pulled up and were hunched over against the wind and rain," she said, "and the ones without hoods had pulled up their sweatshirts, so the neck was over their heads. Those are the ones that really looked kind of headless. The rest looked more like hunchbacks."

I looked at Jack, who had pulled up a chair.

"Did you see them?" I asked.

"Meadow called me over and I got a quick look. Could be. The outlines seemed a little off, but what I saw before was across the street at night. Looked bigger and shadowy. But that could be a trick of the light."

"Or it was an adult in something less colorful than the track team sweats. The kids don't usually run by here?"

"No." Meadow shook her head. "I think it was the storm. They were taking the shortest route back to the school."

"Well, it's something," I said, "and I can tell Officer Webber. But the police will probably want to speak to you."

Jack nodded.

"I'll call Sam and tell him to drop around for some coffee," he said. "It's been a while."

He took the coffee pot and headed back to the counter. Meadow saw my expression and laughed.

"Sam O'Donnell was not always the Eagle Scout he appears to be," she said. "Few people are. Sam and Jack have been friends since we moved here. Now, do you want a little something for later? I see your car's still in the shop."

I placed an order. Meadow's Eagle Scout comment had caused a little ping in my brain, but I couldn't tell why. Jennie Webber showed up right on time to get me to the library for my reference shift. We exchanged information on the way. As expected, the files she wanted were in an off-site storage facility, and would take some time to retrieve. She hoped to have them the next day.

"But I'm going to try to catch Felicity before she leaves town," Jennie said, "and I'll drop by on Vince and Matthew

Prentiss. They're the closest we've got to eyewitnesses to the Douglas drowning unless we turn up another name in those files."

"The newspaper articles might have something."

"Maybe. Call me as soon as you get them. I'm going to have another go at Agnes Jenner about last night."

"Did she see anything?"

"She made a 911 call right around the time of the accident. Said a woman walked into the fog and a fox ran out, and kept going on about fins and metal teeth. She made no sense but kept saying someone was hurt, so the ambulance was dispatched before I called it in. She was incoherent last night, but I'll talk to her now. With any luck she's still sober."

"She was right about the fox," I said, and told Jennie about my encounter.

Jennie sighed. "All right. I'll see what she says today. Maybe she saw a headless ghost, too."

She waited until I was in the door and took off. I had to give her credit. She was hanging in there with the crazier stuff far better than I could have hoped. Most of the village, it seemed, was okay with crazy, at least those that used the library. Something in the water? Or just the atmosphere of the manor?

"She is too fond of books," I quoted, "and it has turned her brain."

Chapter Twenty-Two

～

The first hour of my reference shift was spent dealing with concerned co-workers. Helene offered to take over at the desk, but I told her I needed the distraction. I also needed to pounce on the interlibrary loans as soon as they arrived. Promising to spell me when I needed a break, Helene drifted around the reading room, tidying and filling in displays. She looked as tired and anxious as I felt. Even the unflappable Mary Alice was showing signs of strain. It was a slow afternoon, and we busied ourselves with mindless tasks, glad to feel we were accomplishing something. It should have been routine, but I was not the only one who jumped at every noise, keeping a closer eye on the place than usual. I was glad to see one of O'Donnell's plants. Jennie had admitted there were officers on loan keeping an eye on things, though she refused to confirm my guesses. A miscommunication had resulted in my being left alone the night before. She promised it wouldn't happen again.

I was replaying my conversation with Felicity, thinking there was something I missed, when the bins full of materials our patrons had requested from other libraries arrived. I didn't want to tip my hand to their importance by diving into the pile, so I waited. Mary Alice worked quickly, and I was rewarded in short order.

"Package for you, Greer," Mary Alice called. I put the recommendation cards I was sorting back in their box and went to Circ. There it was, the familiar state library stamp in the corner of the envelope. I tucked it under my arm, told Helene I'd like to take my break, and headed to the office.

I slid the contents of the envelope onto my desk. Clipped to a sheaf of blurry photocopies was a note. *Couldn't get them all and the quality is questionable, but I did my best. Cheers!*

I flipped through the stack, starting with anything related to Carol Douglas. Most told me no more than I already knew, but one of the Albany papers had done a longer article, complete with a photo of the little girl and a shot of the Ravens Kill right below the bridge. I looked at the smiling face and thought of Joanna's girls, and my own nieces. So young. So awful, as Felicity said. According to the article, there had been two witnesses to her death—Matthew Prentiss and Vincent Goodhue. Carol Douglas often trailed around after her brother and his friends, wanting to be included in their games. The two boys had been playing in the woods. No one was sure how Carol had ended up in the water, but they had heard her call out and gone to investigate. Matthew, older and a stronger swimmer, had gone in after her while Vince ran for help. By the time help arrived, Matthew was partway to shore, clinging to rocks and half-submerged branches, and Carol had been swept downstream. Her body was found later that day.

They found her there, in the water.

Felicity's words came back to me. I thought she meant Matthew and Vince found the body, but they had found Carol alive and in trouble. I looked at the blurry photo, and pictured the Raven's Kill, the water high and moving fast from snow melt, as it was this spring. Hypothermia or drowning, it didn't matter. A small child would not last long in the icy current.

I shivered and went back to the article.

There was little else of note, but it did name the local police officers involved. One name jumped out. I was pretty sure Salvatore Cosmopoulos was Pete's grandfather. If so, Jennie should talk to him. I made a note and began reading about the second death, the older woman found dead of exposure on the banks of the Raven's Kill.

These articles were all brief, but those that moved beyond "breaking news" identified her. Marjorie Douglas was in her late seventies and suffering from dementia. She had started to wander in the months before her death, and had apparently let herself out of the house she shared with her son and his family after everyone else was asleep. She was predeceased by her first and second husbands and her daughter Carol, and survived by her son, Matthew Prentiss.

Dementia took many forms. How far gone was she? Still mobile, and with some motor skills, or she could not have gotten out of the house undetected. What did that correspond to mentally? Was there any way to tell for sure? All I knew was that it was a cruel and unpredictable illness. Unpredictable. Joanna's notes said "reno—locks." How secure was the house, and what could Marjorie Douglas still reason through on her own? I would have to do some research.

The only other news item that mentioned Marjorie Douglas was a brief paragraph in the local paper a few years before her death. She had placed some land bordering the manor grounds in a trust. This land, along with a parcel from another relative, was to be used for future expansion of the village library "where she spent many happy hours."

There was nothing else.

I flipped through the pages again, lingering over the last item. Joanna's notes had mentioned a trust of some sort. What had it said? James Family Trust. Felicity's maiden name was James. Had to be related, but how? Another thing to look into, but I could do that in the reading room. I needed to get back to reference.

I pulled out my phone and sent Jennie a quick text.

Got articles. Sal Cosmopoulos officer on scene of drowning. Retired, still alive and in town, I think. Pete's Pizza connection? Also, James Family Trust important!

I stuffed everything back into the envelope and taped it shut. I wasn't letting it out of my sight, but neither did I want to draw attention to it. I grabbed a request card and scrawled Jennie Webber's initials and cell phone number across it, then stapled it to the envelope. If some evil befell me, the packet would go in the queue of requested materials and someone would call her. I grabbed some similar items from my desk, buried the envelope in the middle of the stack, and went out to reference. My phone buzzed in the hall. Jennie.

Thnx. Will check. Stuck downtown. Talk later.

I now knew everything Joanna knew. More, if she had never seen these articles, and I was sure she hadn't. If she had gotten any further with her research there was no evidence of it, and she was a thorough investigator. There would be something. But could the little she had known have gotten her killed? I considered the large life insurance policy and the feud with Ed Dexter. For all I knew, checking up on Dexter was what took Jennie downtown. But those things seemed more and more unlikely. No, everything seemed to center around the Prentiss family tragedy. The answer was here, between the manor and the banks of the Ravens Kill. Vince, Felicity, and Matthew, in some combination, were the only people who kept turning up. Who else knew all the players and had spent their life in and out of the manor?

Millicent?

Millicent disliked Joanna's push for progress. Based on the argument I'd heard between her and Vince, she felt she was being blackmailed. Her passion was local history and the Ravenscroft legacy. Would this trust for a potential library expansion have threatened that? Millicent and Marjorie Douglas would have been close in age, and both had spent plenty of time at the Manor. What was the connection? Who was the other relative who had donated land? I couldn't make anything fit, but I couldn't rule it out. There were too many blanks, and no way to dig into the legal documents from where I sat.

I eyed Mary Alice. She wasn't a lifelong village resident, but she'd been here for decades and her husband was the local doctor until he retired. I trusted her. Still, I thought, glancing around the reading room, I needed to be circumspect. Within minutes, I had trundled a full bin from the book drop over to Circ and started checking them in.

"I ran into Felicity this morning," I said. "We had coffee. She's very upset about Joanna. Says it's just too much on top of everything else. I hadn't realized there was so much tragedy in the Prentiss family. Going back quite some time, I gather."

Mary Alice shook her head.

"She was ahead of Carol Douglas in school, but still. It's a small town. She took Marjorie's death hard. Blamed herself. I was hoping she'd got past it, but I guess losing a friend has stirred up bad memories."

"Why did she blame herself? The woman had dementia, didn't she?"

"Marjorie was living with them at the time. She needed care but didn't want to leave her home. The old Prentiss place was huge, so Matthew and Felicity and the kids moved in. They were renovating it. The place hadn't been touched in years. Anyway, the youngest was just a baby, and colicky. Felicity wasn't sleeping much. At first Marjorie was able to help with the older child, but the dementia got worse and then Felicity really had her hands full."

"Marjorie started to wander, didn't she?"

Mary Alice tsked. "It was heartbreaking. She kept try-ing to get to the Ravens Kill. She thought Carol was calling to her for help. Felicity told me once that everything would seem fine, and then she'd find Marjorie staring out the kitchen window, mumbling how she should have known, she had seen it, she should have done something, and soon after she'd slip out of the house. They put new locks on the doors, some kind of complicated deadbolt. And Marjorie got paranoid, too. She didn't want to leave the grandchil-dren alone with anyone, and then she didn't want Felicity out of her sight. I think in her mind they all became Carol, and she was trying to save them. She was frightened all the time. I remember Dave prescribed some kind of sedative so she would at least sleep through the night, but I'm not sure it was effective. Felicity looked to be on the edge of a breakdown."

"But how was any of this her fault?"

"Well, as I said, she hadn't been sleeping well for a while. As the baby's colic got better, Marjorie got worse. There was a terrible storm the weekend Marjorie died. Heavy snow one night, and the next the temperature dropped and the wind picked up. Felicity had taken a turn shoveling, and was exhausted. She slept like a log all night. And I gather she'd been forgetting things, which is understandable, but there was some discussion of whether everything was locked that night. She was the last to go to bed."

"So, Marjorie got out of the house and froze to death," I said.

Mary Alice nodded.

"She wasn't far from the house—on the path to the water. But she was in her nightgown, so the cold took her fast. They didn't find her until late the next day because of the blowing snow."

"My God, that's awful," I said. I'd read the story, but Mary Alice had made it vivid. I saw it all in my mind. The little girl on a sunny day, playing in the woods, and then in the cold water, struggling. The old woman, her very essence dissolving as her mind shut down, searching endlessly for her lost child, wandering barefoot in the snow, answering a plea only she could hear. And Joanna, fierce and brave, lying cold and still at the bottom of the stairs. That part I had seen for myself.

This wasn't just awful, it was evil. Evil because it was deliberate in some way, and Joanna had guessed, and so had to die.

Nevermore, nevermore.

Whatever, whoever—would be stopped. This would end here.

"Did you know Marjorie Douglas well?" I asked.

"I knew her to speak to, but only because I would help out in the office when Dave's receptionist was out."

"What about Millicent? Were they friends?"

Mary Alice gave a wry smile.

"I'm not sure Millicent has any close friends, but they were friendly, yes. They played bridge together, as I recall."

"Hmph," I said.

"Is there some connection here, Greer?"

"I don't know, but I'm sure Joanna thought so. It all keeps coming back to the same people. Vince and Matthew and Felicity and Millicent, and all of them in and out of the manor their whole lives."

Mary Alice frowned. "That's true, and you could actually see the old Prentiss house from the manor, at least when the trees weren't in full leaf. But I don't know if that tells us anything. What about the little Barrett girl? Any news there?"

I filled her in on what Jack and Meadow told me. Mary Alice thought for a moment and shook her head.

"Still doesn't make any sense to me, but I don't like it. I'm glad the police know, but I'm still keeping a sharp eye on that child when she's here. It worries me that she saw something that night."

"Me too. But I'm not sure what else we can do."

"I'll talk to Dave tonight and see if he remembers anything else about Marjorie Douglas."

The rest of the afternoon passed quietly. I did some discreet web searches related to the new information I had, but found nothing useful. A quick read-through of information on Alzheimer's and dementia only made me angrier, but I made some notes and bookmarked the site. I had some time between the end of my shift and the ride home Jennie had arranged for me, so I checked out a Miss Marple video and went back to the office. In addition to the usual stack of mail there was a box on my chair. It was addressed to "Hogan/Goodhue" care of the library.

Joanna had mentioned in her note that she was ordering some things for the girls. I slit open the box and checked the contents. All books, and all from the list I had given her. I waited for the familiar sadness to wash over me, but felt only cold resolve.

Nevermore.

The raven from my dream cawed in my head. I saw them standing at the end of the hall, Danny in his suit, Joanna in her hoodie.

It's a message. It's the answer.

That persistent whisper again. I had all the pieces. I had to put the puzzle together. A lawyer friend once told me, "Trust, but verify." I checked the time and pulled out my phone.

I had questions for Vince, but delivering the books was out of the question. I didn't have a car and I didn't want to be alone with him. Meeting at the library would be my best bet. Tonight was out but the morning would work.

I called the Goodhue home number and got voicemail. I left a message saying I had something for Vince and wanted to make arrangements to give it to him, asking him to call my cell. With any luck, he'd presume it was the missing flash drive and call as soon as he got the message.

While I waited, I printed out the annotated booklist I had made for Joanna and tucked it in with the books. I resealed the box and stashed it under my desk. My phone rang as I finished.

"Did you find it?" Vince asked as soon as I said hello.

"I'm sorry, I don't have the drive, I have something else," I said, and explained the situation. I implied that I had the box with me and wasn't at work. I didn't want him to stop by and get them after I'd gone for the day.

"So, since I'm busy for the rest of the evening, I was hoping you could come by the library tomorrow morning," I said.

There was a brief silence and then Vince agreed to meet me. We set a time and hung up. I gathered my things and waited by the door for my ride, hoping it would be Jennie. No luck. It was my prom date from earlier in the week, who explained that Officer Webber was tied up elsewhere but would be in touch, and that there would be a police presence on my street all night. I didn't know whether to be flattered or alarmed that I rated this much attention from a small- town force, and hoped someone was keeping an eye on the Barrett kids as well.

I had a lovely dinner with Henri, who listened carefully to what I'd learned. I was hoping he'd be able to shed some light, but after reading through the newspaper articles he shook his head.

"I confess I cannot see the connection," he said, "except, as you say, the players are the same."

"What about this donation of land Marjorie Douglas made? It mentions a previous donation by another relative. Do you remember hearing anything about that? Some sort of trust, the James Family Trust?"

"I believe that Felicity's father and the Douglas woman were related. Cousins, perhaps. Most of these old families around here are. Big farms, lots of kids, everyone intermarried. But all that changed with the wars. When we first came here there were still some working farms, but eventually the land was divided and sold off to developers. It was worth more that way, and people died or moved or simply needed the money."

"Are we talking about a lot of money? A large trust?"

"I cannot say for sure, though both families always seemed very comfortable. I am sorry to say my memory is not what it was, Greer. I would guess a considerable sum, but if I knew, I have forgotten."

It wasn't much, but it was food for thought. Henri walked me to my apartment, leaving me with extra dessert and Pierre to serve as my alarm system. I settled on the couch with the dog, giving half my attention to "A Caribbean Mystery" while my mind spun through the evidence. I sent Jennie a text but got no response. Jane Marple solved her mystery in ninety minutes, complete with appropriate biblical quotation. But she did have an unnecessary death toward the end. There'd be no more of that on my watch.

Nevermore.

Chapter
Twenty-Three

I woke with the sense that I'd made some brilliant deductions overnight, if only I could remember what they were. Adding to my frustration was a cryptic text from Jennie, saying "new developments, talk later." I sent back, "James Family Trust. Checked?" While I was loathe to admit the police could accomplish anything I couldn't, there was no way a lawyer was going to talk to me and finding the original documents at the county clerk's office would be time-consuming even if I could get there.

When I was deposited at the library by my police escort of the day, the manor lot held more than the usual assortment of cars for a Friday morning. I recognized Anita's and groaned. Whatever was going on, I was keeping a low profile. With any luck they would all be gone by lunchtime. I ducked into my office and made sure the box of books was still where I'd left it. With some time to spare before Vince was due to arrive, I decided to do a little discreet information gathering.

Jilly was at the reference desk, getting herself organized before the library opened. Mary Alice was emptying the book drop. The main floor was otherwise quiet.

"So, what's going on?" I asked Jilly.

"Emergency board meeting. I'm taking Helene's reference shift and Anne Marie will do story hour. Hopefully not a big crowd because she's only done it once on her own, and as soon as she's through we've got to put the room to rights because the Friends' jumble sale committee needs to huddle and figure out how to get things back on track without Joanna. What a mess! None of this was on the calendar and we're all scrambling."

"I can help Anne Marie clean up."

"Thank you, Greer, that would be great. There's no telling what kind of crowd we'll get here in the reading room. Everything is topsy-turvy between the weather and the murder, but there are always a few parents who want help with book selection after story hour."

I moved on to Mary Alice.

"Any news?" I asked.

"Not really," she said, "though Dave does remember prescribing a sedative for Marjorie. He recommended Felicity take something but she wouldn't. Said even an extra-strength Tylenol would knock her out and she needed to be alert. He tried to talk them into a home health aide for Marjorie, but Matthew felt his mother would be too upset by a stranger in the house. He was adamant that they would care for her as long as she recognized them and was in any way coherent."

"Hard on Felicity."

"Yes, it was. Dave felt Felicity would have liked the help, but agreed that Marjorie would be frightened. It worked against them in the end, I guess."

I asked Mary Alice about the James Family Trust and Marjorie's bequest, but she didn't know anything more than Henri. My frustration mounting, I got myself some fresh coffee and returned to my cubicle.

Vince Goodhue was sitting in my chair, idly scanning the surface of my desk. He looked awful. Even better, he looked like a man who needed someone to talk to.

"Hi," I said, leaning against the wall and blocking his exit, "thanks for meeting me here. My car's in the shop, and I didn't want to leave the books sitting around. How are you and the girls doing?"

"The girls are with their grandparents and I'm trying to figure things out. Work, the kids, Joanna."

"Anything new about Joanna?" I asked.

He shook his head. "They keep coming back to me with questions. About me, about Ed Dexter, her job, any stories she might have been working on, stuff here at the manor. I'm still a prime suspect, but I guess I'm not the only one. I just want to get on with my life, figure out how to manage. But I can't."

"I'm sorry, Vince. I liked her, and I'll miss her."

"Thank you, she liked you, too. Not everyone really got her, you know?"

"I know, and I know she rubbed some people the wrong way. I feel like I let her down. She left me a note, asking for my help researching something, but I didn't find it right away."

"What was it?"

"There was something about a bequest to the library, some land for an expansion, from a woman named Marjorie Douglas—" I began.

"Millicent!" Vince banged his fist on the desk.

"How do you figure that?"

"Anything that goes on in or around this building, she's involved in. Or at the bottom of," he said through clenched teeth. "I swear, you'd think she owned the place. Some of the things she's pulled—"

He stopped abruptly.

"Was there anything else?" he asked.

"Something to do with a little girl drowning."

"Carol Douglas."

"Yes. I guess she asked you, too, since you were there."

He looked at me.

"She wanted some old newspaper articles. I found them and read them. She was looking into a couple of things, but I can't make sense of them."

"She did ask me about it. I was surprised, because I've never mentioned it. I never spoke about it to anybody, after the fact. Once we talked to the police, we never mentioned it again."

"You and Matthew," I said.

"Yes. Carol was his little sister."

"What happened, Vince? What did you tell Joanna? This could be important."

"I don't see how, after all this time," he said, scrubbing his hands over his face.

I waited.

"All right." He sighed. "But if you read about it, you know the story. Matthew and I were scouts, and we were going to practice tracking in the woods. Carol wanted to tag along, she always did. Sometimes we would let her, but we were trying to earn a badge, so we said no. Then she threatened to tell on us. That was her latest thing, 'I'll tell Mommy.' It wouldn't have mattered, we weren't doing anything wrong, but you know how little kids are."

I nodded. I had employed this tactic with my older sister.

"Time consuming, having to explain yourself to a parent. You could never be sure who they'd believe," I said.

"That's right. My kids do it. Makes me glad I'm an only child."

"So, then what happened?"

"Matthew took her aside and talked to her. They bickered for a bit, then he whispered something to her and she was all smiles. He tugged her ponytail and she headed off toward the house. Truth be told, I think he had taken to bribing her. Money, candy, an ice cream cone here and there. It doesn't take much at that age."

This, too, I knew from experience.

"So, you thought she went home?" I said.

Vince nodded.

"We figured we were clear, so we started talking about where we should go. She must have followed us, or listened and tried to get ahead of us. I don't know."

Vince stopped. He was staring straight ahead, into the distant past. I kept still, waiting.

"It wasn't long after when I heard a scream. I couldn't tell at first where it came from, and then I heard it again. We both ran for the kill. I waded right in, but I lost my balance. The current was too strong. Matthew yelled at me to get out and get help, and that he'd try to get Carol. He was bigger and a good swimmer. He was already partway in when I got up the bank and looked back. I ran to the Prentisses' house, yelling my head off all the way. His mother must have heard me because she was already in the yard. She told me to go in and phone for help and wait for the police. Then she ran toward the Ravens Kill."

"And when the police came? What happened?"

"It was too late."

"Matthew?"

Vince shook his head. "One of the policemen pulled him out. He was clinging to some rocks at the edge. He had swallowed a lot of water. They stuck us both in an ambulance and checked us out. Carol was nowhere in sight. They called in more officers, from all over, but still they didn't find her until hours later."

"The current took her under," I said, remembering the Barrett kids and their twigs.

"It did, and Matthew never got over the fact that he couldn't save her. He hated to fail, even then. When we were in the ambulance, he was sobbing and gulping and spitting up water. It was awful. He asked me never to tell anyone, ever."

"The police?"

"Oh, we talked to them, but after that we never mentioned it. Until Joanna asked, I hadn't thought about it in years. I'd worked at not thinking about it, you know?"

I knew. Nowadays, specialists would have been called in to help the kids process the trauma. Back then, you just didn't discuss it.

"So, you told Joanna all of this, what you just told me?" I said.

"Exactly," Vince replied.

"But what made her ask?"

Vince leaned back in my chair and looked at me.

"Now that I'm not sure about," he said, "though she and Felicity had been spending a lot of time together lately."

I raised my eyebrows.

"Felicity was worried about something," he continued, "Joanna didn't give me a lot of details. But it was something to do with all these old stories being dredged up, and the effect on her kids. She seemed a little afraid."

"And if Matthew were running for office, these things might be reported on again?"

"I didn't know that was common knowledge, but I think so. Felicity feels responsible for Marjorie's death. And she's a private person."

"But where does Joanna fit in?"

There was a commotion behind me. The noise in the hall made it clear the meeting had ended. Vince looked past me and stood.

"I'm sure a lot of it was Friends' business, with the jumble sale coming up," he said, taking the box of books. "Well, thanks, Greer," he added.

I stepped aside, and he left. I heard him greet someone outside the office, and then that was drowned out by the sounds of the arriving story hour crowd. I settled into my chair and waited for the noise to die down. I now knew everything that Joanna had, and a few things she hadn't. It was time, as Poirot would say, to employ the little gray cells.

Chapter
Twenty-Four

I started by making notes about my conversation with Vince, and added in the little details I had gotten from Mary Alice and Henri. I pulled out the copy I'd made of Joanna's handwritten notes and studied it. Kinsey Millhone wrote things on index cards and rearranged them on a bulletin board; I'd have to make do with paper, pencil, and the circle and arrow method. I snagged a big piece of craft paper from Jilly's cubby and got to work.

I listed my suspects. Because the police always put the spouse at the top of the list, I started with Vince. I added Ed Dexter and Millicent Ames, as both had a beef with Joanna. Underneath them went Felicity and Matthew Prentiss, because both were tied into what Joanna had been researching. Which one of these would have a reason to kill her?

Once again, I started with Vince. He had a large life-insurance policy on her, and there was perhaps some professional jealousy there. He had also been seen looking tight with his old flame, Felicity. But still, that didn't hang together for me. Joanna was the brains behind their business, and also had the steady paycheck. Vince was going to be hard pressed to run a small business on his own while raising two young children. While he seemed to be genuinely fond of Felicity, I didn't sense any great passion there. And if it was Vince, who had attacked him and why?

On to Ed Dexter. He and Joanna had fought, and if she was determined to get him fired, she wouldn't rest until she'd accomplished her goal. If he was in line for a promotion to a major network or a bigger market, he couldn't risk even a hint of scandal. With his ego, he might believe assaulting her was justified; he might have intended to scare her rather than kill her. The drugs were a wild card. All bets were off if he were high.

Millicent. A dark horse, in my opinion. While she and Joanna were on opposite sides in the new library debate, I couldn't see her committing murder at this stage of the game. But there was that argument with Vince. I could still hear the venom in her voice when she said "blackmail." Joanna had clearly been nosing around the archives. Did the two of them have something on the infinitely respectable Millicent Ames? I reviewed the vague rumors about wills and deeds. The James Family Trust. Millicent was tied into everything around the manor, according to Vince. Old sins cast long shadows. If there was some physical evidence tying Millicent to a scandal it could explain the attack on Vince and the interrupted search of his pockets. It could even explain Joanna's death—an attack that went wrong. But there was the shoulder issue. I doubted she had the strength. I couldn't rule out Millicent, though my theory relied on a lot of "ifs," and I thought it unlikely that she was the killer.

This brought me to Felicity and Matthew. Matthew was planning on running for a local office, and Joanna had been investigating his past. The only things she had come up with were tragedies. Not only were they already known, if presented correctly they would engender sympathy. Unless there was something more to them.

What were the possibilities? The drowning seemed to be a tragic accident, witnessed at least in part by two people. What if they had goaded Carol into the water to teach her a lesson, with tragic results? Could they have maintained the lie this long? The boys had been questioned by the police at the time and their story had held. Vince acknowledged being first into the water, but Matthew was right there with him and may have saved the younger boy by ordering him out of the strong current. Or so they said. Vince's recital of the events had the ring of truth, as did his statement that he didn't see how it had any bearing. I was inclined to believe he was being straight with me.

Marjorie Douglas was another story. No witnesses. The only other people in the house were two small children and two adults, sound asleep after a day of shoveling and child-care. Mary Alice said Felicity had been exhausted and at the end of her rope for some time. Felicity had wanted help with the old woman, but had been denied. Felicity had been in charge of locking up, and apparently failed to secure the kitchen door. Felicity had then slept through the night, she said, hearing nothing.

Felicity. It was possible. A young mother with a toddler and a colicky infant, saddled with a mother-in-law whose dementia was advancing and who didn't want her out of sight, may have reached her breaking point. Had she decided to set the stage for an accident? She would only be hastening an end that was inevitable, but one that would be excruciating to witness, exhausting to manage and could drag on by degrees for years. Had Felicity planted the suggestion in Marjorie's mind that night, or unlocked the door and left the rest to fate?

I shuddered. I didn't want to think it of her, but I couldn't rule it out. If Joanna had figured it out, or was close, it gave Felicity a motive to silence her. I remembered the file on the flash drive labeled "FEL." I'd thought it was typo, but maybe not. I scribbled my theory next to her name, and went back to my notes.

Everyone had a motive. Some were stronger than others, but motive alone would not give me my answer. So, who could have done it, physically?

I started at the top of my list, ignoring my new prime suspect in the interest of fairness. Vince had been downtown shooting the *Haunted Albany* documentary, but had come back to the village for a forgotten piece of equipment. The timing was tight but he could have done it, especially if the supposedly forgotten item was in his trunk all along. He was strong enough, and knew his way around the building.

Ed Dexter was known to be in the area and had the physical strength. While he had been seen at dinner with his co-workers and later at the Java Joint, not every minute of his time was accounted for. On the other hand, he would have had to arrange a meeting with Joanna in advance, and gotten in and out of the building without anyone seeing him. Unlikely, and equally unlikely that Joanna would ever turn her back to him. Unless they had met, he'd gotten nowhere in changing Joanna's mind, and he'd managed to follow her to the attic. This was a stretch. He didn't know the building and he would have been seen. He didn't match the profile of Sadie's ghost. I labeled him "Unlikely" and moved on.

Millicent was such a fixture in the library that no one would ever remark on her presence. She could have locked the archives, stayed inside, and nipped up the stairs. Again, this would have required a pre-arranged meeting, but that was possible. But did she have the strength? Millicent was pretty spry for a woman her age, but she did have arthritis. I knew her shoulder was bothering her earlier in the week. And she'd been very awkward when closing the windows with her left hand. I would express concern about the state of her joints the next time I saw her, but for now I was labeling her unlikely as well.

Felicity was at the same meeting as Joanna, and almost immediately after was with Julia Wainwright at the Java Joint. The timing was tricky, but if both she and Joanna left the meeting at the same time, she could head for the rest-room or the office and double back, do the deed, and shoot off to meet Julia. I made a note to see if anyone had noticed when Joanna and Felicity had walked out of the meeting room, and where each had gone.

Matthew Prentiss had been home all night. He'd been working in his office after checking homework and putting on a movie for the kids. He had emerged only to put them to bed, and had gone back to practicing a presentation. Felicity had heard him when she got home, but since he didn't like to be interrupted when he worked, she went directly to bed. That was the story both of them told, and from what Jennie said, there was no reason to doubt it. Had anyone questioned the Prentiss children? That kind of thing was tricky with minors, probably requiring parental consent or presence. I'd ask Jennie.

There. Motive, means, opportunity—all charted out. I ran a critical eye over it. Any one of them *could* have done it, a couple of them much more easily than others. The question was who *would* have done it? I have always believed that given the right set of circumstances, everyone is a killer. Who on this list felt sufficiently threatened, and either plotted murder or took advantage of circumstances to get rid of a threat?

My phone buzzed. I pulled it out and saw a text from Jennie. "James Family Trust all went to Felicity Millicent Ames trustee. Land bequest fuzzy. Will call. Be careful."

Well, well, well. Following the money was looking like the best bet after all. It all seemed to come back to Felicity, and to a lesser extent, Millicent. I penciled a little star next to both names on my chart.

I was wild to find out the exact nature of that trust. There's nothing more titillating, or revealing, than other people's finances. The next best thing is their real estate records, also enlightening and usually more accessible. Jennie described the land bequest as "fuzzy." Maybe I could clarify it. I pulled out the article on Marjorie Douglas's bequest. No location for the gifted property, only the statement that it was adjacent to the manor grounds. On the theory that it was part of a larger parcel that was broken up, I checked the address given in her obituary in the local paper and typed it into Google maps.

Nothing.

That was odd. I checked the address again. I had typed it correctly. I checked Felicity's address on the Friends' membership list. If they had renovated the Prentiss house after Marjorie's death, it should be the same.

It was not. Close, but Marjorie Douglas had lived at 1 Barn Hill Road, and Felicity's address was 11 Barn House Road. I popped that into the search box and got an immediate hit. I was studying the overhead view when a harassed sounding Jilly called my name.

"Sorry! Coming!" I yelled, frantically folding my chart and stuffing everything under my keyboard. I threw a few random magazines and files on top, then closed the office door as I raced through. Taking the back stairs, I entered the community room to find Anne Marie wielding a small bottle of solvent in an attempt to remove a paper daffodil from the hair of a crying toddler. The mother was hovering, bleating "Is that organic?" and generally getting in the way.

You couldn't pay me enough. I ducked out and busied myself folding the easel in the hall and gathering scattered bookmarks. Estimating that Anne Marie needed a few more minutes to contain the meltdown, I went to the window. Mary Alice had said that you could see the Prentiss place from the manor when the trees weren't in full leaf. I looked at the hillside across the Ravens Kill. Leaves were budding, but the foliage wasn't too thick yet. There was nothing that looked like a building in sight.

I leaned in closer and looked left. Here the manor grounds quickly turned to a thickly wooded slope topped by a plateau known as Ravensloft. The play on the family name had come about when hikers had discovered the area long ago, and it had stuck. If you braved the trek through the forest primeval you were rewarded with a spectacular view of the village and surrounding area. I spotted nothing that looked like a house. A faint line marked a deer trail going up the hill, but beyond there was nothing but trees. I remembered Sadie's secret paths, and let my eyes drift over the hillside. Nothing revealed itself to me. The woods were keeping their secrets.

Anne Marie gave me the all-clear and I headed into the community room. I stacked chairs while Anne Marie cleaned up the craft supplies.

"Thanks for your help, Greer. You can leave about half those chairs out; the Friends are in here next. We just need to tidy and shift the tables."

"No problem. I understand the scheduling issue. Do you get a break after this or are you going to spend some time at reference with Jilly?"

"Neither, unfortunately. I have to sit in on the Friends meeting and take notes. Helene has a regional directors' meeting and there's so much going on she wants to make sure she doesn't miss anything."

"Just think how good all this is going to look on your resume," I said, eliciting an eye roll from the intern.

"Were you at the meeting the night Joanna Goodhue was murdered?" I asked.

"Yes, actually, I was. Helene thought I should have exposure to the fundraising aspect of the job, and that meeting was all planning for the sale."

"Did you happen to notice if Joanna was alone when she left the meeting?"

"She walked out chatting with Mrs. Prentiss. I was right behind them."

"Did you happen to hear what they said?" I asked, trying to keep my tone casual.

Anne Marie frowned.

"I remember thinking it was strange. Mrs. Prentiss was thanking Mrs. Goodhue for taking her turn sorting through the jumble sale donations, and Mrs. Goodhue said she was glad to help and she hoped the meeting went well. I thought it was weird to have a meeting that late, but then I figured they must be talking about the next day or something."

"Sometimes a few of them will stay late if they have any side business to take care of. They're already out and they have the child care covered."

"I don't think so," Anne Marie said, "because Mrs. Prentiss walked out right ahead of me and got into her car."

"Then you're probably right," I said, "I'm sure it's not important."

We finished the room and I decided to pay a call on Millicent. I found her at her desk in the archives. She looked up with a frown as I came in.

"Oh, it's you, Greer," she said, her face relaxing. "I'm glad to see you and not another curiosity seeker."

We chatted briefly. I expressed concern about her arthritis, and verified that her right shoulder was bothering her, that she was right-handed and so was seeing her doctor that afternoon.

"She looks all of twelve, but she seems to know what she's doing," Millicent said.

I laughed and offered help if she needed anything, then took my leave, mentally scratching Millicent off my suspect list.

The jumble sale committee was milling about in the community room when I went by. I peeked in to see if there was anyone I wanted to talk to. Most were wearing yoga pants and tees that proclaimed them regular worshipers at the shrine of Our Lady of Perpetual Pilates. A few had on their new FOL sweatshirts. They were virtually indistinguishable from the doorway as they chatted and opened boxes of baked goods. I thought longingly of a doughnut but there was no one I needed to speak to and I had to get back to my suspect list. My phone was ringing as I reached my cubicle. I patted my pocket—it wasn't there. I started flinging things around on my desk until I unearthed it, managing to answer before the call went to voice mail. It was Jennie Webber.

"Can you talk?" she said without preamble.

"I think so, just a sec," I said, taking a quick look around the office and making sure the door was closed.

"Yes," I said, "go ahead."

"You got my text?"

"I did, and some new information, too," I told her.

"You are supposed to be keeping your head down and your mouth shut." I swear I could hear her teeth clenching over the phone.

"I am. This is just some gossip I picked up."

After a little internet research, and some discreet questioning, I added silently.

A small, exasperated noise reached my ears.

"So, what is this gossip?" Jennie asked.

I peeked around the corner of my cubicle again, just to be on the safe side, then filled her in on everything I'd learned. She let me run on until I got to my conversation with Vince.

"So, you were questioning one of our chief suspects?" she said, sounding more than a little annoyed.

"He stopped by to get something." I explained about the package from Joanna, and added, "I made sure he came when there were a lot of people around."

"You should have let us handle that, but since it's already done, what did he say?"

I told her, and ran through all my theories, ending with Felicity as killer. There was a brief silence when I was done.

"You may be on to something," she said, a note of respect in her voice, "though I don't think we could charge her with anything in the old lady's death. It doesn't sound like there were any signs of elder abuse or neglect at the time. If Felicity snapped and decided to do away with her mother-in-law, she left a lot to chance."

"True, but she'd have more than one opportunity. And what about the money? How big is that trust fund?"

"That's where it gets complicated. Felicity and her sister are the only surviving members of the James family, and the sole beneficiaries of the trust."

I could hear pages flipping as Jennie checked her notes.

"The two girls got certain property outright, as well as some cash. Half the income from the trust and anything Marjorie owned went to Felicity, and was then supposed to pass to any offspring of Felicity and Matthew Prentiss. There's more to it, but that's the bottom line."

"Nothing to Matthew?" I said.

"According to Marjorie's will, he was left well-off when his father died. Long line of lawyers there, so that's no surprise. Anything from the Prentiss side went to Matthew, and anything from Marjorie's side went to Felicity. Including the house they lived in and the building where Matthew's office is."

"Huh." That was odd, particularly the house and office. "What about the land bequest?"

"Unclear. The will describes the parcels generally, and refers to an addendum and some other documents. Those were either never filed or are missing. The attorney who handled it all is retired. Sam is pressuring the firm, but it's going to take time. I was hoping you could help with that."

"Really? The police would like my help?"

"Unofficially," she qualified.

"You're throwing me a bone and trying to keep me busy and out of trouble."

"Out of trouble, yes, but this is the kind of research you know how to do, and you can do it from where you are without anyone being the wiser. I don't have time. I'm on my way to talk to Sal Cosmopoulos about that drowning. Something feels off there. Then I need to have another chat with our friend Vince."

"Ok, give me what you have," I said.

She rattled off some information and I repeated it back.

"And stay away from these people, Greer. I mean it. Don't get caught alone with any of them."

I promised to behave and hung up.

Chapter
Twenty-Five

～

I spent the next forty-five minutes toggling between government webpages, real estate sites, and mapping search engines, and made little progress. Addresses, parcel numbers, deed holder name—every system needed something different. I cross-referenced as much as I could, but something was off. I looked at those two addresses I'd found earlier and wondered.

Going back to a mapping site, I typed in the Prentisses' address and switched to the aerial imagery view. I found myself looking at the roof of an old barn. I panned out, looking at the immediate area, then switched to street view. The barn had been renovated into a dwelling, and sat at the end of a winding road with a few other homes, all recent construction. The whole area was what I called faux rural—rustic on the outside with all the mod cons inside. I always found it a little pretentious, though I had to admit some of the repurposed old buildings were lovely. This neighborhood was well done, though the barn was obviously the only original structure. Barn House Road indeed.

I went back to aerial view and scrolled around, trying to place the Prentiss home in relation to the manor. Barn House Road led in the opposite direction, snaking down into the village, but I could trace a line through the woods between the two old buildings. Unless I was missing something, there was no way to see one from the other. Unlikely, too, that the Prentiss family had been living in a partially renovated barn at any point in this saga. I must have missed the house somewhere.

I went back to the barn house and began the painstaking process of examining the area between it and the manor systemically in as much detail as I could manage. Marjorie's bequest was becoming secondary; there was something here that didn't make sense, and all my girl detective instincts were telling me it was important.

My eyes were watering and my stomach growling by the time I found something. Directly across the Ravens Kill, from the window I'd looked out that morning, was a clearing, and in that clearing I could detect the faint outlines of a building foundation. The whole thing was overgrown, but the vegetation wasn't as dense in some areas, and those areas were too regularly shaped to be natural. The wilderness will reclaim anything in time, but a stone foundation would stay visible for a while. A sparse river of grass led from the clearing toward the street leading to the manor, disappearing into a knot of shrubbery. If that had at one time been a road, then the land to the south of it would be the parcel Marjorie Douglas had bequeathed to the library.

I leaned back and studied the image on my screen, the sense that I had discovered something important growing stronger. Ideas whispered at the edges of my mind; whispers I could hear but not quite make out.

"*Trust your instincts,*" Jennie said, "*because your instincts keep you alive.*"

If only I could figure out what they were telling me. My rumbling stomach reminded me that a girl could not live on instinct alone, and that my reference shift would begin whether or not I had eaten. I blanked my screen and hid my notes, the pile now too unwieldy to tote around with me. Maybe some food and a change of scene would give my subconscious a boost.

I headed for my favorite perch. It was occupied. I didn't recognize Anne Marie until she turned around at the sound of my footsteps.

"Hi," I said, as she made room for me on the bench, "I thought you were one of the Friends."

I gestured to the brightly colored hoodie she was wearing. It looked at least a size too big.

"This was my welcome present. They gave it to me at the meeting last week. They were all wearing them and wanted me to feel like part of the team."

Anne Marie shoved at a too-long sleeve.

"Apparently, they run a little big, so I leave it here for when it gets chilly. Like today. It looks like I missed the sun," she added, glancing at the overcast sky.

We chatted about the weather for a few minutes and then Anne Marie left, saying she was going to take advantage of the quiet office to finish a paper and would be happy to cover my break at the reference desk. I pulled out my sandwich and studied the landscape in front of me.

If I had oriented myself correctly, I should be staring straight toward the clearing where I had spotted the foundation. There were breaks in the trees at the top of the hill, and some gaps in the foliage. I spied the little trail I had seen from the window, tracing it from the Ravens Kill to one of the breaks in the trees. That had to be where the Prentiss house had been.

I finished my lunch and scattered some crumbs for the ravens. No matter what I had promised Jennie, I was going to have to ask some questions.

After a quick stop at my desk, I headed for the reading room, passing Millicent in the hall. She told me she was off to the doctor, the archives were locked, and that she would be gone the rest of the day. I'd have to tell the page to keep an eye on the second floor.

I checked in with Jilly and made a circuit of the reading room. Fantasy sports guy was in his usual spot with his laptop. A few other people were drifting around, but the place was quiet.

I was glad to see Dory at the Circulation desk. She had taken over from Mary Alice mid-day, and since Millicent was both off limits and unavailable, Dory was my best source of quick information.

"So how goes the snooping?" she asked.

"Not too well, I'm afraid, but I'm hoping you can help."

Dory leaned forward, her eyes bright.

"I'm not sure it has anything to do with the murder," I said, "but I'm curious. I know Marjorie Douglas left some land to the library, and I know she was Matthew Prentiss's mother, but I can't figure out exactly where that parcel is. I know Matthew and Felicity moved in with her a while before she died, but their address is nowhere near the manor grounds. Do you know anything about it?"

"I'd forgotten about that," Dory said, "but I can tell you where the land is. It runs between the Ravens Kill and Agnes Jenner's place. It's where Barn Hill Road used to be."

"Barn Hill Road?"

"Yes. The road that led to the old Prentiss place on the hill."

"But I thought that's where Matthew and Felicity lived. I thought they had renovated it."

"Well, I think that was the idea," Dory said, "but the house was old, and it held a lot of sad memories. Once Marjorie passed, they decided to just knock it down. It needed an awful lot of work. They took it down that spring, as I recall. They moved into the big old Victorian where Matthew's office is, and started building the new place right away."

A vague idea was forming in my mind as I listened to Dory. It didn't make sense, but I went with it.

"Were you ever inside? In the old house, I mean."

"A couple of times," she said, "Marjorie was in the garden club until she started to fail. Why?"

"I was wondering about the kitchen. Which way did it face?"

"Toward the back. It was the typical big farmhouse kitchen. It opened to the garden."

"So, you could see the manor from the windows?"

"Well, from some of them maybe. Why do you ask?"

"It's something Mary Alice said. Marjorie Douglas would look out the kitchen window and start thinking about her daughter that drowned."

Dory nodded.

"I'd heard that. It was why she kept trying to get out. You could see the Ravens Kill and the manor from the kitchen, but only when the leaves fell. You could ask Felicity."

"She might find it too painful. Besides, she's out of town."

Dory frowned.

"Really? I could have sworn I saw her car when I was on my way here. Of course, whoever it was, was going awfully fast, so maybe I'm wrong."

Dory's lead foot was legendary. If she thought someone was going too fast, that someone had to be breaking the sound barrier. That didn't sound like Felicity.

We were interrupted by a patron wanting to check out, so I made my escape before Dory could ask any more questions.

For the next hour and a half, I employed my little gray cells. I took the occasional book request, answered a few simple questions, and tried to channel every single one of my favorite detectives. After skimming through all the articles one more time, I discreetly studied my suspect chart, and once again pulled up the aerial view of the old Prentiss place. I printed a few screen shots. I had all of the pieces, but I couldn't make them fit together. What was I missing?

I tucked everything away and got up. Prowling around the library, I paused in the children's area and stared out at the main staircase. I did a little straightening, plucked out a Scouting handbook, and went back to my desk. I skimmed the section on outdoor adventure, snapped it shut and turned to my computer. I looked up dementia, finally finding some reliable information on how it intersected with paranoia, suggestion, and hallucination. A phrase from Joanna's notes leaped out at me. *Gaslighting, reno, locks.* Not what I'd originally thought. A few quick checks on real estate values and state inheritance laws, and I was done. I now knew three things for sure.

Vince had lied to me.

Felicity knew more about her mother-in-law's death than she was telling.

Either Joanna knew more than I thought, or someone believed she did.

The picture forming in my mind all day became clearer. I was horrified and angry. Greed, pride, lust, or even envy — one of these had led to murder more than once. My wrath grew. I drummed my fingers against the desk. I still needed a couple of answers.

Jennie Webber's admonition flashed through my mind. Leave it to the professionals. Well, the police had protocols and procedures that had to be followed. Greer Hogan, Girl

Detective, could lie and threaten with impunity, and if it got the desired result it was all to the good.

I made my plan and phoned Anne Marie, asking her to cover the desk. All my evidence, new and old, went into the big envelope. Making sure I had my phone, I went in search of somewhere I wouldn't be overheard. Jilly was in the librarian's office, on the phone, so I tried Helene's office. Finding it unlocked and unoccupied, I slipped in.

My first call was to Felicity. I didn't expect an answer but it was worth a try. She was already so tightly wound that one or two pointed questions might rattle her enough to shake loose the answers I needed. After a couple of rings, it went to voicemail. On a whim I tried her again from the phone in Helene's office. Same result.

Vince was next. This one went to voicemail, too. I waited for the beep.

"I found the flash drive and I know what's on it. Call me."

It didn't take long.

"It's me," Vince said, sounding weary, "where did you find it?"

"Where Joanna hid it before she died," I said, "because she knew someone was after her."

Silence.

"That can't be right," he said, "that's horrible."

He sounded both stunned and appalled. If he was faking it, he was a better actor than I'd given him credit for.

"It looks that way," I said.

"Where was it?"

"I'll get to that, but first I have some questions. The day Carol Douglas drowned, you said you and Matthew were practicing tracking. Were you together the whole time?"

"No," he said, still sounding confused, "that's not how it works."

"I'm a city girl. Spell it out for me."

"We took turns. He was going to be tracker first, so I got a head start and he had to follow my route. We started from the footbridge."

"How long were you apart?"

"A few minutes."

"How many minutes?" I was impatient. "Three? Five? Ten?"

"Five or ten. Not quite ten. It's hard to remember."

"And when you heard the screams, you ran toward the kill?"

"Yes. I couldn't tell at first where they were coming from, but after the second scream I could tell, so I started running."

He'd said that before. At least he was consistent.

"How long did it take you to get there?"

"Not long. I had doubled back on my own trail to try to confuse Matthew, so I was close to where I started. That's why we got there at the same time. He was coming off the bridge as I ran down the bank."

"And that's when he pulled you back?"

"He didn't pull me back. He yelled to me. He was on the other side. She was closer to the other side, I think. He was wading in as I left. Why is this important, Greer? Why are you doing this?"

"Because Joanna thought it was important, and now she's dead, Vince. Because someone may have tried to kill you, and someone nearly killed me. Now answer my questions."

I was relentless.

"Who else was in the woods that day, Vince? Anyone? Another child, or an adult? Anyone who could have seen all this?"

"No, at least, I don't think so. The first person I saw was Mrs. Douglas."

"And then the police."

"Yes."

"When Joanna asked about it, you told her what you told me the first time? Without all this detail?"

"She didn't ask all these questions."

But she would have eventually.

"Between the time you talked to the police and when Joanna asked, you really never told anyone? No one at all?"

There was silence, and then a sigh.

"I'd promised, but I started having nightmares. It was years later, but I started dreaming about it."

"That's understandable. You were a child when it happened. You needed to talk to someone. So, who did you tell?"

"Felicity," Vince said. The rest came out in a rush.

"It was when we were dating, in high school. I started having the dreams. One night we were both a little drunk. She'd taken a bottle of wine from her parents. She knew about the nightmares and said I'd feel better if I talked about it. She asked a lot of questions, just like you did, and I answered her. But I swore her to secrecy. She said she'd never repeat it."

"Felicity and Joanna were spending a lot of time together. Do you think they talked about it?"

"Joanna would have come back to me on it, so no, I'm sure they didn't."

That part didn't fit, but the rest did.

"What about the drive?" he said, "Where was it?"

"In the archives. The police have it now. Have they talked to you yet today?"

"No."

"They will." I hung up.

Chapter
Twenty-Six

❧

I sat and replayed the conversation. It was almost, but not quite, what I had thought. Almost there, but I was missing something. Maybe Jennie had made progress. She'd be livid if she found out I'd talked to Vince, but if I could hand her the murderer, figuratively at least, I might be in the clear. I sent a text.

Back in the reading room, I found the usual Friday afternoon rush had begun, a little earlier than usual due to the increasingly threatening skies. I went through my ritual of hiding the evidence and spotting the undercover cop, then began dispensing recommendations, books, and DVDs. I gave it only half my attention; my mind was still spinning through various scenarios, trying to make one work.

Half an hour before we closed, Jilly let me know she was leaving, but that Anne Marie would be here until we closed if I needed her. Fifteen minutes after that, the page told me she'd finished everything she could while the library was open, including the second floor, and would it be okay if she left before the rain started, since she'd ridden her bike?

I checked with Dory, who looked around and gave a nod. Everything was under control, and there was always Anne Marie. I told the girl to go.

My phone buzzed. I stepped into the hall. It was a text from Jennie.

"Developments. On my way to Vince. Pick you up in 30 min. Have someone wait with you."

I responded with an ok and got busy with closing. I made a sweep of the building, veering into the raven room when I spotted a wrapper on the floor. Who had been in here?

Scooping up the wrapper, I gave the windows a quick check and spun slowly to see if everything else was in order. The stuffed raven caught my eye, his expression as inscrutable as always.

"What am I missing?"

He remained silent, but his compatriots on the lawn rose with indignant cries. I looked out.

Crows. Too many and too small to be ravens.

They all look alike to me.

Now where had I heard that?

"Ms. Hogan? Can you help me find something?"

"Sure," I said to the child standing outside the door. Once my young patron was in line with an armload of books, I reminded the few stragglers that we were closing shortly. It was only drizzling outside, but the wind was picking up. I could hear the telltale rattling of a window not properly latched. I worked my way methodically around the room, ending at the back and peering out in the hope that Jennie had arrived early. No luck. There were a handful of cars in the lot, and a few kids in colorful anoraks—including the Barretts—zooming around on their bikes, but no Jennie. One hard core cyclist paused to adjust a strap. A blond woman, the one I thought was a cop. The only other activity came from the birds. They swirled and chattered, agitated by the gusts of wet wind. I hadn't seen so many since the day of Joanna's memorial.

I turned back to the reference desk, shutting down computers as I went. I wanted to be out of there as soon as Jennie showed up, so I decided to check in the books and movies I was done with, grab my stuff from the back and help Dory finish closing.

My hand closed on the Marple DVD and I stopped. The picture of a woman in a colorful shawl floating face down in the water swam up from my memory, a woman struck down from behind on a dark, rainy night. I went hot and then cold, as I had when I found Joanna's body. I turned and looked out the back windows, where the various black birds were still swooping and cawing. I had watched them from the stone bench on the day of the memorial, and thought how they mimicked the anxious excitement of the crowd. I had shared that same bench with Anne Marie, this time talking of the weather rather than ravens and crows.

Unkindness and murder.

I put the DVD back on the desk. I made a fist of my trembling hand. I knew who had killed Joanna Goodhue, I knew how, and I knew why. It was too fantastic, but it was the only answer that fit.

How often have I said to you that when you have eliminated the impossible, whatever remains, however improbable, must be the truth?

Sherlock Holmes. I wished he'd shown up sooner.

"I'll be right back," I said to Dory, and raced for the office.

I got to the office and found no sign of Anne Marie. Damn! I grabbed my things and wheeled back around, colliding with her in the doorway.

"Sorry!" she said breathlessly, wiping her wet face with the sleeve of her oversize sweatshirt, "I was trying to get all my project stuff in the car before the rain got heavier."

"No problem. Listen, you got your hoodie at the meeting last week, right? Everyone was wearing them because they had just come in?"

"Yes." She looked confused. "Why?"

"I think they must have some smaller sizes. I'll ask. You've been such a big help. You deserve one that fits. Now, if you could check downstairs and make sure everything is locked and shut off in the staff room, we can all get out of here."

"Okay, but I have to put away the story hour books, and I told Dory I'd finish some holds."

Interns were too conscientious.

"I'll take care of it. You get your stuff and get moving."

I snatched a stack of picture books out of her hands and began backing through the door. She stared at me.

"I'm absolutely starving," I said, "and it's been a long week. So, check the staff room, turn off the lights, and meet me by the back door. I need to wait for my ride. Don't forget to turn off the coffee pot," I yelled as the door swung shut.

I grabbed everything I'd stashed at reference on my way by and dumped the whole pile at Circ. Dory eyed it.

"I was just about to shut down," she said, gesturing to the computer, "everything else is done. I need to get to the store. Grandkids tonight."

"I'll do it. I need to take care of something. I'm desperate to get out of here. Anne Marie is taking care of the staff room. I'll only be a minute. Someone needs to wait with me for my ride. She should be here in a few minutes."

I got to work while Dory gathered her belongings. I heard a tsk.

"I must have left my umbrella downstairs. Do you mind if I go look?"

"Nope, I'll be right behind you," I said.

A deafening rumble shook the building. There was a blinding flash and the lights flickered and went out. Two seconds later they were back. I stood blinking, and when my vision cleared saw the computer rebooting.

Damn, damn, damn.

I briefly considered leaving everything for the Saturday shift. I looked at the time. Only five after, so I had ten minutes. I'd see how long the reboot took. Keeping an eye on the screen in front of me, I changed my shoes and put on my jacket. As the system popped back to life, I heard the outside door clang. If Jennie was early, I was leaving everything for tomorrow.

I scooted to the back window. I stared in disbelief as Anne Marie got in her car and took off down the drive. Dory's Cadillac was nowhere in sight. There was only one car left in the lot. I recognized it, and it wasn't Jennie Webber's.

It belonged to Felicity Prentiss.

Chapter
Twenty-Seven

❧

I stood rooted to the spot for a heartbeat. The beeping of the Circ computer startled me into movement. I pulled out my phone and dialed Jennie. Voicemail. I began to panic.

Think, think, think.

911. I'd call 911 from the library phone. I moved quickly to the reference desk. Every line was blinking, signaling it was in use. If the phones were out, the set would be dark. Someone had taken them off the hook elsewhere in the building. That someone was either waiting outside, or was in the manor with me.

I moved back to the window and looked out. My heart dropped. Sadie Barrett was at the bottom of the drive on her bike. She was circling, looking at the building. Farther down the road I spotted her brothers, and the blond cyclist. *Please be a cop.* I still couldn't risk going out there. If I stayed put and called 911 from my cell, the sirens would alert the killer, and Sadie stood between the manor and escape. I was stuck.

I checked the time. Seven minutes until Jennie was due to arrive. Seven minutes hadn't been enough the last time. This time it would have to be. I said a brief prayer for Jennie's punctuality, and decided to bluff.

Moving back to the Circ desk, I yelled into the hall.

"Almost done, Anne Marie, be right there."

Back at the desk, I looked at the motion sensors. They weren't showing anyone but me. Unless someone was standing completely still, I was the only one in the reading room and there was no one in the hall. If I was going to leave a trail of breadcrumbs, I needed to do it now.

I pulled out my suspect chart and highlighted a name, then folded it into a neat square. I was tucking it into the Miss Marple DVD case when I had an idea.

I grabbed the keyboard and opened the borrower menu. Bingo. Jennie Webber was there with an e-mail contact. I created a hold on her account for the DVD and scanned the barcode. The machine printed out a label and the system automatically sent an e-mail. Putting everything together with a rubber band, I filed under 'W' on the hold shelf.

I checked the time again. Five minutes. Still nothing on the motion sensors. Whoever was stalking me was waiting to grab me on my way out, but they weren't going to wait forever.

I moved into the children's area, going directly to fairy tales. I flipped through *The Complete Works of the Brothers Grimm* until I found the story I wanted and marked it with my finger. Back at the desk I folded some of the newspaper articles and tucked them into the book. I generated another hold and added it to the shelf. I repeated the process with the scouting book and created a hold for Sam O'Donnell.

The lights started to go out.

This was no outage. Someone was working their way through the main control panel by the door. First the lights in the hall went out, and then parts of reading room. Only Circulation and the doorways were left on. I was spotlighted in the center of the room.

Two could play that game. I went to the auxiliary light panel and killed every light in the building. I blacked out the computer screen and grabbed my phone. Hoping Sadie was gone from the parking lot, I dialed 911. As soon as the operator answered, I whispered, "Raven Hill Library. Emergency! Send the police!" Then I muted the volume. I wanted to maintain the connection without the sound and light telling the killer where I was. I stuffed the phone in my bra. I wanted it with me, but not obvious.

I checked the alarm panel. Something was moving near the back door. I had to time this perfectly. I picked up my bag and worked my way around the stacks, angling toward the front entrance to the reading room. I waited, peering into the gloomy hallway, until I saw a shadowy figure slip in the other entrance.

I stepped carefully down the hall, avoiding the creaks I knew about, fighting the urge to sprint. Once I got to the far entrance, I'd have enough of a head start to take off, but not until. I catfooted my way along, barely breathing, accompanied only by my distorted image in the antique mirrors that lined the hall. Almost there. I eased left, away from the dim light spilling into the hall from the arched doorway to the reading room, and prepared to bolt.

A ghoulish image loomed out of the darkness, startling me and sending me off balance. An arm went around my throat and I teetered for a moment, looking at my own murky reflection caught in the grip of a figure in black, a hood pulled tightly forward to reveal nothing but two glittering eyes. I regained my balance and the arm tightened around my throat.

"I know who you are, and I know what you did," I said to the image in the mirror. "You can't pretend anymore. Too much has happened. Once Joanna died, it was too late."

"Bitch!" snarled Matthew Prentiss. He swung me around to face him. "You should have minded your own business," he said, yanking me toward the door. "Now you've got to go, too."

He shoved me into the parking lot. Still no sign of the cavalry. Time to stall.

"You'll never get away with this." I pretended to stumble.

"Watch me," he said, pulling me back to my feet and dragging me to Felicity's SUV. He shoved me into the driver's seat, knocking my head against the steering wheel. I saw stars, and by the time they cleared he was next to me, a thin, sharp blade with a delicately jeweled handle held against my neck.

He reached over and started the car.

"Now, you are going to drive down this winding road in this terrible rain and you and my lovely wife are going to have a tragic accident, an accident resulting from an argument when you accuse her of murdering Joanna Goodhue in order to cover up the fact that she arranged my mother's death. Knowing she's been found out, she will attempt to stab you with the little knife she has always kept on her desk. In the struggle, the car will go off the road and both of you will be killed."

"Felicity?"

He jerked his head toward the back seat. I turned and saw a lumpy bundle under a blanket.

"Do you think anyone is going to believe that?"

"Of course." He smirked. "You spelled out the evidence so cleverly in your little chart. You really shouldn't have left that on your desk, Greer. You never know who's wandering around in that building. Now give me your bag and drive."

The egotistical bastard really thought he was going to get away with it. I needed to buy time and distract him before he realized the evidence was not in my bag. I'd worked for this type of arrogant ass more than once. I knew how to get under his skin.

"Matthew, you're not nearly as smart as you think you are. Honestly, you couldn't even kill the right woman on your first try. You didn't even recognize your own wife. You're a joke."

"Shut up and drive!" he screamed, pressing the blade harder against me.

I eased the car into drive, and rolled slowly through the lot.

"That wasn't my fault," he said more calmly, "that was a last minute change of plan. If my stupid wife had been where she was supposed to be, none of this would be happening."

"Oh, but she's not stupid, Matthew. She's the smart one. She always was. Everyone knows she got your law firm off the ground. She figured out what you'd done to your sister, and then to your mother."

He was breathing heavily. I kept my eyes on the road ahead. We were moving toward the last dip in the road before the bridge. Coming toward us, straight down the center of the road, was a large, black bird.

"You're nothing but a lifelong failure, and pretty soon everyone will know it," I said.

"SHUT UP!!!" he screamed. "Shut up, shut up!"

"Loser, loser," I sang out.

Out of the corner of my eye I saw him draw back the hand with the knife in it, ready to plunge it into my neck. The raven flew at the windshield, screeched, and went up and over.

Nevermore.

I pulled the wheel hard to the left and hit the gas. The car spun, hitting the water that had pooled in the road and hydroplaning. Matthew was flung sideways into the door, losing the knife as he tried to catch himself. The car came off the road and skidded to a stop on the bank. I threw myself out and ran toward the footbridge. I gained some traction as I got off the wet grass and put on a burst of speed, but it wasn't enough. I had reached the bridge when I was caught from behind.

I struggled, but I was outmatched. Matthew was dragging me closer to the edge. In seconds I'd be in the frigid water, and unless help arrived immediately, either the current or the cold would get me.

I made a decision. I had one last trick up my sleeve. I threw my weight forward against Matthew's arms, pulling him off balance. As soon as he tried to compensate, I hurled myself backward, pushing off with both feet and launching us against the rickety rail. I heard it crack, and we were airborne.

I was going into the kill, but I was taking Matthew Prentiss with me.

Chapter
Twenty-Eight

The shock of hitting the icy water sucked the air from my lungs. The current pulled me under and spit me out hard against the stone piling of the bridge. I clawed at it, disoriented, and slipped under once more. Opening my eyes briefly in the murky water, I managed to right myself. I kicked against the frigid darkness, trying to move toward the glimmering light above me.

I broke the surface in the shadow of the footbridge. I clung to the uneven stone, gulped in air and blinked to clear my vision. The gnawing cold had me shaking uncontrollably as my body grew numb. I had to get out. I searched along the piling and tried to find a handhold. My scrambling feet had found purchase against the deadfall wedged between the pilings when a splash and a curse to my left sent me shrinking back into the shadows.

It was Matthew Prentiss. He was working his way toward the bank, strong swimmer's strokes moving him between rocks he would grip and push off from. He paused once, scanning the bank and the stream. I stayed still. Over the rain and rushing water I heard the faint sound of sirens. So did Matthew. He struck out again for the bank, his eyes fixed on the still-running SUV so close to the water. There was a chance he would escape.

I would not let that happen.

I edged around the piling, keeping low to the water in the shadow of the bridge. I pushed against the deadfall with my feet, kicking loose roots and branches that shifted and sent up bubbles of fetid air. Breathing through my mouth against the stench of rot that surrounded me, I gained the bank just behind Matthew. As soon as his back was to me, I struck. Lunging from the water with my arms outstretched, I clawed at his jacket, pulling him back down the slippery slope.

He turned his head, eyes wide with shock. With a snarl he jabbed his elbow into my chest, sending me flying. I hit the ground half in the water. I got my face clear but couldn't drag myself out. Just when I knew I was done, that the cold and the pain were too much, warm hands touched my shoulders. They gently rolled me over and eased me up the bank and away from the kill.

It was the young officer who had accompanied me home a few nights before. Behind him was a haze of flashing lights. Jennie Webber was pounding across the bridge. A string of police cars lined the road, an ambulance right behind, blocking any escape.

Jennie reached me and helped me sit up, thumping my back as I choked and sputtered.

"Felicity," I gasped, "car. Backseat."

Jennie yelled out some orders and other officers sprinted toward the SUV. But where was Matthew Prentiss?

I stood, swaying, and looked around. Jennie kept her grip on me as I craned my neck, trying to spot him. There was a commotion near Felicity's car, and I saw Matthew bolt toward the Ravens Kill with a policeman on his heels.

"No!" I croaked, and then screamed it, my lungs clear at last.

I watched as Matthew gained the center of the stream, using the current and his own strength to try to get to the woods on the opposite side.

"We'll get him," said Jennie, "don't worry."

"No," I whispered, my eyes on the fleeing figure.

With a groan, the accumulated deadfall broke loose from the footbridge and swept downstream, flying apart and scattering. It slowed Matthew, but he kept moving. A tree limb popped to the surface, bobbing along behind him, twigs like small fingers snagging his jacket and hair.

I was inspired.

"Matthew!" I screamed, "It's Carol! It's Carol, she's calling to you! Can you hear her? Matthew!"

He heard me. His stroke faltered and he looked back, his face so contorted with rage it was unrecognizable. Somewhere, a knife slashed through a portrait, and here, tiny branches plucked and grabbed at the monster in the water. He shuddered, and tried to push them away. The slight delay was enough. The tree limb caught him, branches tangling in his jacket as more of the debris roared toward him. He struggled, and disappeared beneath the water. He would not surface again. I had it on good authority that the currents have always been strange in the Ravens Kill.

"Let justice roll down like waters, and righteousness like an everlasting stream," I said.

Only Jennie Webber heard me. She turned her head, her hand still on my arm, as I stared at the kill.

"Book of Amos," I added. And then I did the unthinkable.

I fainted.

Chapter
Twenty-Nine

～

Sunday morning found me stretched out on the large flat stone that crowned the Ravensloft. I woke with the birds and left the carriage house before the parade of concerned visitors and callers commenced. There were things I needed to think about, and I didn't want to be disturbed. My scraped and bruised face was bare, my hair loose. Even a ponytail hurt. I ached in every limb. I paused at the end of my road, remembering Sadie's advice, and the path I'd only glimpsed before revealed itself. I walked slowly through the quiet, thick woods, my bruised and aching body loosening as I went, glad to be moving and breathing at all.

I'd been lucky. No concussion, no broken bones, not even a sprain. I'd been released from the hospital late Friday night. Jennie brought me home. Henri and Pierre had greeted me with kisses and containers of food. While I showered, Jennie warmed the food and brewed tea. No whisky, but I let it go. She wouldn't be there all night.

Over dinner, Jennie brought me up to date. Felicity was alive but in the hospital. She'd been drugged and knocked around, either by Matthew or by being unconscious on the floor of the SUV. Probably both. She regained consciousness in the ER. Since no one was sure what Matthew had given her and her kids were safe with her sister, she didn't object to being kept for observation.

Matthew's body had been found early Saturday morning in the same place as his sister's decades before. It took longer for the Ravens Kill to spit him out, and it gave him quite a beating. Poetic justice, in my opinion.

Jennie and Sam O'Donnell had spent all of Friday night piecing together what had happened, using what I found and talking to everyone involved.

"Felicity believes Matthew either killed his little sister, or made no effort to save her," Jennie told me. "And she's sure her mother-in-law believed it, too. When the dementia set in, Marjorie would start talking about the day Carol died, just odd comments and crying. Taken individually, they made no sense but added to what Vince had told her. Felicity heard enough and she got nervous. She mentioned some of the things Marjorie said to Matthew, and that's when he decided there would be no outside help. It was shortly after that the old lady started getting out."

"Matthew planted the idea in his mother's mind," I said, "I'm sure of it. Then he let her out the night she died."

Jennie nodded.

"We'll never prove it, but it seems likely he used one of his mother's sleeping pills and drugged Felicity that night. He'd made hot chocolate after dinner and she thought it tasted funny, but he told her he'd added brandy and cinnamon."

"Then he let her believe it was her fault," I said.

"She never completely bought that, but she was afraid. She had finally decided to leave him but wanted a clean break and no chance of him seeing the kids unsupervised."

"So, she confided in Joanna, who volunteered to try and dig up some proof and cover for her while she met with the lawyer," I said, "but Matthew suspected something and decided to get rid of his wife. After all, he'd staged two successful 'accidents' so why not a third?"

"Joanna was in the wrong place at the wrong time," Jennie said, "and from the back, in the dark, he thought it was Felicity. He was going to get rid of the one person who suspected the truth, and get control of the money to fund his political career."

"So, he killed the wrong woman, Felicity got even more suspicious, I started nosing around, and the police didn't buy the accident set-up."

"Not for a minute," Jennie said, "though your comment about the light switch is what clinched it for Sam. Matthew decided both you and Felicity had to go, and he waited for his chance. Anne Marie told Dory she would wait for you, and then Matthew told Anne Marie that Felicity was your ride home. She feels terrible."

"She couldn't have known," I said, "she had no reason to suspect him."

Jennie ran through a few more details, and then left to tie up some loose ends.

Now I had to do the same.

I stretched and sat up, dangling my legs over the side of the big stone. The Village of Raven Hill spread out below me, the kill winding its glittering way around and through it. The manor stood sentinel over it all.

A hawk cried out, and I looked up. Its shadow crossed my face as it circled lazily. I drew in my knees and thought of Joanna, my courageous and funny friend, now silenced. I thought of Danny, who asked for my help, and whom I also failed. The shadow of the hawk passed over me again. I felt the tears come.

After I'd had a good cry, I wiped my face and looked once more at the village and the sunny sky.

"I'm sorry," I said, "so very, very sorry."

A breeze ruffled my hair. The sun warmed me, and the shadow of the hawk crossed me for the third time. A great weight lifted. I knew what I had to do.

I had found Joanna's killer. If I had failed her, I had done my best to make things right. Not so with my husband. Danny had asked for my help and I'd put him off. Then he was dead, and the man in jail for the crime swore he didn't do it. I could hear his voice in my head now.

"He was alive when I left him, I swear it. I didn't hit him that hard, and only the one time. I didn't kill him. Someone else was there after me. I swear it."

I believed him.

I am ashamed to say I always had. Too many things didn't add up, but as long as my secret was safe, I didn't care.

I cared now. It was time to find the truth. I would have to be so careful. I didn't know who to trust. But I knew where to begin. How it would end was anybody's guess, but that no longer mattered to me. All that mattered was the truth.

I stood. The hawk flashed past me, in a silent dive toward its prey. I walked to the trail. Turning my back to the sun, I stepped into the welcoming shadows. The trees whispered as the darkness closed around me. I inhaled the green-scented air and relaxed into the forest's cool embrace, the soothing caress of leaves as I followed my secret path downward. My mind hummed with possibilities and questions.

I felt more alive than I had in years.

The game was afoot.

Acknowledgments

This book would not exist without the help and encouragement of many people. Special thanks to my husband, Mark, who encouraged me to attend my first writer's workshop; my agent, Julie Gwinn of the Seymour Agency; agency intern and author assistant Lauren Ash; and beta readers Lisa Pellegrino and Connie Novak. Nothing is created in a vacuum—constructive criticism and suggestions on everything from plot to word choice are invaluable as a novel is being written. For this kind of help, I credit Lorin Oberweger and the staff and students at Free Expressions Breakout Novel Intensive Workshop Orlando; Jason Sitzes, Carol Dougherty, and the staff and students at the Writers Retreat Workshop San Antonio, and the staff and volunteers of Killer Nashville 2019. Many thanks to you all.